MURDER IN MONTMARTRE

THE MAGGIE NEWBERRY MYSTERIES
BOOK 24

SUSAN KIERNAN-LEWIS

SAN MARCO PRESS

Murder in Montmartre. Book 24 of the Maggie Newberry Mysteries.

Copyright © 2024 by Susan Kiernan-Lewis

DESCRIPTION

Make new friends. But kill the old.

Reunions are great. Especially if everyone makes it home alive. After twenty years living in France, Maggie's proud of her language skills and her ability to adapt to a foreign culture, so when four women from her Atlanta high school invite her to get together for a mini reunion in Paris, Maggie can't wait to show them how she's changed.

Unfortunately, after two awkward days and a miserable Seine River tour Maggie realizes what she should have remembered—three of the four girls were never really nice to her in high school—and the fourth one didn't know she existed. Everything changes dramatically however, when, on the morning that Maggie decides to leave early, one of her friends is found brutally murdered in her hotel room.

The police suspect the killer is one of the four surviving friends with Maggie's name topping the list. Determined to prove her innocence, Maggie plunged into the secret pockets and hidden quarters of Montmartre and the nontouristy parts around the Sacre Coeur to find out the truth. In the process she discovers that each of her friends had reasons for wanting Christy dead.

As suspicions deepen and tensions rise, what started as a fun reunion in the City of Light, becomes an intense game of life-and-death as Maggie races to unmask the killer and the decades-old secret that drives her—before she kills again.

Murder in Montmartre is a riveting international whodunit about the snarled perceptions of old friendships, and the treasures - and tragedies - that can arise when a terrible past that won't die collides with the lies of the present.

Free Falling
Going Gone
Heading Home
Blind Sided
Rising Tides
Cold Comfort
Never Never
Wit's End
Dead On
White Out
Black Out
End Game

The Mia Kazmaroff Mysteries
Reckless
Shameless
Breathless
Heartless
Clueless
Ruthless

Ella Out of Time
Swept Away
Carried Away
Stolen Away

1

F orget Lupin. Forget Ponzi. Forget Madoff.
Life's most relentless thief is time.
That's what Maggie was thinking when she caught
her reflection in the train window, noting the lines that hadn't
been there in high school and the silver streaks in her hair
she'd chosen not to dye. The last time the "girls" had seen her,
she'd worn her hair long and past her shoulders. It was shorter
now. Easier to take care of. These days, that mattered.

She felt the train begin to pull away from the Aix-en-
Provence station and, as it gathered speed, she couldn't help
but feel as if she were rushing toward a moment that had
already passed. Four women she'd known in high school when
they'd all been starry-eyed girls. Four friends she hadn't seen in
forever. A life time. *Four* lifetimes. Four friends who had each
taken their own separate and very different paths. They were
all bound to have changed.

After all, haven't I?

Maggie looked out the train window, watching the buildings and landscape blur into a fast-moving panorama. The
rattling hum of the train provided a rhythmic soundtrack as the

fields of Provence spun by as she made her way towards Paris. She felt a blend of anticipation and nostalgia. The memories of their school days filled with laughter, shared secrets, and dreams of the future brought a smile to her face.

When Monica called last month to suggest they get together for a mini reunion in Paris, Maggie had been surprised but beyond delighted at the idea. So much had happened in the intervening thirty years. She felt a tingly sense of anticipation at the thought of seeing her friends again. She was fairly confident she would hold up in comparison. It was true, she'd gained weight. And her chin was a little softer. Now that she thought about it, Monica had probably had work done. Maggie was sure Monica would look amazing.

But there were other hallmarks to reflect upon. Maggie spoke French fluently. She'd raised three children into three relatively happy adults and was instrumental in the running of a successful vineyard. For years she'd written an expat newsletter that had helped her connect with the surrounding villages and brought in a decent revenue. Not bad. But of course none of those world-shaking accomplishments. After all, Christie had been short listed for a Pulitzer. Beth had just retired from a career as an international human rights lawyer. Maggie felt an unwelcome flinch of doubt that was interrupted by the sound of her cellphone vibrating on the train seat next to her. A picture of her best friend Grace VanSant appeared on the screen.

"Hey," Maggie said, answering her phone.

"Are you on board yet?" Grace asked.

Maggie smiled. Her closest friend for over twenty years, Grace now ran a bed and breakfast just a few miles away from Maggie's home in St-Buvard.

"The train just left the station," Maggie said.

"I'm so glad you're taking some time for yourself this weekend," Grace said. "You deserve a break to let your hair down and indulge in a few Lemon Drops."

Maggie laughed. "Trust me, I intend to."

"I honestly didn't even know you had such great pals back in high school. You never talk about them."

"Well, we weren't really besties or anything," Maggie said, glancing out the window as she watched the Aix suburbs recede from view. "We all belonged to different clubs and were on different tracks. One of us was hell-bent to get into an Ivy, another just wanted to get married."

"You know these reunions are all about regret and redemption, right?" Grace said.

Maggie laughed. "If you say so."

"It's true. The prom queen grows old trying to stay the belle of the ball only she's always the one who ends up alone. The high school brainiac wishes she'd spent more time developing hobbies. The wallflower is always the one who found true love."

"You seem to have done some studying on this."

"It's a basic trope," Grace said. "But in any case, they are going to be blown away by you."

Maggie felt a flush of love for Grace. Leave it to her best friend to zero in on the one tiny iota of insecurity that Maggie was feeling, then lock in and destroy it.

"Don't be silly," Maggie said. "Why would they?"

"Because you speak French like a native for one thing!" Grace said. "And you haven't aged a day since high school for another."

"Okay, now I know you've broken into the cooking sherry," Maggie said with a laugh. But she felt a warmth infuse her at her friend's words. "Trust me, I can't compete with these ladies. One almost won a Pulitzer, and another had a New York Times Bestselling novel sell like a bazillion copies worldwide. *Death Breeze*?"

"Never heard of it. Sounds ghoulish. Anyway, darling, I hope you have a wonderful visit. While you're there, could you find a moment to check in on Zouzou?"

Grace's youngest daughter had moved to Paris four years ago to get her degree in French pastry arts. Since then, she'd found a job as *sous* pastry chef in various small restaurants. But at twenty-five, Zouzou was not settled. Or at least not in the way that Maggie knew Grace would prefer. She came home every few months to *Dormir,* Grace's *gîte,* but of course the visits were never enough for Grace.

"I've already texted her," Maggie said. "We're meeting for dinner this evening."

"Oh, thank you, darling. She's been impossible to get a hold of lately, and when I do, she never has time to talk. Well, I won't keep you. I know part of the therapy for this kind of respite begins the minute you get in your train seat. So just lean back and let the world go by. Don't think about anything back here."

"I won't, Grace."

"Don't forget those Lemon Drops."

"I won't. Talk soon."

"*Ciao,* darling."

After disconnecting with Grace, Maggie opened her bag and took out a travel pillow, a pashmina she always packed in case the air conditioning got too cold, and a pair of noise-cancelling headphones. She smiled when she saw the small bag of *chouquettes* tucked into her bag. That of course was Laurent's doing. Like many French people, her husband had strong views about food and its powers to strengthen and cosset. This was his way of sending love and support on her trip north.

Maggie plucked out a few *chouquettes,* careful not to get the powdered sugar onto her jacket. The explosion of sugar on her tongue was immediate and she quickly ate two more before putting the bag away. Then she pulled out the paperback book she'd brought for the trip and settled in for the next four hours. A few minutes later, when the catering cart came by, she bought a coffee and ate a few more *chouquettes*, surprising herself when she realized she'd eaten nearly the whole bag.

Laurent will be so pleased, she thought with a smile. Instead of worrying about any extra pounds she might have gained in the last twenty years, he was only concerned with her enjoying food—usually those dishes he prepared himself.

As she sipped her coffee, Maggie found herself looking away from her book to gaze out the window, taking in the changing landscape. She was well aware that a big part of the attraction of this reunion weekend was the unique perspective on the past it afforded. It was a dive back into her past—a past that over the years she had spent very little time thinking about. When she first moved to France with Laurent all those years ago she remembered how homesick she'd been for Atlanta. She'd only agreed to come for a year and after that Laurent promised he would settle in Atlanta with her. As the first glimpses of the Parisian skyline began to peak over the horizon, Maggie found herself smiling at the memory.

After three children, one grandchild and a bustling family vineyard business, that was not how things turned out.

It was true what she'd told Grace—she hadn't been all that close to the women she was traveling to Paris to meet. But when Monica suggested the reunion Maggie hadn't hesitated. It was just the much needed break from the preparatory work of the coming harvest or her routines at home—caring for a feisty five-year-old was exhausting.

Maggie gazed out at the undulating landscape. No, the main reason she'd decided to come was because of the curiosity she'd felt when Monica invited her. The more she thought of it, the more she found herself wondering how seeing her old friends after so many years might crystalize her reflection of her own life choices. Not that she was sorry for the road she'd taken. In fact, she was generally happy with the path she'd chosen—however she'd fought it at the time. But that didn't mean she didn't think of those other paths from time to time.

When she was in school, Maggie had planned to be a world-renown journalist working for the *New York Times* or the *Washington Post*. Throughout her teen years, she'd revered the stories of those journalists who'd literally changed history by their dedication to uncovering the truth.

Even when, after graduating, Maggie took a job in an ad agency—instead of accepting the low-paying internship when it was offered at the *Atlanta Journal-Constitution*—she always thought the agency job detour was just a stepping stone to her career as a famous writer. It wasn't until that summer when she went to the south of France to find her sister Elise and her little niece Nicole and met Laurent that everything changed for her.

Seeing these women again would remind her of the kind of person she'd aspired to be back then. Back when she was young and full of hope and brimming with excitement about the future.

She didn't believe she was doubting herself or regretful about how things had turned out—even without a Pulitzer. Not at all. Or at least not really. But she was hoping that the weekend might allow her a glimpse of the road not taken. And that having seen it, she would still be okay with her choice.

2

By the time Maggie's Uber let her out in front of the hotel that she and the other women were staying at in Montmartre the rain was a soft drizzle, barely more than a mist. As she pulled her roller bag out of the car, she looked up at the façade of Hôtel Belle Vue. It was a carefully restored 19th-century building with ivy crawling up its stony exterior, which Maggie thought gave it a sense of timeless elegance.

After dodging the raindrops into the lobby, Maggie checked in and went up to her room where she quickly unpacked. As she was leaving her room, she got a text from Monica saying that they were all in the hotel bar. Maggie hurried down the wide spiral staircase to the lobby.

Situated opposite the lobby, the hotel bar was small and dark. It was decorated with several vintage chandeliers, each casting a warm, inviting glow over the room. The furniture was a mix of plush velvet armchairs and wooden bistro-style tables, creating an atmosphere that was both cozy and chic.

"Maggie! Over here!" a voice called out.

Maggie turned to see four women seated at one of the bar's

back tables. A tall woman with blonde hair wearing an elegant twinset of a cream cashmere stood up to greet her. Monica had been their school's senior year prom queen and the undisputed leader of the group of girls back in school. And to Maggie she looked almost exactly the same.

Maggie hurried over to the table.

"Oh my God, you still look sixteen!" Monica gushed as she gave Maggie a quick hug.

Maggie felt a flash of something undefinable as she suddenly remembered that Monica had always been the master of giving a compliment that could be taken two ways.

"So do you," Maggie said.

That was nearly true as Monica's skin was stretched tautly across her cheeks.

Maggie turned to the others at the table. The first person she saw was Christie McCoy who, with her auburn hair and strident personality, had always been a stark contrast to Monica. Professionally, Christie was the one Maggie had always envied. Although she'd never married, she had succeeded in doing what Maggie had always dreamed of—excelling in a career as an investigative journalist. Maggie had followed Christie's career through social media over the years. She had written for all the big papers and had been short listed for the Pulitzer. Smiling at her now, Maggie suddenly remembered that beneath Christie's vivacious and confident exterior was a quick temper and a penchant for dramatics.

Beside Christie was Beth. Unlike Christie and Monica, Beth was a picture of demure sophistication in a sleek black dress. Shot with threads of silver, her dark hair was pulled back into a neat chignon, her make-up subtle and elegant. She nodded in acknowledgement of Maggie but made no other gesture of welcome. That was fine. Maggie hadn't been close to Beth.

Lastly, there was Lisa, the one of the four of them who always exuded an easygoing charm and exuberance.

"You're here!" Lisa exclaimed as she jumped up from the table and threw her arms around Maggie. "You look amazing!"

Lisa was another friend who Maggie followed on social media. It was partly for that reason that Maggie knew about Lisa's exciting round of acclaim from the novel she'd written a decade earlier. As Maggie recalled, the book had even been optioned to be turned into a movie from one of the big streaming giants, although she didn't remember if was ever produced.

"You look just the same," Maggie said as she sat down next to Lisa. "What's your secret?"

Lisa snorted with humor.

"Stay hungry, basically," she said.

"I hear you moved back to Atlanta," Maggie said. "Tired of the big city life?"

Lisa laughed.

"Something like that. You remember my big book, *Death Breeze*?"

"Of course. Congratulations, by the way. That was amazing."

"Yeah, well, much less amazing was the fact that the two other books I wrote after that never earned their advances back, so my publisher dropped me and then my agent did too."

Maggie felt instantly uncomfortable hearing Lisa relate her failure so bluntly and so quickly upon seeing each other. It was almost as if she wanted to get it over with. Or perhaps she thought Maggie already knew about it and she didn't want to appear to be living in a golden moment of the past. The other women at the table must have heard the story before because they simply began chatting among themselves.

"And then the divorce, you know?" Lisa said to Maggie. "So, after life royally dumped on me I came home to Atlanta. I have a daughter."

"I saw that on Facebook," Maggie said, eager to latch onto something Lisa might be proud of. "How is she?"

"Oh, fine. She graduated from Georgia and met this wonderful young man. I'm a grandma! Twice over!"

Lisa pulled out her phone and began scrolling through it for photos.

"Are you working?" Maggie asked as she took the phone to admire a series of pictures of the two adorable grandchildren.

"If you can call it that," Lisa said with a sigh, taking the phone back and gazing at her grandchildren. "I mean, it's impossible to find any real work at our age, you know? My last job was as a communications specialist but trust me, Maggie, that title means something totally different from when you were in the game."

Maggie realized that Lisa didn't know what Maggie had done after college.

"In fact, I was laid off just before I came on this trip," Lisa continued. "But I don't blame them. I was so far behind the curve, I couldn't figure out any of the tik-tokking insta-crap they needed me to know. That's a young woman's game. Or at least a millennial's."

"I am so sorry," Maggie said.

"They said AI could do my job better." Lisa laughed. "I wouldn't mind if they said it could do it cheaper, you know? But they said *better*."

Christie leaned across the table and tapped Maggie's wrist.

"Give me a hint," she said. "We were in fourth period Algebra class together?"

Maggie saw Christie's eyes dance with malicious delight. She found herself surprised to realize that in this way at least, Christie seemed not to have matured much since high school.

"That's probably it," Maggie said mildly.

"Oh, Christie, don't be an ass," Monica said, turning to Maggie. "Ignore her. She's jet lagged."

"I'm serious!" Christie said with a laugh. The sound was abrupt and loud and, now that Maggie remembered, often inappropriate.

"I had to keep asking the other girls to remind me again who Maggie Newberry is?" Christie said, laughing again and looking around the table as if to invite the rest of them to enjoy the joke.

"So I hear you've also come back to Atlanta?" Maggie asked her pointedly.

"It's temporary," Christie said, her smile dissolving from her face. "Who knows where I'll go from there?"

"You're not doing investigative journalism anymore?" Maggie asked.

"What makes you say that? Just because I'm not attached to a newspaper, I'm still digging for a good story. In fact, I've got a couple of book ideas I'm pitching."

Maggie saw her glance around the table, and she wondered if Christie had already shared the specifics of those projects with the group.

"But what have *you* been up to?" Lisa asked Maggie. "You're not on Facebook?"

"Not really," Maggie said. "What with the vineyard and all... plus we're raising a five-year-old and she keeps me pretty busy."

"In any case," Monica interrupted, "we need to be thinking about dinner." She turned to Maggie. "We held off on reservations until we had you here to speak French for us."

Maggie frowned.

"It's probably a little late for reservations," she said, "but I do know of a—"

"Look, there's a great place right on this street," Christie said. "I read about it on TripAdvisor. And you don't need reservations."

"Honestly," Maggie said. "No reservations on this street means it's probably a tourist trap."

"Okay, Maggie," Christie said sarcastically. "We know you're the French expert and all, but I think we can manage going to a restaurant without you holding our hands."

"Suit yourself," Maggie said, picking up her purse. "Unfortunately, whatever you do, I'll have to hear about it tomorrow. I have an engagement with the daughter of a friend."

"Really trying to rub it in that you know people in Paris, aren't you?" Christie said with another barking laugh.

"Oh, stop it, Christie," Lisa said. "Maggie's lived in France for twenty years. Of course she knows people here!"

"That's the point she's making, though, isn't it?" Christie said.

Maggie kept her smile nailed in place and stood up.

"See you ladies at breakfast?" she said.

As she turned to leave, she heard the conversation behind her fill up in her absence like a wave rushing in to cover the shore. A niggling memory in the back of her mind jostled its way to the forefront when she found herself recalling that these women hadn't listened to what she had to say thirty-two years ago either.

3

La Petit Paradis was an old-style *brasserie* located in a neighborhood between Montmartre and Pigalle, wedged between a dry cleaner and a small grocery store. At first glance, it looked like it was closed, but Maggie had known too many almost Michelin star eateries in France that looked abandoned. As soon as she stepped inside, she felt a warm, inviting ambiance engulf her—complete with rustic wooden tables, and cozy red velvet banquettes lining the walls.

She immediately spotted Zouzou at a corner window table. Next to her was a handsome young man, his hand resting casually on Zouzou's. Zouzou bounced out of her chair.

"Aunt Maggie!" she squealed.

Maggie felt a wave of delight at the young woman's joyful affect, and she quickened her steps, reaching the table and pulling Zouzou into her arms. The girl's hair was shaved on both sides forming a dyed green mohawk down the middle. Maggie couldn't help but wonder if Grace had seen Zouzou's hair.

"You look adorable, *mon vieux*," Maggie said, kissing her, and realizing with surprise that she actually did.

"I was afraid you'd faint when you saw my hair!" Zouzou said. "Aunt Maggie, I want you to meet Pierre."

The young man had gotten to his feet and stood beside Zouzou now, smiling awkwardly. Maggie turned to him and smiled.

"Hello, Pierre," she said. "I'm so glad to finally meet you."

"*Moi aussi*," he murmured bashfully.

The two young people stepped back, their hands reaching for each other. Both of them were dressed casually yet stylishly, their youthful elegance fitting perfectly with the relaxed atmosphere of the restaurant. Maggie sat down since it was clear Pierre wouldn't sit until she did.

"So tell me everything," she said to Zouzou. "It's been ages since you've been home."

"Oh, I know," Zouzou said. "I'm missing all of you so much. Oh, Aunt Maggie, can we speak French? Pierre doesn't know any English."

Maggie turned to him and smiled.

"*Naturalement*," she said, switching to French. "What is it you do, Pierre?"

She'd read somewhere that asking what one did for a living was a quintessentially American thing to do. The French tend to ask where you're from instead. But the intense debriefing that awaited Maggie when she returned home would be from an American mother who would require employment facts rather than whatever area of France Pierre came from.

boyfriend. "It's a huge multinational publishing company in Montmartre. He got the job over about a hundred other applicants."

"*Chérie*," Pierre admonished, blushing as he shook his head in embarrassment. He looked at Maggie.

"I have always loved literature," he said. "But I am not a

good writer myself. This seemed the best way I could get paid to read."

"Sounds logical," Maggie said with a smile.

"Pierre is so clever," Zouzou said. "He's only been there a year and already they're giving him big projects. Tell her, *chérie*."

"No, *mon cher*, it is boring for her, I am sure." He turned to Maggie. "How are you liking Montmartre? Have you been before?"

"Yes, a couple of times," Maggie said. "But I'm with old friends this trip so it'll be interesting seeing it through their eyes."

"They do not speak French?"

"No. I'm sort of their default translator," she said.

"Oh, Aunt Maggie, you'll need to take them to *Sobo's*!" Zouzou said. "The tourists haven't discovered it yet and it's amazing. There are only six tables! We love it, don't we, *chéri*?"

Zouzou's gaze drilled onto Pierre's face with an intensity that surprised Maggie. As they waited for the waiter to take their orders, Maggie couldn't help but be impressed by how the two of them seemed lost in their own private world. She found herself wondering how long it had been since she herself had felt swept away like that. She and Laurent had been married over twenty years. Rapt gazing had long since given away to grocery lists and mundane routines.

Maggie couldn't wait to report back to Grace that Zouzou seemed to have found a good one in this young man.

Despite the tension lingering from her meeting with her schoolmates back at the Hôtel Belle Vue bar, Maggie couldn't help but feel a sense of calm wash over her. It was partly the ambiance of the restaurant itself—nobody creates a better tableau for romance than the French—and partly just being on the front row of a love story unfolding before her eyes. The restaurant, the happy couple, and the feeling of her first evening in Paris all came together to create what felt to Maggie like a beautifully captured moment in time.

Ah. To be young and in love in Paris.

For a moment, Maggie felt an intense longing to be sitting in this charming little *brasserie* with Laurent. But as much as the fantasy wanted to develop in her brain, she knew the magic of this moment wouldn't hold for him and so it wouldn't for her either. Although born in Paris, Laurent had no love for the city. As a result, they rarely came here. On those rare times when they were able to get away from the vineyard, Laurent much preferred vacationing on the Côte d'Azur or even the States.

"How long have you known each other?" Maggie asked, redirecting her attention back to the couple after the waiter had taken their orders.

"I don't know," Zouzou said as she idly traced a finger along the rim of her wine glass, her mesmerized gaze focused on Pierre.

"Perhaps six weeks?" Pierre suggested.

Maggie smiled at the answer. Yes, she could see they were both infatuated and there was definitely a time for that in a young person's life. It was a heady, intoxicating feeling and she was glad Zouzou was experiencing it. On the other hand, whatever this Maggie smiled at the answer. Yes, she could see they were both infatuated and there was definitely a time for that in a young person's life. It was a heady, intoxicating feeling and she was glad Zouzou was experiencing it. On the other hand, whatever this was could easily flame out in another couple of weeks. The intensity of this stage of their relationship couldn't possibly be maintained for long. Perhaps they would simply mellow out, slow down, and continue on.

She liked the thought of that since Pierre seemed so stable and good natured. The fast-burning fires always snuffed out the quickest, she thought with sadness. She hoped that Zouzou didn't get her heart broken again.

Later, after the meal was winding up, Pierre excused himself to use the facilities and Zouzou leaned across the table brimming with excitement.

"Well?" she said in English. "What do you think? He's amazing, isn't he?"

Maggie hesitated.

What would I want Grace to say to Mila if our positions were reversed?

She didn't want to throw water on Zouzou's happiness, but she did want to suggest taking a breath.

"You've got your whole life ahead of you," Maggie said. "Enjoy getting to know each other."

Zouzou pulled back, a petulant frown on her face.

"I already know him," she said.

Maggie smiled.

"I'm sure you think you do, but there's always more to learn. Why not enjoy the process? Take your time."

"We are taking our time," she said. "I asked him to move in with me."

Maggie was surprised and tried not to let her face show it. She must have failed in the attempt by what Zouzou said next.

"How long did you know Uncle Laurent before *you* moved in with him?" Zouzou asked.

"Nearly a year," Maggie said, outright lying.

She glanced in the direction where Pierre had gone. She wasn't sure how Grace felt about Zouzou living with a man before marriage as she and Laurent had done. The experience for her had given her the time she'd needed to be sure she wanted to marry not just Laurent but a man from another country with all the complications that would bring. Even then, after a year of living together, that first year of marriage had come very close to being their last.

But of course everyone was different.

"Look, Zouzou," she said reasonably, "all I'm saying is take your time. You're in no hurry."

"You're right," Zouzou said, leaning back in her chair and crossing her arms in a close approximation to a sulk. "I guess I'm not in any hurry as long as it doesn't matter if the baby is born in wedlock."

4

The next morning, Maggie stood outside the hotel waiting for the rest of her group to assemble. The weather—overcast and raw—seemed to mirror her feelings.

As she waited, she felt a swarm of emotions come over her. She had been stunned by Zouzou's news last night, but also grateful that she'd gotten back to the hotel too late to fit in a phone call to Grace. As it was, she'd responded to an early morning text from her saying Zouzou was well, happy and in love and that she'd call later with a full report. But she wasn't at all sure she should tell Grace what was really happening.

"We're here! We're here!" Lisa called as she and Monica, Christie and Beth emerged from the hotel entrance.

Maggie smiled at them as they joined her on the front steps.

"You guys look like you had a late night last night," Maggie said.

"Oh, you missed a good one, Maggie," Lisa said. "But you were right about the restaurant. We waited forever and the food was awful!"

"Not as bad as the service," Beth said. "They did their part to ensure the continued reputation of rude French waiters."

Christie wore sunglasses and carried a can of diet cola. Maggie remembered she'd been drinking one when they met yesterday too. She'd read that some people were addicted to diet sodas.

The five of them moved off the steps and headed for the neighborhood's historic center. Despite the years since Maggie had last visited Montmartre, she noticed that the neighborhood streets had retained their timeless charm. They were still lined with bohemian cafés, sidewalk art, and the iconic Sacré-Cœur Basilica ever present, visibly perched atop the hill of Montmartre.

As they meandered through the streets, Maggie fell into step behind Monica who appeared to be attempting to make up for her hangover by walking quickly. Maggie was about to remind her that the cobblestones could be deadly if one chose to ignore them when Monica tripped and grabbed for Beth's shoulder to stay upright.

"Hey!" Beth said indignantly.

"Sorry!" Monica said with a laugh. "I think I'm still drunk!"

Maggie turned at the sound of wheels clattering against the ancient cobblestones to see a young teenager pushing a stroller toward them. She knew this must be Sophie, the teenager Monica had hired to accompany her to Paris to look after Monica's granddaughter Emily. The baby, nearly two years old sat awkwardly in the stroller, her eyes glazed and drooping.

"Hello, little one," Maggie said to the child with a smile. "You don't look quite awake yet."

"Ugh," Monica said, turning to glower at Sophie. "She's been up for hours as I can personally attest. I probably should've gotten Sophie her own room, but Jason didn't want to spend the money."

Monica's husband Jason had also come on the trip.

"Hurry up, Maggie!" Lisa called from where she waited at the foot of a steep hill of stairs. Laughter from Beth and Christie who had walked on ahead seemed to echo off the ancient stone buildings. It was a familiar sound that seemed to transport Maggie back to their high school days.

Once Maggie, Sophie, and Monica had caught up with the others, they passed a *patisserie* doing a bustling business with a line of people snaking out the door. Instantly, all five women reacted to the enticing aroma of fresh pastries.

"Oh, Maggie, darling," Monica said. "Would you mind? The rest of us just end up pointing at the display case like a bunch of baboons. Can you get a *pain au chocolat* for me? Anybody else?"

Lisa turned to Sophie who was leaning heavily on the handlebars of the stroller as if exhausted.

"You should try one, Sophie," she said. "It's all a part of your Paris education."

"Okay," Sophie said with a shrug.

"Anyone else?" Monica asked. "Girls?"

"I'll take one, I guess," Beth said squinting into the bakery window. "Is it filled with chocolate?"

"You've never heard of *pain au chocolat*?" Lisa asked with a laugh.

"I guess things got lost in my cultural education," Beth said sharply, "while I was busy working for a living."

"Now, now, girls," Monica admonished. "Christie? Although I can't imagine eating one with a Diet Coke."

"Yeah, get me one," Christie said. "But can she bring them to the church? I want to make the climb while the weather is not too hot."

"Maggie, darling?" Monica said to her. "Do you mind getting them and meeting us at the church."

"Not at all," Maggie said, feeling a spasm of annoyance.

"I'll stay with you," Lisa said. "Sophie? Want to stay with us?"

"Sure," Sophie said listlessly, pushing the stroller toward the *patisserie* while the others moved on ahead. She looked in the bakery window.

"We'll wait for you outside," Lisa said to Maggie. "Need some euros?"

"No, I've got it," Maggie said.

As soon as she turned to go inside, she opened her purse to pull out her wallet and was jostled from behind by an unmindful tourist. Her purse tumbled to the ground and its contents scattered across the cobblestones. Maggie watched in dismay as her hotel keycard skidded into a sewer grate before she could grab it.

She quickly jammed everything back in her purse—nobody near her made any attempt to help—and then went to stand in line, wondering not for the first time that day why in the world she'd come on this trip.

Twenty minutes later, pastries bought, Maggie rejoined Lisa and Sophie on the sidewalk. Lisa was now holding Emily who was squinting into the sun and looking around.

"I think she's looking for Monica," Lisa said as she patted the baby's back. "Are you looking for your mama?"

"She never sees her mama," Sophie said. "Her real mama, I mean."

"What do you mean?" Lisa asked.

"Well, Miz Williams asked me if I could move in to take care of Em full time and I asked why not her mother? And Miz Williams got real upset and said it's because Em's real mom doesn't live with them anymore."

Lisa gave Maggie a questioning look.

"I'm sorry to hear that," Lisa said, continuing to pat the baby's back.

"But I can't move in. I've got school. And my parents need me at home."

"Of course they do," Lisa said. "Is it a lot of work? Taking care of her?"

Sophie smiled at the baby.

"No, ma'am. Me and Em get along great. She's like my own little sister. If I had a little sister."

Lisa put Emily back in her stroller and began pushing it toward Sacré-Cœur while Maggie handed out a pastry to Sophie and a small piece of one to Emily.

"Oh, my gosh, this is so good!" Sophie said, her eyes wide. "I've never tasted anything this delicious! It's like the chocolate is exploding in my mouth!"

Maggie laughed. "Welcome to France," she said.

After a moment, the climb got steeper, and Sophie took over the stroller from Lisa. Lisa fell back to walk beside Maggie.

"I'm sorry about what Christie said earlier," Lisa said. "You know, expecting you to get the pastries and then not waiting for us."

"It doesn't bother me," Maggie said.

"It's just so rude."

"So Emily's mother isn't in the picture?" Maggie asked, preferring to change the subject.

Lisa squinted in the direction of Sophie pushing the stroller up the steep hill.

"I knew Monica's daughter was in and out of rehab," Lisa said. "Honestly, I never heard Monica do anything but complain when her daughter was young. But I admit I didn't know she wasn't living at home with them any longer."

"Raising a baby is hard work at any age," Maggie said. "But especially at our age."

Lisa gave her an odd look and then shrugged.

"If you say so," she said. "I'd like nothing better than to

babysit my grandkids full time. But Jenny says they're happy in day care."

Maggie realized that Lisa seemed to have forgotten that Maggie was raising a child herself at her age.

"Beth is so quiet," Maggie said. "Remind me. Has she always been that way?"

"Oh, yes," Lisa said. "But maybe more so now. She's had some hurdles along the way, you know. Sophie, do you need me to take over? I'm pretty rested now!"

Sophie gave her a thumbs up to indicate she was fine.

"She went to work in DC after law school, right?" Maggie asked.

"Beth? Yes, she did. She worked there for twenty years in some kind of think tank. I don't know the details and Beth isn't really the chatty sort. I heard she married a guy, but it didn't last."

"But she's married now?" Maggie asked.

"She is. Second marriage. From what she says, they seem happy."

"But no kids?"

"No, and I think she regrets that. He's got kids. But it's not the same."

After that, as they mounted the steps to Sacré-Cœur, Maggie and Lisa fell into a comfortable silence, each lost in their own thoughts, each focused on saving their breath for the climb. Once at the top, Maggie marveled at the sight of the city stretched out before them, bathed in the soft mid-morning light.

"It's really beautiful," Lisa said surveying the sight.

"It is," Maggie said.

Her face felt warm from the climb. Christie had been right about doing it before it got too hot. It was already starting to get uncomfortable.

"Have you been to Paris often?" Maggie asked.

"This is my first visit if you can believe it," Lisa said. "I've thought about coming—especially once I started following you on Facebook. Your life just seems idyllic."

Maggie laughed. "Hardly that."

Lisa looked at the crowd of tourists and then pulled out her phone.

"I thought we were supposed to meet the others up here," she said. "I can't believe Monica just takes off and leaves Sophie to fend for herself."

"Well, she's with us," Maggie reminded her.

Lisa snorted and started texting on her phone. Maggie looked down at the city again and found her thoughts going back to Zouzou.

Pregnant by a man she's known six weeks.

How was Maggie ever going to tell Grace?

"Monica says they were at the top," Lisa said with disgust, "and now they're down below looking at all the artists' paintings. I can't believe they didn't wait for us."

Sophie rolled the stroller over to them.

"Any more of those chocolate pastries left?" she asked, eyeing Maggie's bag.

Maggie laughed and handed her the whole bag.

"Help yourself," she said.

Later, after walking back down the rue du Chevalier de la Barre to the Place du Tertre, Maggie and Lisa met up with the other three. Christie and Monica appeared to be in the process of haggling with a street artist over a painting. Maggie saw the artist become agitated as the negotiations continued but she held back from getting involved. First, she wasn't thrilled about being aligned with Christie and Monica who were both acting like the epitome of rude tourists. Second, she didn't feel inclined to help Christie—who of the two was being the bigger ass—out of a difficult situation.

As Christie's voice grew shriller, Maggie caught Sophie's eye and the two of them turned to wander to a different part of the square while Lisa hurried over to see if she could help the fractious transaction.

"So are you enjoying your trip to Paris?" Maggie asked as Sophie pushed the stroller and gawked at all the activity around them.

The square teemed with life and color, its cobblestone paths lined with artist stalls. Faint melodies of a street musician's guitar floated through the air. They stopped to watch an artist at his easel, his brush dancing over the canvas with a life of its own.

"I am," Sophie said hesitantly.

"The work isn't too demanding?" Maggie asked.

"I mean, Emily is so sweet. I just love her to pieces."

Maggie wondered if she would say more but Sophie stopped short of complaining about her employer and Maggie respected her for that. She'd already heard Monica admonish the girl twice this morning—quite harshly she thought—and she imagined there was more where that came from within the privacy of their hotel room.

"Is Mr. Williams around much?" Maggie asked.

"Not really," Sophie said. "He leaves first thing in the morning for his conference. Did you know he was at a conference here?"

Maggie shook her head.

"And I guess he had dinner with them last night."

"How about you?" Maggie asked. "What did you do for dinner?"

"Miz Williams ordered room service for me. Once Em was asleep, I watched Netflix on my iPad and ate cheeseburgers."

As they walked back to where the others were waiting for them, Maggie realized that despite the years and the distance between them all, the essence of her friendships with the other four was largely unchanged. She didn't know what she'd expected from this weekend. But it was pretty clear that whatever they hadn't had back in high school as a group wasn't going to magically blossom into something forty years later.

"Looks like Miz McCoy got her painting," Sophie remarked.

Maggie looked up to see that, sure enough, Christie carried a loosely wrapped painting under one arm. Maggie had been surprised that it was Christie who'd wanted the painting. Not that there wasn't a good deal of talent in the place de Tertre, but the subjects were all strictly tourist level—Sacré-Cœur, the Eiffel Tower, the ubiquitous flower carts—and Maggie would've thought Christie might have considered herself too sophisticated a world traveler for such clichés.

"Hello, children!" Monica called to Maggie and Sophie. "We have returned from the Battle of the Grubby French Artiste!"

"And won!" Christie said, hoisting her purchase up in victory.

"So we see," Maggie said. "What next?"

"How about food?" Beth said, a frown of impatience across her face. "I'm not used to doing ten thousand steps before lunch. I'm starving."

"I know!" Lisa said as she clapped her hands in exuberance. "That windmill restaurant looks popular. There must have been fifty people on the terrace."

Maggie nearly groaned at the thought of a crowded and overpriced tourist restaurant. But before she could make a different suggestion, Beth chimed in.

"Done!" she said. "Let's go."

Maggie decided it wasn't worth arguing about and turned to tag along behind them. Christie raced off to find a post office to mail her painting home, saying she'd grab a slice of pizza from one of the street vendors while the rest of them headed to the famous Moulin Rouge restaurant.

Nearly two hours later, after a long wait to get seated

without reservations and then a tense meal after which Monica and Beth fought over who owed what on the bill in front of an impatient and openly derisive waiter, the four exhausted and ill-tempered women walked back to the hotel with the teenager behind them dutifully pushing the stroller.

Maggie's own meal had been an uninspired duck *confit* with green salad. Even now she felt it churning in her stomach— whether from nerves of the day or the meal itself, she couldn't tell. The baby had slept the entire afternoon away and Maggie found herself wondering if the poor thing had been drugged to keep so docile. Even Mila when she was little—who was a generally compliant child—would not have been so tractable confined to a stroller for a full day. Maggie couldn't help but think of Zouzou as she looked at the baby, wondering if there was any way the girl was ready for this level of relentless responsibility.

Sophie managed well with the child but of course she knew the hardships of the job were temporary. She could always sign off and go back to being a teenager whenever she liked. Zouzou wouldn't have that option.

As they trudged up more stairs on the Escaliers du Calvaire on their way back to the hotel, Maggie found herself wondering how much of Zouzou's secret was Maggie's responsibility.

More than that, she wondered if she should tell Grace.

Or if she should just let this particular family matter sort itself out without her input.

After all, at this point, what was done was most emphatically done.

5

Maggie's walk back to the hotel that afternoon was tiring with her brain swirling with indecision and worry. The day had been a whirlwind of stimulating sights and sounds, but the vibrant beauty of Montmartre had been overshadowed by her worry over Zouzou, and the constant bickering and ill-tempered exchanges among her companions as they got increasingly worn out and overheated from the day.

Christie had mentioned at least twice during the day how she still couldn't remember Maggie from high school, as if the running gag was enormously funny to everyone. Maggie forced herself to smile at her comments knowing that to show Christie that she was getting on her nerves would just encourage her to double down.

Once back at the hotel, the group parted—most to take naps and shower—with plans to meet up in the hotel lobby before tonight's Seine boat trip. Before going to her room, Maggie stopped at the receptions desk to get a new key card. When she did, she noticed that Sophie and the stroller were still in the lobby. The girl looked exhausted. Maggie looked around wondering if Sophie was alone when she saw Monica's husband Jason appear from somewhere and walk over to the girl. He handed her a soft drink and put his hand on her shoulder. Maggie thought she saw Sophie flinch.

"*Oui*, Madame?" the desk receptionist prompted Maggie.

Maggie dragged her attention away from Sophie and Jason. "Uh, yes. I'm afraid I've lost my room key."

The man made a brief grimace and then turned without a word to open a drawer and extricate a plastic card. He quickly punched in a code on his key duplication machine and handed the new key card to Maggie. She thanked him and then turned back to look for Sophie and Jason. But they were gone.

She frowned as she headed to the elevator. She remembered Jason very well from high school. In those days, he'd skated by on his good looks and his moderate athletic ability. He wasn't the best on the basketball team, but he rarely warmed the bench. He'd been homecoming king to Monica's queen—something that everyone assumed had clinched the notion that the two would wed after college. Jason was still handsome forty years later, Maggie noted. But there had definitely been something in the way he'd interacted with Sophie that had felt wrong to her. She decided that at the first opportunity she got with her, she would ask the girl if everything was okay there.

As soon as she stepped into her room, the space seemed to welcome Maggie with its soft, ambient lighting and even a faint scent of lavender. She could almost feel the stress seeping out of her as she slipped off her shoes and sank into the armchair by the window. Outside, the city was transforming in the late afternoon sun, the light casting long shadows on the cobblestone street. The breezes off the Seine would be a little cooler tonight, Maggie knew, but the thought of spending another moment in the tense company of the women with whom she'd just spent the day was far from appealing. Her eyes drifted to the inviting image of the clawfoot bathtub in the adjacent room. She would feel more like the evening's activities after a nice soak, she decided.

An hour later, wrapped in a fluffy Terry cotton robe, her hair pinned up off her neck and the pleasure of her hour-long soak truly restorative, she picked up her phone and saw she'd missed a call from Laurent. She called him back.

"Hello, *chérie*," Laurent said, his voice a purr of honey over the line that still made Maggie's insides tingle. "You are having a good time?"

"Pretty good," Maggie said. "I'm already pooped though."

"I never loved that American colloquialism."

Maggie laughed.

"I saw Zouzou last night," she said. "And her new boyfriend."

"*Ah* oui?"

"He seems nice enough. He's got a decent job at a publishing house so he's not some itinerate musician or actor, which is a step up."

"Is he respectful to Zouzou?"

"Yes, and he seems very much in love."

"So what is the problem?"

Maggie nearly laughed at how well Laurent knew her. He could tell, in spite of her glowing report, that there was indeed a problem.

"She's pregnant."

There was a silence on the line.

"Laurent?"

"She is too young."

Maggie knew that Laurent was doing what she herself had done most of the day: remembering Zouzou as a toddler, remembering her as the chubby, insecure teen she'd been too. But just because they remembered Zouzou as a child didn't mean it wasn't time for her to grow up.

"She hasn't told Grace yet," Maggie said.

"Has she asked you to tell her?"

"No," she said. "Not exactly."

"Stay out of it," he said.

"Grace is my best friend."

"She needs to hear this from Zouzou."

"I don't think Zouzou is in any hurry to tell her."

"That is not your affair. Stay out of it."

"I'll think about it."

"You haven't already told her, have you?"

"No, Laurent," Maggie said with exasperation. "I haven't even spoken to Grace yet. But she's waiting for a report from me. If I do tell her, it'll be face to face. Meanwhile, how are things at home?"

"The house has not burned to the ground. The animals are all alive. Amèlie too."

"That's a win."

"And your school friends? Are you enjoying your visit?"

"I'm not really sure. I think I forgot how...contentious they could be."

"*Tant pis*. You should enjoy your weekend away. Harvest will start in a matter of weeks."

If harvest time wasn't Laurent's favorite time of the year it was pretty close. It was the culmination of a yearlong cultivation of his grapes—of all the hours of tending, staking, feeding, watering and weeding—not to mention all the hours of talking and arguing about the grapes with the other vintners in the area.

Even though Maggie didn't do any actual picking herself, harvest time was still a time of upheaval and commotion for her. In the past, she'd often enjoyed the excitement of it—especially when the children were small—but lately she found herself wishing they could do it every *other* year. Laurent always housed the pickers—usually refugees and gypsies—in the mini houses that he'd constructed specifically for this purpose. Many of the people who lived in the little houses now had been pickers for Laurent in years past. They'd either settled into village life and found other ways to make a living the rest of the year or earned their bread at the nearby monastery which used transient labor for its gardens and renovation efforts.

But during harvest time, while the pickers had work in the daytime and a place to lay their heads at night, it was up to Maggie to feed them. That involved full picnic tables of pizza, grilled chicken and roasted vegetables. The grill stayed hot all day and into the early evening. When the harvest was over, Maggie usually felt as if she'd finished a marathon. This would be the second year that they'd have Amèlie with them during the harvest. The child was still too young to be involved but Maggie knew it was an exciting time for her. Their own children had been an enormous help during harvest time—especially Luc and Jemmy—doing everything from hand harvesting to sorting and cutting.

This year, Maggie knew that Laurent was just hoping that Amèlie wouldn't fall down a well, annoy the pickers or get bitten by a snake. The child was unlike anything they were familiar with before. Maggie smiled at Jemmy's comment on the phone last week when they told him how Amèlie had tried to paint one of the dogs with mud.

"Bet you're reevaluating how much trouble I was as a kid *now*, aren't you?" he'd teased her.

The fact was, Jemmy had never been any trouble as a child or as a teen. Not like Mila, who had been extremely *difficile* during the teen years. But those times were far behind them now with Mila's cheerful weekly phone calls and boundless enthusiasm making both Maggie and Laurent miss her keenly every day.

There was nothing in Maggie's life she valued more than the years she had spent raising her children and the pleasure they gave her now as adults. Maggie found herself feeling sorry for Beth and Christie, both without children.

"Mila called," Laurent said as if reading Maggie's mind. "She said she'll be home for a couple of weeks this summer after all."

"Oh, that's wonderful!" Maggie said. "I was hoping she could manage it."

After graduating from the University of Florida with a degree in tourism and hospitality with a specialization in business management, Mila had taken a position as a tasting room manager for a winery in California. The plan had always been for her to come back to France to work with Laurent in the vineyard, but they understood that Mila wanted to see a bit of the world first.

"What about Luc?" Maggie asked. "Have you heard from him?"

Luc had married the year before in Napa and Maggie and Laurent—along with little Amèlie—had gone to California for the wedding. The plan at that time was for the couple to come to France for Thanksgiving, but Maggie held out hope that Luc —who had studied vineyard management in school—might come home for the harvest.

"No," Laurent said. "We will see them in November."

After that, they talked about what Jem was doing. He'd had a bit of trouble with the police a couple of years back in Atlanta where he lived and since then he'd been careful with alcohol. Jem was was a smart, capable young man who often made poor decisions. She couldn't help but think that having a steady girlfriend would be a good first step for him. And then she reminded herself that Zouzou's having a steady boyfriend wasn't necessarily the happy answer they were all hoping for.

After talking with Laurent, Maggie felt much more encouraged about the evening boat trip. Without saying so in words Laurent had reminded Maggie that she had a strong and loving family to fall back on. It didn't matter how tense or annoying or even exhausting the upcoming evening was. In the end, Maggie would be going home to a place where she was loved and respected.

I have a lot to be grateful for, she thought as she got up to get dressed for the evening.

And she didn't need four contrary school chums to remind her of it.

6

As Maggie waited at the base of the gangplank to board the boat, a gust of wind sent leaves swirling in tiny whirlwinds. The evening air was cool against her skin, which was a pleasant contrast to the warmth of the day. She pulled her pashmina tighter around her shoulders. She hadn't really needed it, but knew she'd be glad to have it once they were on the river.

They'd all dressed up a bit for the dinner cruise. Like Maggie the others seemed to have recovered from the cranky end of their day of sightseeing although Maggie was sure the day's conflicts were likely not forgotten. Monica wore a belted Halston jumpsuit and had traded her kitten heels for ballet flats for traversing over the lumpy cobblestone streets. She stood next to Beth making *sotto voce* comments while Christie and Lisa, both dressed in floral cotton dresses and flats, studied their cellphones.

Maggie couldn't help but think that despite their differences, the five of them shared at least one common thread: the air of unresolved issues among them.

Sophie was not included in the boat ride tonight, having

been tasked with babysitting Emily in the hotel room for the evening. Maggie found herself wondering why *Jason* wasn't babysitting the child. She wondered if he had plans of his own tonight.

Or was he babysitting *with* Sophie tonight?

Maggie turned her attention to the river. She had taken the Seine River cruise many times but not for years. She imagined it was still magical. How could it not be?

As the group made its way up the gang plank and onto the boat and then across the main deck toward the dining room, Maggie saw where softly lit, intimate tables had been set up. They found their table in a prime spot marked by a placard that read *Buckhead High School Reunion* and which afforded a panoramic view of the riverbank.

As she took her seat, Maggie gave a surreptitious glance at her wristwatch. It was eight o'clock. The cruise was scheduled to end by nine thirty. In spite of her good intentions, the duration seemed interminable.

She tried to focus on the menu, but her brain was buzzing with a myriad of uncomfortable thoughts—the most prominent one being the fact that she now remembered that three of the four women at the table had never been particularly kind to her in high school. She shook her head in rueful amazement.

How could I have forgotten that?

"Why can't I have a different wine?" Monica asked the server, a young woman who stood at the table with her order pad in hand.

"It is all fixed, Madame," the girl said.

"Well, I'll pay you to unfix it," Monica said.

"I am sorry, Madame. This is the only wine we have."

"That's just not true. I know it's not true. Where's the manager?"

"Oh, for heaven's sake, Monica," Beth said. "Let it go. Who cares? Get your special wine when we get off the boat."

"I know it doesn't matter what *you* drink," Monica snapped. "But some of us have standards."

Maggie turned away from the bickering in an effort to concentrate on the cityscape which was slowly transforming into an enchanting spectacle under the shroud of wispy darkness. The iconic landmark of the Eiffel Tower was cloaked in a fading glow, its lighting strategically placed to cast dramatic silhouettes that reflected off the gently rippling water, creating a mesmerizing tableau.

"I'll have hers if she doesn't want it," Lisa said, shoving her now empty champagne glass across the table at the hapless waitress.

Maggie realized that Lisa was well on her way to becoming drunk.

She must have started drinking in her hotel room.

"Maggie, tell this stupid girl that I want a different wine," Monica said. "She's being deliberately obtuse."

"This is a *price fixe* menu," Maggie said, giving the waitress an apologetic smile. "If you looked at it online, you'll have seen—"

"Why would I look at it online?" Monica interrupted, a pinched expression on her face.

"Well, that's what normal people do," Christie said, "when they want to know what they're buying."

"Oh, shut up, Christie," Monica said and then waved the waitress away with an irritated gesture. "*You* don't care what kind of swill you drink. Where's your Diet Coke?"

"Could you please shut up about the damn wine?" Beth said hotly. "Nobody cares, Monica."

"Well, excuse me for having a modicum of taste!" Monica said, folding her arms across her chest in a huff.

Maggie turned from the group again and this time she closed her eyes to better appreciate the cool breeze off the river. She wondered if she tried hard enough if she could pretend she was on the boat by herself. Monica got up and took the empty seat next to her.

"I feel like we haven't had a chance to catch up," she said.

Maggie was surprised and slightly discomfited by Monica's sudden attention.

"Well, you certainly have your hands full with little Emily. She's adorable, by the way."

"Honestly, she isn't half the work the babysitter is," Monica said.

"Really?"

"Oh, Sophie doesn't steal or anything like that, and she's usually on time but she's such a klutz."

"I haven't seen that," Maggie said.

"All day today I was afraid she was going to drive the stroller right into the river."

"Surely not," Maggie said with a frown.

"Well, I exaggerate a little," Monica admitted. "But she's got two left feet. Let me just say that. She tripped over a stuffed animal left on the floor in our living room last spring and broke her foot. Un-believable."

"She seems to be very loving with Emily."

"Yeah, she likes her. Although I would've thought that was the minimum requirement for a babysitter."

Maggie was astonished at how harsh Monica's assessment of Sophie was.

"It's just impossible to find childcare in Atlanta," Monica said. "No teenager wants to work. It's also why none of the restaurants in town can get wait staff."

"I would do anything to change places with you," Lisa gushed from the other side of Maggie. "I miss my grandbabies so much, you know?"

"Excuse me," Monica said, moving back to her own seat and leaving Maggie with Lisa. Maggie noted that Lisa's cheeks were flushed and her eyes held a glassy sheen as if she were fighting back tears. It was as if the alcohol had peeled back the layers of her inherent cheerfulness revealing a raw, broken Lisa underneath.

"My grandbabies are my whole world," Lisa said. "You don't have any yet, so you don't know. They're the whole reason why I'm here."

Again, Maggie noted that Lisa had forgotten that she did in fact have a grandchild—one she was actually raising.

"Here in Paris?" Christie asked sarcastically.

"No, here in my life," Lisa said earnestly, oblivious to Christie's sarcasm. "I really think I was born to have a hand in creating them. You don't have children, Christie, so you wouldn't know."

"At least I know when I'm about to get sloppy drunk," Christie said. "Does that count?"

"I'm sorry, Christie," Lisa said, her eyes wide with embarrassment as if she'd suddenly realized what she'd said. "I forgot..."

"What, Lisa?" Christie interrupted harshly, curling her lip. "*What* did you forget? Did you forget how to string two words together? Did you forget how to hold onto your husband? Or maybe you forgot how you got dumped at the Junior prom!"

"Stop it," Maggie said sharply to Christie. "She's only trying to enjoy the evening."

"Is she, Maggie?" Christie said, jerking her head around to regard Maggie. "Is *that* what she's doing? Wait a minute!" She snapped her fingers and pointed at Maggie with malicious glee dancing in her eyes.

"Now I remember how I know you! I slept with your brother Ben!"

7

The rest of the boat trip was an unalloyed trial. Maggie sat stiffly, fuming and waiting for the whole thing to be over while the waiters moved deftly around the room, serving their meals under the star-studded sky. The clinking of cutlery against fine china and the soft murmur of conversation from the other diners added to the strained ambiance.

Maggie was so annoyed with Christie at this point—and uninterested in pretending that she wasn't—that she didn't even see Paris unfolding around her in all its nighttime glittering glory. She looked at her watch so many times that when she caught Beth giving her a disapproving look Maggie simply glared back at her.

As dinner was mercifully coming to a close, Maggie noticed that Christie had been drinking steadily from the bottomless champagne bottle as evidenced by her voice becoming louder and louder until she finally knocked over a full glass of champagne. The waiters came over to sop up the mess, their faces showing no hint that this was anything out of the usual in their typical evening's work.

"This reminds me of junior prom!" Christie said as she leaned back in her chair, nearly toppling over in it.

"Christie, leave it," Monica said, her voice suddenly hard.

Maggie could see that Monica was drunk too but appeared in no hurry for the evening to end. It occurred to Maggie that Monica might be resisting the idea of going back to the hotel where she would once more be called upon to be the responsible adult to a teenager and small child.

And who knows? Maybe even to a wayward husband.

Monica's reluctance to return to the hotel was at least understandable, Maggie thought, if Jason really was spending all his time at his conference instead of helping out with the baby.

"Oh, come on, Lisa," Christie said, giving Lisa a rough nudge. "Don't be such a sore loser."

Maggie thought that an odd comment given the evening. She watched Christie's gestures become exaggerated as she swung her champagne glass recklessly in one hand. Beth and Monica exchanged uneasy glances.

"Man, I wish we'd had cellphones back then, you know?" Christie said. "That night—the look on your face, Lisa, when Jeff didn't show! Priceless!"

Beth laughed softly and Christie snapped her head around, grinning at her.

"See? Even Beth remembers! It was classic, wasn't it?"

Beth looked at Lisa and shrugged.

"Come on, Lisa. You have to admit it *was* classic."

"Thanks a lot, Beth," Lisa said bitterly, slurring her words.

"Oh, Lisa, don't be that way," Monica said. "They're just teasing you."

Maggie tried to remember what had happened at junior prom that year. She hadn't been able to go because her uncle had died the week before and she'd been in Jacksonville, Florida for the funeral. She looked at Lisa who was staring at the table setting in front of her, her hand tightly gripping a now empty glass of champagne.

"Oh, God, Maggie doesn't remember," Christie said, her eyes wide with excitement at the opportunity to relate it.

"Just shut up, Christie," Lisa said, her lips curling into a snarl.

"No way!" Christie said. She turned to Maggie. "So do you remember Jeff Dixson? He was one grade ahead of us? Super cute?"

Maggie saw Lisa's jaw working like she was biting the inside of her mouth. Her eyes seemed to drill into Christie as if she were watching a car accident that she was powerless to stop.

"Well, we talked Lisa into asking him to the prom," Christie said. "And you can't believe what *that* took! I thought she was going to have a nervous breakdown. Remember, Monica?"

Monica laughed, hugging herself as she shook with drunken mirth.

"Aw, come on, Lisa," Christie said. "I can't believe you're still so sensitive about it! It was just a prank!"

Lisa stood and glared at Christie.

"You are evil, Christie! Personified evil," she said.

"Oh, listen to the big words from the big author," Christie cackled.

"I wish to God you would die!" Lisa screamed, throwing her napkin at her. "I wish you would die a horrible death!"

With that, she wobbled away from the table. Maggie thought about getting up to follow her but decided the boat railings were tall enough to prevent any mishaps. She turned to look at Christie, who appeared unaffected by Lisa's reaction. She was finishing off her champagne and looking around the room to try to catch the eye of one of their servers. Maggie realized that Christie had lost interest in telling the story. She assumed it wasn't as amusing without the victim there to hear it.

That night after they'd finally docked and made their way back to the hotel, only Monica bothered saying goodnight. Everyone else just trudged into the hotel lobby and headed to the elevator and their rooms. Maggie took the stairs. Twenty minutes later, she climbed into bed exhausted and drained. Whatever she'd imagined she'd get out of this weekend had not happened on any level. Worse, it was reminding her of some latent memories that she'd clearly buried about high school. And it wasn't improving her life to be reliving them now.

Before coming to Paris this weekend Maggie had hoped that seeing these four again might serve as a catalyst to rediscover parts of herself that she had forgotten or put aside. She'd even envisioned this time as possibly helping to remind her of those parts of her personality she had suppressed. Perhaps even using her schoolgirl passions as a way to realize new desires and goals.

But that had been folly. It was true that she and these women had walked away from each other thirty plus years ago and taken drastically different paths. But more than that, it turned out that she'd never been close to them.

How had she not remembered that?

8

The next morning, Maggie was up and dressed and packed. She was already rehearsing what she was going to say to the others at breakfast about why she was leaving early. She considered lying and saying that Laurent had called with a minor emergency at home but in the end she thought that was more effort than she needed to expend. She didn't want to insult anyone, but she also didn't think her absence from the group would matter to them either. Not to anyone except possibly Lisa.

Just as she was about to open her room door, she noticed an envelope lying on the floor where someone had obviously slipped it under her door. She bent to pick it up and saw it was addressed in an elaborate hand with the large letter *M* complete with curly-cues and scrolls.

Maggie was about to open it when she heard a noise in the hallway., She tucked the envelope in her purse, stepped out into the hall and shut the door behind her, the click of the lock echoing in the silent corridor. Immediately, she saw Beth standing outside Christie's room door, which was beside Maggie's. Beth was rapping sharply against the polished wood door with an urgency that instantly set Maggie's nerves on edge.

"Christie?" Beth called through the door. "If you're not ready, I'm not waiting for you."

When Maggie approached, Beth turned to her, a grimace of annoyance on her face.

"Can you believe this?" Beth said. "Does she think I'm her personal turn-down service?"

"Why are you bothering?" Maggie asked. "So she misses breakfast. So what?"

Beth gave her a scathing look.

"Because she *asked* me to, last night," Beth said. "And because that's what friends do."

I guess friends who were too drunk to set their alarms on their cellphones.

Maggie turned toward the elevators.

"Our rooms have adjoining doors," Beth called after her. "I'm going to go back to my room to see if her side is locked."

There was something in the way Beth said it—even the fact *that* she said it, that made Maggie think she wanted her to accompany her.

"Do you want me to come?" Maggie asked.

"Would you mind?" Beth said. "In case she needs help or something?"

Maggie was mildly surprised. Beth hadn't addressed two words to her all weekend. It was for that reason alone that she turned and joined Beth in walking down the hall toward her room.

"It just bugs me when things don't go the way they're supposed to," Beth said. "I mean if you ask someone for a favor, be there when you say you will."

It occurred to Maggie that perhaps this little kindness toward Beth might win her a round of forgiveness after she told everyone she was leaving, at least from Beth. And then she found herself wondering why she cared. Beth used her key card to enter her room and then strode past the bed to the connecting room door. Maggie looked around Beth's room and wasn't surprised to see that the place looked as if the maids had already come through. The bed was made, not an item was visible on top of the desk, even Beth's shoes were tucked away in the closet.

Beth knocked on the adjoining door.

"Christie? This is your wakeup call! So wake up!"

Beth twisted the door handle and pulled it open. Christie's room was filled with a thick, oppressive heat as Beth entered with Maggie right behind her. In spite of herself, Maggie felt a chill run down her spine. It felt as if the air itself was holding its breath, waiting for something to happen. There was a slight odor to the air that prompted an irrational compulsion in Maggie to open a window. Her eye was drawn away from the bed where Christie lay to a slight movement under the desk. Maggie suddenly saw a small mouse lying on its side. It had a tiny notch out of its tail. She made a mental note to mention it to the hotel staff.

Beth walked over to the bed. Christie was dressed in panties and a t-shirt and was partially under the covers. Her hair spread out across the pillow. Beth stood beside the bed without touching Christie.

"Christie, what is your problem?" Beth said with annoyance and then immediately, she sucked in a gasp. "Christie?"

Maggie turned to look at Christie who was lying on her back, her mouth open. Suddenly, Beth grabbed Christie's hand and then dropped it, backing up and knocking into Maggie.

"Call somebody!" Beth shrieked, turning to Maggie, the veins standing out in her neck and her face bone white. She pointed toward her bedroom. "Hurry! I think she's dead!"

9

As the crackle of police radios filled the air, the once serene hotel lobby was now the hectic scene of a confusing frenzy. The arrival of the police marked the onset of the grim reality for Maggie and the other three women, turning the morning's shocking incident into a tangible nightmare.

She sat in the lobby with Beth, Monica, Lisa and Jason along with Sophie and the baby in her stroller. The police had requested they sit apart and not speak. Maggie wasn't sure how the rest of them had interpreted those instructions, but she knew them to be what they were: a warning that at least for now they were considered suspects.

From where she sat in her corner of the hotel lobby, her body numb with shock, the plush velvet upholstery beneath her feeling oddly unreal. It was as if she were stuck in a twisted dream. The opulent surroundings of the lobby, from the gleaming marble floors to the soft glow of the crystal chandeliers, seemed to mock her with their tranquility.

This was a place for cocktails and dressing up before a night on the town. Not death.

The image of Christie lying lifeless in her bed was seared into Maggie's brain. She had seen sudden death before but there was something about this image that felt particularly traumatic. Someone Maggie had known, spent time with, and someone alive and vital, had been reduced to a cold, lifeless form. The shock of it felt like a tidal wave that threatened to swallow her whole.

As she sat there with the other women, a sense of dread crept over Maggie. She could see they too were all in a state of shock, their faces pale and their eyes wide with incomprehension. But underlying that fear was an undercurrent of something else. Suspicion.

Maggie's mind raced with questions. Did Christie die naturally? Had she had a hidden medical issue? How could someone be so alive one minute and then the next...?

The wait for the police interviews to start was agonizing. Each ticking second seemed to stretch into an eternity. Maggie hugged herself in an attempt to ward off the invasive dread that was slowly seeping into her bones.

A detective had arrived minutes after the ambulance and the uniformed police. He was the one—Detective Bernard Benoit—who'd told them all to stay in the lobby and not talk to each other. He appeared to be in his late fifties, Maggie decided, a seasoned officer with a stern demeanor and sharp, observant eyes.

After moving them to the lobby and closing the hotel, Benoit and his team had gone upstairs to Christie's room. In the meantime, a team of forensic experts showed up—dressed in white jumpsuits and booties carrying the forensic tools of their profession. Maggie was surprised to see them. She knew their job would be collecting evidence, photographing the bedroom from every angle, and marking out the positions of key items.

Were they treating it as a crime scene?

Maggie glanced around the lobby. Jason, his face unreadable, was intently reading something on his phone. Lisa sat stunned and clearly hungover, wearing only a robe and sweatpants and slippers. She had obviously not been intending to meet for breakfast. Sophie held the baby on her lap, jostling and hugging her and looking around in complete bewilderment.

Beth alternately wept into her hands and stared unseeing into space. Monica's face was bleached white with shock, making the black eye she sported even more noticeable.

"What happened to your eye?" Maggie called to her from across the room.

Monica jerked her head up as if she'd been slapped. She lifted a hand to touch her face but stopped herself.

"No talking, please," said a female police officer who stood in the lobby, nearly invisible behind a potted fern.

As Maggie stared at Monica's black eye, she remembered that while Christie's room connected with Beth's room on one side, it connected to Monica and Jason's on the other.

A heavy tension hung over them all as they waited to be told how Christie died and to tell their version of what they knew about it. Every time Maggie closed her eyes, she saw Christie lying on the bed, immobile and lifeless. She felt Beth's hysteria punch into her over and over again as Beth had frantically tried to get a pulse from Christie. Maggie heard and reheard the shrill panic in Beth's voice as she screamed for Maggie to call for help.

Finally, Detective Benoit and his sergeant came downstairs and entered the lobby. Jason was the first one on his feet, but the detective held up a hand indicating this would be done his way and in his own time. Jason returned to his seat. Maggie seemed to remember he hadn't been particularly forceful back in high school either.

After that, one by one, each of the women were called into an empty room off the lobby to provide their statements. When

Maggie saw Lisa go in, she found herself wondering if she would tell how she'd stomped off the boat last night not speaking to anyone—particularly Christie. She wondered if Lisa would mention the fact that she had screamed at Christie that she wished she would die.

Maggie wondered if anyone else would mention it.

10

The room the young policewoman led Maggie to when it was her turn was a stark contrast to the opulence of the lobby. It served as a sobering reminder of the grim business at hand. The room was small and windowless, its walls painted a sterile white that seemed to magnify the harsh glare from the fluorescent lights overhead. A long wooden table dominated the narrow space, its surface scarred with the ghosts of countless meetings and coffee cup rings. On one side of the table were two metal chairs, as unyielding and cold as the situation Maggie now felt herself in.

She was the last person to have her statement taken. Monica and Beth had gone before her after Lisa. All three had left the room in tears. As each woman had been led into the room, the door would close with a soft, yet final, thud, behind them, a disconcerting reminder to Maggie of their isolation. Now that it was her turn, Maggie noticed that the air in the room was heavy and still, and the only sounds were the low hum of the overhead lights.

The policewoman who'd led her into the room, indicated a chair opposite where Detective Benoit sat, with the table between them. Maggie had been formally questioned by the police before but something about this situation made her anxious in a way that was different from her other encounters with the law. The detective's sharp blue eyes were all but hidden under a pair of bushy brows. Even so, Maggie felt as though his gaze was analyzing her every facial expression.

Detective Benoit opened to a new section in his notepad and asked her name.

"Margaret Dernier," Maggie said.

She tried to keep her voice even, though her heart was pounding in her chest. He frowned at a piece of paper in front of him.

"Try again," he said.

Maggie remembered that Monica had booked the rooms and had likely put Maggie's name down as Newberry, not her married name.

"Maggie Newberry," she said.

"And you are in room fifty-eight?"

"Yes."

He wrote something down and then tapped a pen against his notebook before looking up at her. Maggie knew her own room was one of the rooms near Christie's. If Benoit was looking at Christie's death as suspicious, surely, she would be down the list from the two rooms that flanked the victim's?

"Was she murdered?" Maggie asked.

His eyes narrowed at her.

"Why do you ask that?"

"Because the police don't normally take formal statements from witnesses if it's a natural death or an accident."

"Is that what you think you know?"

His mouth tweaked as if he was thinking of smiling. Maggie knew it would not be a nice smile.

"That's what I assume," she said. "My father died in his bed like Christie and the police didn't hold us all hostage while they went through a checklist of who was where when."

The detective tilted his head as if suddenly more interested in Maggie and she silently cursed herself for talking too much.

"I just want to know if Christie was murdered," Maggie said. "Or if …if she did it to herself."

"Was your friend suicidal?"

"I didn't think so."

He nodded gravely, never taking his eyes off Maggie.

"Tell me about the boat ride," he said.

Maggie knew that Lisa, Beth and Monica had already told him about the boat ride, and she was aware that if she inadvertently left something out that they had thought important to relay, it would look suspicious for her.

"We went on the Bateaux Parisiennes Seine River cruise," she said. "The tour was two and a half hours long."

"I'm told people drank too much," he commented. "The victim?"

"Yes. I think Christie was pretty drunk."

"But not you?"

"I'm not in the habit of drinking to excess."

"How moderate of you."

Maggie wasn't sure if that was a sarcastic comment. The detective's face gave away nothing.

"I'm a vintner's wife," she said and was sorry she offered that up. She'd just wanted to assure him that she was responsible around alcohol.

"Where?" he asked.

"Provence."

He ripped a piece of paper out of his notebook and slid it and a pencil across the table to her.

"Name of vineyard and address, please."

Maggie wrote down *Domaine St-Buvard* but found herself getting flustered. The last thing she wanted to do was make

Laurent a part of what was happening here. Because of his past, things got quickly complicated when Laurent was involved. What did Christie's death have to do with where she came from? How did a vineyard eight hundred kilometers from Montmartre matter in Christie's death?

She pushed the piece of paper back at him. He studied what she had written.

"What time did you find the body?" he asked.

"About eight o'clock. I was on my way to breakfast."

"How is it you entered the victim's bedroom?"

Maggie took in a long breath.

"I passed Beth Robinson in the hall as she was knocking on Christie's door. Christie wasn't answering so Beth thought she should go in through the connecting door from her room to see why."

"Why did you accompany her?"

"She asked me to."

Maggie thought for a moment. That wasn't true. Technically, Beth didn't ask her. She'd merely acted as if she wanted Maggie's company.

"When you saw the body, did you touch it?" the detective asked.

"No. I immediately called the hotel medical service."

"Why did you not use your cellphone?"

"I didn't want to use the emergency number for all of Paris. I thought calling from the hotel phone would be more expedient for getting someone to respond immediately."

"Why did you not use the landline in the victim's room?"

Maggie frowned as she thought back to what she'd been thinking at the time.

"I...I don't know. I don't think I saw one there."

She felt a sudden wave of exhaustion sweep over her. Everything had happened so fast that she really hadn't had time to process most of it. She hadn't taken a moment to register that

Christie was dead and that she and Beth had been the ones to find her body.

But what she did know from past experience was that the ones who found the body are always right at the top of the investigator's list of likely suspects.

She wondered how Beth had held up when Benoit spoke to her. The sight of Beth leaving this room in tears a few minutes earlier had done nothing to clarify to Maggie that the truth had been useful to the detective in any way. Maggie found herself remembering Beth standing with the detective when he first showed up on the scene. She'd stood with her face in her hands, completely shaken.

After Maggie had dashed into the adjoining bedroom to call the concierge medical staff and then the police, Beth had come to sit next to her on the bed, her face pale with shock, her hands shaking.

She kept saying over and over again as if dazed, "I can't believe it. I can't believe she's dead."

That was the image Maggie had in her head now as the detective stared at her from across the table, not as one who was interested in hearing information to help him determine what happened—but rather as one who was looking for someone to blame.

11

L ater that afternoon, Maggie, Monica, Beth and Lisa met at a café down the street from the hotel. Monica had sent Jason, Sophie and the baby to a nearby park. The café the women had found was a small, cozy place tucked away in a side street of Montmartre. Twinkling fairy lights were strung around the edges of the café's terrace awning, giving the place a warm, inviting glow amidst the cool, grey wash of the rainy day. It was exactly what Maggie needed after the terrible start to this day.

As they stepped inside, they were immediately greeted by the comforting aroma of roasting coffee beans and of freshly baked pastries. The interior was a hodgepodge of mismatched wooden tables and chairs, each bearing its own story in classic *brasserie* style. A stone fireplace crackled at one end of the room, lit even in late summer, its warmth a solace against the chill of the rain-soaked streets.

As the women claimed a corner table, Maggie was keenly aware of a palpable sense of disquiet in the air. Looking at her friends' faces, she saw the signs of shock and fear, their eyes wide, each lost in her own whirlpool of thoughts, the words of the detectives no doubt still ringing in their ears.

They ordered coffee and waited for the waiter to leave before speaking.

"They think one of us killed her," Lisa said.

"Don't be ridiculous," Monica said, her gaze fixed on a point outside the window, her face ashen under the shocking bruise around her eye. "She must have had a heart condition. The autopsy will show that."

"Tell me again how you got the shiner," Maggie asked.

"How dare you," Monica said, glaring at her and blinking back tears.

"That's not appropriate, Maggie," Lisa said in an admonishing tone.

"I'm sure the detective asked her the same question," Maggie said.

"And I'll tell you what I told him," Monica said in a raised voice. "I walked into the bathroom door this morning."

The waiter returned with their coffees and disappeared again. Maggie absently added sugar to her cup and stirred her coffee, the spoon clinking against the porcelain cup like a metronome marking the passing seconds.

Black eye or not, the fact was that Lisa was right. The cops did act as if Christie's death was not an accident or self-harm. And that meant they thought that someone around this table was not just a shocked and frightened woman, but a murderer.

"She always wanted attention," Beth said suddenly.

"Beth!" Lisa said. "You shouldn't speak ill of the dead."

"Why not? *She* would if the positions were reversed," Beth said. "You know she would."

Maggie noted that unlike the rest of them, Beth had ordered a whiskey with her coffee. After a couple of quick sips, the alcohol had already put some color in her cheeks. She now looked almost recovered from her earlier trauma.

The others seemed to digest Beth's comments for a moment. And then, as if a dam—long straining and fragile—finally broke and with it, the last particle of reserve among them.

"I don't know if you remember her that well back in school," Lisa said to Maggie, "but Christie was definitely the school slut."

Maggie started in surprise.

"I don't remember that," she said, although she reminded herself that Christie had bragged last night about sleeping with Maggie's brother.

She quickly dismissed the uncharitable thought. Christie might have slept with Ben, or she might not have, but telling Maggie about it would have been for no other reason than to throw it in her face. That wasn't being a slut. That was sociopathic.

"Well, you weren't really in our crowd," Monica said. "Not properly. We all knew about it. I heard she was sleeping with Mr. Beavers, the math teacher."

"I'm not sure what any of that has to do with her death," Maggie said.

"I'm just saying," Beth said with a shrug. "She wasn't a nice person."

"Being a slut doesn't mean she wasn't nice," Lisa said. "In fact, it means she was too nice."

She giggled.

"They asked me if I'd spoken to her last night after the boat trip," Beth said.

"They asked me that, too," Monica said.

Lisa and Maggie both nodded to indicate they'd been asked as well.

"But I hadn't," Beth said. "I mean, aside from telling her I'd knock on her door this morning, I was ready to see the back of her."

"Ditto," Lisa said.

Maggie glanced at her. She was tempted to ask if anyone had mentioned Lisa's outburst about wanting to see Christie dead but didn't have the nerve. Not at the moment any way. She couldn't detect any rancor in Lisa's face this morning. But maybe that was understandable. An uncomfortable thought came to mind then where Maggie was reminded that Lisa had done some acting during the years she'd lived in New York.

Monica signaled to the waiter and then turned to Maggie.

"Can you ask him to bring menus?"

Maggie sighed. This was Montmartre. Although he probably wasn't *fluent* in English, she wondered if Monica knew that *menu* was probably one of the few words he'd definitely recognize. When he came to the table, Maggie asked for four menus and another round of everything they were drinking.

"Did the cops ask you not to leave town?" Monica asked her.

Maggie nodded.

"They asked me not to leave the country!" Lisa said in an indignant tone.

"Well, same difference really," Maggie said to her. "Did they take your passports?" She looked around the room and all three women nodded unhappily.

"It's just a formality," Maggie said. "Until they can rule us out."

"I have things to do back home," Monica said. "I have about six different committees I chair, and I can't just blow off a week hanging around Paris doing nothing!"

Maggie found herself wondering if Monica had ever even liked Christie. She didn't seem very sad about her death, just annoyed at the inconvenience Christie's death was causing her. She found herself wondering why Monica had even invited Christie on this trip. After the waiter returned with menus, they each ordered their food, had Maggie relay the information to the waiter, and then Monica and Beth excused themselves to find the toilet. As soon as they left the table, Lisa leaned over to Maggie to whisper conspiratorially.

"Did you ever hear the rumors about Christie's senior year?"

Maggie shook her head.

"It seems she went to Switzerland to quote practice her skiing, unquote," Lisa said, "and she didn't come back until everyone had graduated. That's a lot of ski lessons—in May!"

"Are you saying she was pregnant?" Maggie asked.

"Well, I'm sure Monica probably knows the details, but yeah, that's pretty much what everyone figured."

Maggie wasn't sure what this information meant by itself. Christie had been the consummate career woman and unlike Beth had never mentioned within Maggie's hearing any thoughts of being sorry she hadn't had children. It did tell her a little more about Christie and what she must have been going through during that last year of high school, however.

As far as Maggie could make out, Christie had grown into a hard and ruthless woman. But honestly, she had seen the bones of that woman forming years before.

12

Later, after they returned to the hotel—a return which was prompted by a group text message from the Paris detective—they found the lobby still transformed from its usual welcoming ambiance. Several uniformed officers were scattered across the room, their stern expressions and assertive postures a stark contrast to the hotel's usual clientele —none of whom were in evidence at the moment.

Detective Benoit stood in the center of the lobby, flipping through his little notebook, his brow furrowed in concentration while his sergeant, also in plain clothes, was in quiet conversation with the hotel manager, who looked visibly upset.

As the four women entered the hotel, the activity in the lobby seemed to pause momentarily, with all eyes turning towards them. The officers' gazes were not unkind, but they held a degree of scrutiny that made Maggie feel like an intruder in a place that had, until that morning, felt like a sanctuary.

Benoit addressed them without preamble, telling them that Monica and Beth would need to book different rooms as theirs were now connected to a crime scene. Maggie took a sharp intake of breath at that. It left no doubt that he was viewing

Christie's death as suspicious. He then reiterated again that none of them were to leave Paris until released by him personally.

"I appreciate your cooperation while we work to find out the full details of the death of your countrywoman," he said to them.

It was a stilted speech and all the more chilling because of it, Maggie thought. While she appreciated his effort at delivering it in English, it was still an order with an undercurrent of threat in it.

The alcohol Beth had consumed at lunch had apparently made her less meek such that after Benoit's speech, she turned and stomped unsteadily over to the reception desk to book her new room.

"What about our things?" Monica asked the detective in bewilderment. "Our clothes?"

"I am sorry, Madame. They have all been taken for forensic analysis."

"This is unbelievable!" she said angrily. "I'm calling the American embassy. This is appalling treatment of a...of an ally!"

Benoit simply nodded in acceptance of her frustration, glanced meaningfully at Maggie, and then turned to leave with his entourage of officers.

"I guess we're the lucky ones," Lisa said as Monica pulled out her phone before hurrying to the reception desk to find a new room.

"Looks like it," Maggie said.

As the two of them made their way toward the elevator to go back to their room, Lisa sucked in a quick breath as if she'd just remembered something.

"Did you hear about Christie's inheritance?" she asked.

Maggie frowned.

"What are you talking about?"

"I told the cops about it," she said. "It seems Christie told Monica that some spinster aunt of hers had left her a million dollars."

"No, I didn't know," Maggie said. "I'm not sure it means anything though."

"Maybe not, but it's still a lot of money. Worth killing over for sure."

"Did the detective appear interested when you told him?"

Lisa laughed.

"I think I could've confessed to killing her myself and he would still have just jotted in his little notebook without a change of expression."

"Christie didn't have kids," Maggie said. "And no siblings or parents. Who would be in line to inherit that money?"

"I have no idea. I just always hear on television crime shows that you should follow the money. And a million dollars is a lot of money."

As soon as she was back in her room, Maggie called Laurent. She'd already spoken briefly to him on the way to the cafe after her interrogation with Detective Benoit to tell him what had happened. At that time, he'd strongly suggested that he come to Paris and Maggie had talked him out of it.

"I'm fine," she said now as she kicked off her shoes and settled on her bed. "Besides, as soon as the police say I can leave, I'll be on the next train south. And you know how upset Amèlie gets when one or both of us is gone."

Amèlie was the five-year-old daughter of a woman who'd been murdered two years ago—a woman who it had only recently transpired was Laurent's daughter, a child he'd never known about and now would never know. Maggie and Laurent had adopted Amèlie—Laurent's biological granddaughter—and were raising her at Domaine St-Buvard where they'd raised their three other children. But Amèlie was an angry and mulish child. She had lived the first three years of her life in squalor and poverty—and physical abuse. It was taking time for Amèlie to feel loved and safe, but Maggie and Laurent were determined that she would have that if nothing else.

"And now what?" Laurent said. "Is it murder?"

"It's leaning that way," Maggie said. "None of us are allowed to leave the city."

"I will make a phone call."

That surprised Maggie. Not that he didn't know a wide range of people. As the head vintner in Provence for many years, of course he did. But with his history—largely criminal —that had stretched from St-Tropez to the Italian border, Maggie knew of no contacts of his within the police that he still had—unless they were crooked.

"That's not necessary," Maggie said. "I didn't kill her. The facts will speak for themselves, and I'll be on my way home in a few days."

Just then Maggie received a text from Zouzou.

<need to see u urgently. Can meet 2nite?>

"He is an old friend," Laurent said. "Retired from the Paris police department. His name is Antoine Berger. At the very least he will be able to tell you what the police are thinking."

Maggie had to admit that could be helpful. She texted Zouzou back that she would meet her at Café Nemo on rue Houdon at six o'clock.

"I'd like to know what he knows about Detective Benoit," she said to Laurent. "If he's trustworthy or bent."

"I will ask him. Once I find the number, I will text it to you."

Maggie smiled when she heard that. Laurent was famously anti-tech and she tried to remember a single time he'd actually sent a text message to her.

"Fine," she said, wishing irrationally that Laurent *would* come to Paris after all. "But I'm sure I won't need it."

———

13

Café Nemo was tucked away down a side street off the heart of Montmartre leaning toward Pigalle. When Maggie arrived at the café at twilight, she shook the rain off her umbrella, and was pleased to see the interior of the little restaurant was bathed in a soft, golden light, from strategically placed lanterns. Patrons huddled outside on the terrace, their laughter and conversation melding with the rhythmic drumming of the rain on the café's striped awning overhead. Despite the weather, or perhaps because of it, the café buzzed with a cozy energy.

Maggie quickly spotted Zouzou hunched over a small corner table in the back of the café. As soon as she saw her, Maggie's stomach tensed. Gone was the happy, effervescent girl she'd had dinner with just two nights ago. When Zouzou lifted her eyes to greet Maggie, she immediately burst into tears.

"Darling girl!" Maggie said, hurrying to the table. "Whatever has happened?"

Zouzou struggled to control her tears and wiped her eyes with her fingers as she caught her breath.

"It's nothing," Zouzou said. "I don't know what's the matter with me."

"Hormones," Maggie said, patting her arm. "You need a big cup of tea."

"Ugh," Zouzou said.

When the waiter came, Maggie ordered a glass of wine for herself and a cup of English Breakfast tea for Zouzou along with a plate of shortbread cookies. As soon as he left, Maggie leaned over and gave Zouzou's arm a reassuring squeeze.

"Now tell me," she said. "What's going on?"

"It's nothing," Zouzou said again. "You're probably right. My mood is all up and down these days. I don't know whether to laugh or cry."

Maggie studied her for a moment and then waited for the waiter to bring their drinks before speaking.

"You know, darling, maybe now would be a good time for a visit back home."

"I can't," Zouzou said. "This is the restaurant's busy time. I'm lucky to get a night off."

Maggie hesitated and considered her words carefully. She wanted to tell Zouzou that a young woman on her own whose life was about to change as drastically as Zouzou's needed her mother. But she stopped herself from saying that. That might be the thing that would make Zouzou dig in her heels. Besides, the fact that Zouzou—who was usually fairly close to Grace— didn't know she needed her mother right now seemed to Maggie to be an astonishing example of self-deception.

"Have you told your mother?" Maggie asked. "About the baby?"

"No. She hasn't even met Pierre yet. I want to do this in the proper order."

Too late for that.

"Sure," Maggie said. "Only I wouldn't wait too long."

In Maggie's mind, time was of the essence. She could only

imagine how hurt and worried Grace was going to be when she heard the news, especially late and second-hand.

"What does Pierre think?" Maggie asked. "Is he excited about the baby?"

"Of course he's excited. What are you suggesting?" Zouzou crossed her arms, color rising in her cheeks.

Maggie took a beat. The only sound was the soft clink of spoons against china and the sound of the rain outside.

"Darling, I'm not suggesting anything," she said. "It's just that this has happened very soon in your relationship. In fact, just when you are both getting to know each—"

Zouzou burst into tears again, shocking Maggie into silence.

"What is it, darling?" Maggie asked, suddenly sure this was not just hormones.

"He...he isn't answering my texts," Zouzou said, sobbing into her hands now.

Maggie's heart sank. Zouzou's words hung in the air between them, each one a painful barb sinking into Maggie's skin. She reached over and took Zouzou's trembling hands and held them in her own.

"Dear girl," she said, "I'm sure there's a good explanation for that."

Zouzou snatched her hands away and glared at her through her tears.

"He hasn't left me!" she said. "Something has happened."

"Of course. I'm sure that must be it," Maggie said, watching her with concern.

"Why are you looking at me like that?" Zouzou asked petulantly. "You think he took off because of the baby? That's not it! He found out I was pregnant yesterday, but he was *happy* about it! I knew I should never have confided in you!"

Maggie ignored the girl's hostility. She gave Zouzou a moment to collect herself. The droplets against the window near their table traced rivulets down the large glass window, distorting the view of the street outside.

"When did you last hear from him?" Maggie asked.

"Last night," Zouzou said. "He said he needed to get some things from his apartment and that he'd stay there for the night."

"Did you call his office?"

Zouzou nodded. "They said he called in with a family emergency."

Maggie frowned. To leave for a family emergency without telling your pregnant girlfriend was just not believable. Unless of course he was dumping said pregnant girlfriend.

"This isn't like him," Zouzou said, her voice cracking. "Something has happened." She sagged back into her chair.

After that, the rest of the evening was a refrain of Zouzou's worries and tears juxtaposed with Maggie's attempts to reassure her. There was little that Maggie could tell her that Zouzou hadn't already thought of, beyond going to Pierre's apartment in the morning which Zouzou was already planning on doing.

"I'm sure there's a perfectly logical explanation," Maggie said to her as she paid the bill and they stood up from the table to hug.

"Hang in there," Maggie said. "And let me know what you find out, okay?"

"I will, Aunt Maggie. I'm sorry if I was contentious."

"Don't be silly. You have every right to be upset."

Maggie smiled at her and gave her arm a final squeeze before they parted ways in front of the cafe. As Zouzou hurried down the street, Maggie couldn't help but think that she wasn't telling her everything. For a moment she considered that that might actually be a blessing.

After all, what I don't know, I can't tell Grace.

As she walked back to the hotel, her mind churned with

anxiety and warring emotions about Zouzou and her missing baby daddy as well as with thoughts about Christie and Maggie's burgeoning fear that she'd been murdered by one of the other women in the group, Maggie found herself glad at least that she hadn't needed to share with Zouzou what was happening at the hotel. The girl had enough on her plate at the moment.

Just as the hotel came into view, Maggie felt her phone vibrate in her jacket pocket. She looked at the screen but didn't recognize the number.

"Hello?" she said.

"Madame Dernier? This is Detective Benoit of the Paris Homicide Montmartre Division."

Maggie caught her breath and felt her anxiety spike. She stopped walking as if unable to move and speak to the detective at the same time.

"Yes, Detective," she said. "How can I help you?"

"I will need to see you again," he said, his voice formal and cold. "Shall we say eight o'clock tomorrow morning at the downtown station?"

When Maggie hesitated, he continued.

"Do you need directions?"

"No," she said. "No, I can find it."

After hanging up, Maggie stood for a moment longer, her skin vibrating ominously as the man's formal tones echoed in her brain.

14

The Paris police station on rue Louis Blanc in Montmartre was an imposing edifice of stone and glass, standing in stark contrast to the typically iconic architecture everywhere else in Montmartre. Maggie hesitated only briefly on its threshold before entering. Inside, the station was a whirlwind of activity. The air was heavy with the scent of strong coffee. After giving her name to the receiving desk sergeant, she sat in the waiting room, her heart thumping in her chest like a drum, her palms growing steadily clammier as her apprehension mounted.

Eventually, a young, uniformed policewoman appeared and led her to a small, austere room with a single bulb hanging from the ceiling over a metal table and two chairs. Maggie wasn't surprised to find the room devoid of any warmth since that was largely its purpose. As she took the seat indicated, she clenched and unclenched her hands in her lap.

Despite her nervousness, Maggie was well aware of how important it was to keep her composure. She reminded herself that she had done nothing wrong, had simply been a part of the unfortunate incident in which Christie's body was found.

She'd actually been in a few situations like this in the past and she knew that it was a singular situation—when someone found a body—and with it came all kinds of compromising ramifications. She took a deep breath in an attempt to steady her nerves.

Detective Benoit entered the room suddenly. Today he wore a crisp white shirt tucked into tailored trousers, with a dark blazer which added to his authoritative presence. His hair was meticulously combed back, revealing his stern, hawk-like eyes. Despite his somewhat handsome features, there was that same impermeable wall of professional detachment that Maggie had seen in him back at the hotel—one that bordered on unfriendly.

He seated himself across from Maggie at the table, flipping through a case file in front of him before setting down his notepad, a couple of sharp pencils, and a small tape recorder on the table. His face was unreadable. Maggie cleared her throat.

"I did give my statement to you yesterday," she said. "Can you tell me why you need to see me again?"

He glanced at her and closed the file in front of him.

"How well did you know Christine McCoy?" he asked.

"We hadn't been in touch in a few years. I knew her in school."

"You were good friends?"

Maggie had known this question was coming. She'd debated lying but, in her experience, if the truth could be given it was usually better to go that route. Even if the truth caused more questions in the end.

"I wouldn't say good friends," she said.

"But good enough that you agreed to meet up in Paris?"

"I live only three and a half hours away by train. It seemed like a good excuse for a holiday. Can I ask you why you seem to be treating this as a suspicious death?"

"You are married to a Laurent Dernier?" he asked, not looking at her.

The question surprised Maggie but she realized it shouldn't have.

"I am," she said slowly. "But I'm not sure how that's relevant."

But of course it was relevant. Laurent had been a con artist in his younger days always staying just out of reach of an arrest. He'd quit the business before that could happen, but he'd been well known on the Côte d'Azur in his time. Maggie was mildly surprised to learn he might have made a name for himself stretching all the way to Paris. But naturally with today's technology, nothing was purely regional anymore.

The detective's eyes drilled her, and she thought she saw the faint flicker of a smile on his lips before it was extinguished.

"Did all of you and your friends get along?" he asked.

"Are you asking me if one of us could have killed Christie?"

He looked at her for the first time and raised an eyebrow as if in answer to her question.

"We are all old friends, Detective Benoit," she said. "We went to school together."

"Were you aware that Madame McCoy recently came into money?"

"How would that be relevant to me? None of us were related to her."

"Inheritance is not the only way money may be transferred," he said. "Blackmail is another option."

As soon as he said the word, Maggie felt perspiration pop out on her brow. She knew he was fishing. But she also knew he knew more about Christie and her past than she did. And she knew enough about how some detectives work to know that laying traps in order to increase case clearance rates was not unheard of.

"I have no idea what you mean by that," she said, willing her voice not to wobble.

"What do you know about Monica Williams?"

"Monica is an old school friend," Maggie said. "I don't know much about her life today."

"But you knew enough to meet with her for the weekend?"

"As I said, I only live a few hours away. She suggested a mini-reunion in Paris. It sounded like fun."

"Why did you go into the other bedroom to call for an ambulance?"

"I did it without thinking. There was no particular reason. Can I assume by all these questions that Christie died under suspicious circumstances?"

He picked up his note pad and pencils, none of which he'd used, and stood up.

"I don't have to remind you not to leave the country," he said, "as you are a resident of France. But I will ask you not to leave Paris."

"For how long?" Maggie asked. "I have a family I need to get back to."

"Hopefully not long, Madame Dernier," he said, nodding to the uniformed officer standing in the room.

The detective exited and the other policeman motioned for Maggie to follow him. He led her down the hall and back through the waiting room. As soon as she stepped outside, her breathing began to slow a bit. When she turned to glance behind her, she was discomfited to see that Benoit stood in the large picture window of the station's waiting room, watching her.

15

K nowing that she needed some time to process what had just happened, Maggie checked her phone for the nearest city park and plotted a pedestrian walking route to the Jardin Partage de la Butte Bergeyre. From the police station it was only a three-block walk. It was a bright day, not raining for a change, with the sun casting long, dappled shadows through the leaves of the trees.

As she entered the park's entrance, she immediately began to feel a release of tension in her shoulders. She strolled down a long looping gravel path, stopping by a small pond to watch the ducks glide across the water, their calm movements helping to bring a sense of peace to her mind.

All of her takeaways from her conversation with Detective Benoit were uncomfortable to say the least. She hated that Laurent was even peripherally involved in what was happening. As soon as the police learned of him—and his notorious record—they usually wanted to pile up all available incriminating evidence at his doorstep.

Even though he was eight hundred kilometers away at the time of the murder!

While Maggie really couldn't imagine how they could implicate Laurent in Christie's death, it still made her nervous to have them ask about him. In fact, everything about her interaction with Benoit today had made her nervous. Were they looking at *her* as a possible suspect? She did find the body. But surely, they could find no motive for Maggie to want to kill Christie?

Maggie suddenly felt too hot. She turned in search of a refreshment kiosk and spotted one twenty yards away and headed in that direction. Before she got halfway there, she saw someone she recognized.

Monica's husband Jason stood in the middle of the park path next to Sophie and the stroller. Jason was wearing a baseball cap and a loose cotton shirt. He stood next to the teen with his hands on his hips looking very relaxed. The sight of them instantly transported Maggie back to that moment in the hotel lobby when she'd first seen them together. There had been something about their interaction then that had unsettled her and seeing them now only confirmed it—it was an undercurrent of something inappropriate.

She watched the way Jason's eyes lingered on Sophie a moment too long after she turned away, and how Sophie pushed the stroller, her shoulders tense and rigid as if prepared to repulse an assault—or an unwanted touch. Maggie felt a knot forming in her stomach. The comforting sounds of the park faded into the background, replaced by the rush of blood in her ears. She waited for them to walk on, Jason following behind, his hands clasped behind his back as if he didn't know what to do with them.

Or was trying to prevent himself from doing anything.

Maggie knew she needed to talk to Sophie to see if Jason was in fact bothering her. She wasn't sure what she'd do if he was. But she'd do something. When she was sure they'd left the park, she gave up on the idea of a cold drink and instead found a bench by one of the duck ponds to try to sort out all the things coursing through her brain. She sat down and squared her shoulders. Yesterday, she'd mentally censured Monica for not taking time to process poor Christie's death but in fact Maggie had done very little of that herself. In all honesty, she didn't know Christie very well anymore and there was an argument to be made that she hadn't even back in school.

The cold fact was that for the brief time she'd been with Maggie and the others, Christie had been antagonistic. Maggie didn't know if that was Christie's default personality or if there was something about the chemistry of the five of them that had brought out the worst in her. But her manner had been mocking and derisive, in fact, nearly intolerable.

Had one of the other women thought so too?

Christie had humiliated Lisa back in high school—an experience Lisa clearly wasn't finished processing—and Christie had done everything she could to rub that into Lisa's face this weekend.

Was it enough for Lisa to want her dead?

Maggie had no idea of the tenor of the relationship between Christie and Monica except for the fact that they seemed to have kept in touch all these years. Now that she thought of it, they were the only ones who had. If Monica had a reason to want Christie dead, it wasn't obvious what it was.

And Beth? A dark horse and she always had been. She hadn't been particularly friendly to any of them, but neither had she shown any specific animosity against Christie that Maggie had noted.

She sighed and pulled out her phone. She wanted to call Laurent, but she didn't want to hear him insist again that he was coming to Paris. Amélie needed him at home. Instead, Maggie looked up the number he'd sent her for Antoine Berger. After getting her thoughts in order, she put the call through.

"*Allo?*"

"Monsieur Berger?" Maggie said. "This is Maggie Dernier. I'm the wife of—"

"I know who you are, Madame Dernier," the voice said— smooth and deep and reassuring. "Laurent and I have spoken."

"Oh," Maggie said. "Well, good. He gave me your number in case you might be able to help me with some information over this...suspicious death that's happened at the hotel where I'm staying."

"Can we meet?" he asked. "Laurent said you were in Montmartre."

"Yes, that would be great. Whenever is good for you."

Antoine gave her the address for a cafe not far from the park and they arranged to meet there in an hour. As soon as Maggie disconnected, she felt better. Now, instead of talking with three women who she really didn't know—and one of them possibly a killer—she would have someone who was trusted by Laurent to help her process what had happened. Better than that, he would be able to get her inside information. And he should be able to tell her what he knew about the enigmatic Detective Benoit.

She glanced at her watch, glad that she didn't have to jump up and rush over to the cafe. She needed some time to just sit and stare into space, to listen to the children playing and the birds in the trees. When she opened her purse to slip her phone back in it, she saw the envelope that she'd found the morning of the murder on the floor of her room.

So much had happened since then that she had totally forgotten about it.

The envelope was from the hotel. It was made of heavy-weight parchment, the color of old ivory. The sender had sealed it and, on the front, had written the letter *M* in a nearly comical cursive flourish. Maggie frowned. It couldn't be from the hotel, she reasoned. She hadn't told them she wanted to check out. It had to be from someone staying in the hotel.

Inside was a single sheet of paper. It was the identical parchment quality as the envelope. Maggie had a pad of the same stationary in her own room. She did not recognize the handwriting but stiffened when her eye dropped to the signature and saw it was from Christie. She sat up straight, her heart pounding, her mouth suddenly dry.

Christie had sent her a message? When had she delivered it? Maggie turned the envelope over again to look at the front. Sure enough, it was addressed to *M*.

Immediately Maggie knew it wasn't for her. Christie and she were not on nickname terms. It didn't take that much more effort to write out the rest of Maggie's name. She read the letter, her mouth dropping open in shock as she did.

Dearest Monica,

As per our last discussion, please see the enclosed article. I may not be able to punish you in the courts for what you did to me, but I can still ruin your life. In case you're thinking of suing me for libel, please be aware that publicly accusing anyone of a shameful act or crime would first need to be proven as false and even if you were ultimately successful, your image would still be damaged beyond repair.

Win-win for me.

As we speak, the article included in this message has been sent to every community newspaper in Atlanta including Buckhead, Dunwoody, Brookhaven, Chamblee, Decatur, Roswell and East Cobb. In addition, I've taken the liberty of cc-ing it to the members of the Buckhead Women's Club, the Buckhead Garden Club and the Atlanta Junior League..

Basically, you can kiss your squeaky-clean reputation goodbye, Monica.

And trust me, this is just the beginning.

You pal, Christie

16

The day had turned hot, Jason thought, and yet somehow the weather was still glorious. He ambled down the park path, listening to the chatter of the French children all around him, their sing-songy words seeming to blend with the musical chirping birds. Would he begin to see cartoon bluebirds? He grinned at the thought.

He turned his attention to Emily now toddling beside Sophie in front of him, her tiny hand secure within Sophie's, the teen's ponytail bobbing with each step ahead of him. As he watched her from behind, he couldn't help but note how she'd grown in the past year. She was no longer the gangly thirteen-year-old who'd first come to babysit for them. Her features had softened into those of a young woman. Her braces gone, her complexion clear and rosy. Her figure no longer stick-straight. In some ways she reminded him of Monica back in high school. There had been a grace about her then, a lightness in her step that had always drawn the eye.

Sophie's laugh brought him back to the present and he watched her pick up Emily. He admired her energy, her youthful zest in every movement. She was a breath of fresh air, a reminder of the carefree days of his youth. He swallowed hard and tried to shake the thoughts from his brain.

"Sophie, wait up," he called out.

The girl turned around, her eyebrows raised in a silent question.

"I just wanted to say..." He hesitated, his words hanging in the air. "I know it's been a hard week, especially with what happened to Mrs. McCoy, but you're doing a great job. Emily adores you."

A soft pink hue spread across her cheeks.

"Thanks, Mr. Williams. I love babysitting Em."

There was an awkward silence then. Jason glanced at his granddaughter and then Sophie, his gaze lingering on her a moment too long. He knew it. Did she?

"I'm hoping you'll consider continuing to sit for us after school starts," he said. "I know Monica talked to you about it."

"Yeah," Sophie said shyly. "I'm just not sure."

"Is it the money? What is Monica offering you?"

"No sir, it's not that," Sophie said hurriedly. "My mom wants me to just do school. It's...I'm not a great student."

"I'm sure you're a very good student," Jason said earnestly. "Maybe you just need a tutor."

"Maybe."

"And it doesn't have to be full time," he said, feeling his hands become damp. "You could work a few hours a week."

"Maybe," she said.

He looked around at the other children laughing and running about the park. Emily wasn't at that point yet, but she would be. He knew he didn't have the energy to run after her and climb the monkey bars with her. He imagined Sophie climbing the monkey bars.

"Well, I hope you'll think about it," he said, wiping a sheen of perspiration from his forehead.

"I will."

"I think you're quite a mature and sensible young woman, Sophie."

Sophie's blush deepened, her eyes widening slightly. She offered her same shy smile but was looking down at her shoes.

"Thanks, Mr. Williams," she said, her voice barely audible.

"Jason," he said. "Call me Jason."

Sophie giggled, and Jason felt a flush creep up his neck, accompanied by a prickling sense of guilt that he always had around her. Emily's soft coo broke the moment. He turned to glance at the child and felt a pang of shame.

They continued walking, Jason forcing himself to keep his eyes straight ahead, focusing on the path. But the troubling thoughts lingered, like an unwelcome guest. The seeds of doubt had been sown, the suspicion cast.

What is the matter with me?

Should he be worried? He swallowed hard and rubbed the perspiration from his palms on his jeans.

17

The café where Antoine suggested they meet wasn't far from the park. When Maggie arrived, she saw it was a quintessential Parisian establishment, hidden away on a side street away from the hustle and bustle of the city's main thoroughfares. The exterior was adorned with creeping ivy, and the soft, warm light filtering through the stained-glass windows gave it an inviting, almost ethereal glow.

Laurent would love this place.

Inside was a charming blend of elegance and rustic comfort, with mahogany tables, velvet-upholstered chairs, and antique light fixtures overhead. Soft jazz played in the background, its irresistible rhythm weaving seamlessly through the murmur of hushed conversations. Paintings of Parisian landscapes adorned the walls, their vibrant hues adding a touch of local whimsy to the café's ambiance.

Maggie spotted Antoine at a corner table, seemingly absorbed in a tattered paperback. He was an older gentleman as Maggie had guessed he'd be. His hair was silver, neatly combed back, and his piercing blue eyes held an immediately discernable spark of intelligence. His clothes were simple yet elegant—a crisp white shirt, a well-worn tweed jacket, and a pair of polished leather shoes.

As he looked up from his book and caught sight of Maggie, a warm smile spread across his weathered face. Maggie couldn't help but think as she approached that this was a man who had seen much, experienced much, and yet retained a keen interest in the world and its mysteries.

"*Cher* Madame Dernier," he said, standing and extending a hand towards Maggie, his grip firm. His voice was a gravelly baritone, each word carrying the weight of his years.

"Thank you so much for meeting with me," Maggie said as she seated herself.

"A request from your husband is not easily refused," Antoine said. "Not that I would want to. How can I help you?"

Maggie quickly outlined what had happened at the hotel and how she and the other women were not being allowed to leave. He nodded as she spoke making it clear to Maggie that he knew even more than she did about the incident in the hotel.

"I guess I was hoping you might have some information for me about what's going on. The police won't tell us anything."

"Your husband has given me the pertinent facts," Antoine said. "And I have made a few inquiries."

Maggie felt her pulse quicken with excitement. "Do you know what happened? Is it murder?"

"Let us order a drink first, *oui*?" he said, signaling to the waiter. When the man appeared, Antoine ordered for both of them. After the waiter disappeared, he turned to Maggie.

"Your friend, Madame McCoy, died from cyanide poisoning," he said.

Maggie took in a quick intake of air even though she'd been prepared for something like this.

"How?" she asked.

"The poison was found in her system," Antoine said, "and also in the can of diet soda found next to her bedside."

"So it was suicide?" Maggie asked.

Christie had acted the least like anyone contemplating suicide that Maggie could imagine. Antoine waggled his hand as if to say that was unclear.

"There were no other fingerprints on the can but hers," he said. "And the detectives cannot understand, if someone else did open the can, why she would drink from it?"

Maggie thought about that. She had to admit she couldn't imagine opening a soda can for someone else unless they were handicapped or a small child.

"Plus, there are less complicated ways of killing yourself," she said.

"*Exactement.*"

"So the police *don't* think it's suicide?"

"They're not making any proclamations just yet but they're leaning toward murder."

Maggie took in another sudden intake of breath. She didn't know why she was surprised. She herself had been thinking this exact same thing. Christie was not suicidal. And there was no way that cyanide is accidentally ingested.

Just then the waiter returned with their drinks. Antoine waited patiently for the man to lay down cocktail napkins, a small bowl of nuts and spiced olives before leaving.

"Additionally," he said, "there is a video that the victim took of herself around midnight that same night."

A video? Maggie found herself getting excited as Antoine found the video on his phone and showed it to her. It was short, just a few seconds and there was no audio. The video showed Christie in a long t-shirt and knit boxers—the same clothes Maggie had seen her in yesterday in her bedroom. Behind her was the digital clock on her bedside that read twenty-two hundred hours.

In the video, Christie rolled her eyes and mimicked shooting herself with her index finger while a text rolled across her chest reading: *trapped in Paris with the same crew I couldn't wait to get away from in high school!*

"She posted it to Instagram," Antoine said. "That in itself is unimportant but as you can see, the soda can is visible beside her on the desk. Unopened."

Maggie grimaced. It was awful seeing Christie—so snarky yet so alive—and yes, the unopened diet soda can behind her —the cause of her death—was like a ticking time bomb in the room with her.

"So she opened it herself," Maggie murmured.

"Forensics say her fingerprints are on the pull tab on the can. She definitely opened it herself. The finger positioning suggests that there is no believable way it could have been staged or manufactured. And before you ask, the rest of the can was intact. There were no pinholes or breaks in the seam anywhere that the poison might be introduced."

But then how did the poison get into a sealed, unopened can?

"Additionally, this gives the police a time frame," he said.

Maggie nodded. Even without the clock showing in the video, the video itself was time stamped at midnight and the can of soda was still unopened. Whoever put the poison in the can had not yet come. Maggie thought again of the fact that the door to Monica's room connected to Christie's. She was also reminded of Monica's black eye. But how did that fit?

How does one fight with someone and then coerce them to drink a poisoned drink?

Antoine sipped his drink thoughtfully and Maggie watched him and found herself wondering about his relationship with Laurent. She knew Laurent had not been to Paris in years and although it was true that he was naturally secretive, she found it hard to believe he would have made the effort to keep up with all the cronies from his past. His present was much too complicated and demanding. And yet Antoine had dropped whatever he was doing and responded immediately to Laurent when he reached out.

Had they been adversaries? Did Antoine hold a grudging respect for Laurent for all the years that Laurent was simply uncatchable? Or was there something else? Maggie hated to admit it but another way Antoine and Laurent might know each other would be if Antoine was a cop on the take. She didn't like to think of him like that, but it was worth considering.

"And you are wondering now," Antoine said slowly, "about whether the policeman you are dealing with can be trusted, no?"

Maggie blushed darkly, astonished that he had read her mind so well.

"The policeman?" she asked, stalling for time.

"Detective Benoit?" he asked, raising an eyebrow at her.

Maggie blushed again and it was then she realized that if Antoine hadn't interpreted her thoughts before, he certainly had now.

"Oh, right, yes," she said. "Is he trustworthy?"

"That depends on who you are," Antoine said smoothly. "I believe the liar and the opportunist can trust him to do everything in his power to accommodate them if it is to his advantage."

"What about the victim of a terrible crime?" Maggie asked, holding Antoine's gaze.

"I believe the victim can trust him, too, to do everything he can to apprehend the guilty party. That would be to his credit."

"So, he's not crooked."

Antione smiled. "I did not say that."

"So, you're saying he might be bent, but he'll still try to do his job."

"*Et voila.*"

"I guess I'll have to live with that," Maggie said with a sigh. "At least we both want the same thing."

She addressed herself to her own drink. She needed a moment to process the idea that Benoit could be both good and bad. The concept was difficult for her. She knew it came second nature to Laurent—and possibly to Antoine too—but she struggled with it. Finally, she turned back to him.

"One of the women I'm traveling with has a black eye as of yesterday morning."

Antoine's eyebrows shot up.

"She said she got it walking into the bathroom door," Maggie said.

"Is she the one traveling with her husband?"

"Yes, but trust me, she didn't get it from Jason. He's extremely nonassertive."

Antoine shrugged.

"I have heard this many times about abusers in domestic violence cases."

"I know, but in this case, I think it's true. Jason is the least aggressive person you'll ever meet."

"You would rather believe she ran into a door?" Antoine said, his eyebrows still arched dubiously.

"I'm not sure I believe that either," Maggie admitted.

"You think she fought with the victim?"

At this point, Maggie reached into her purse and pulled out the letter Christie had written to Monica. Antoine unfolded the crisp paper. His eyes quickly scanned the neat lines of ink. As he did, Maggie saw his brows furrow deeper, his relaxed demeanor replaced with an expression of stark surprise.

"This is motive," he said, still looking at the letter. "What *terrible thing* does the victim believe this woman did to her?"

"I have no idea," Maggie said.

"You must find out," he said.

He reread the letter again and then waved it in the air.

"The intended recipient never received this?" he asked.

"It was meant for Monica Williams. Christie must have slipped it under the wrong door. My door."

"And your hotel room door is next to Madame Williams' room?"

"That's right."

"The victim writes *as per our last discussion*," Antoine said with a frown.

"Right. So it sounds as if Christie threatened Monica before writing the letter. This was her making good on her threat."

"It is a strong motive for murder," Antoine said again.

"I know," Maggie said. "Did you happen to find out if Christie's body showed signs of having been in a struggle?"

Maggie hadn't seen any, but she'd not looked closely either.

Antoine shook his head. "None."

"Well, so that's weird, right?" Maggie said. "If she fought with Christie, why would Monica have a black eye and Christie be unmarked?"

"You have a good mind," he said, smiling and tilting his head. "These are good questions."

"I've got another one for you," Maggie said grimly, reaching to take the letter back. "What do I do with this? I've already spoken formally to the police twice, and I never mentioned this letter—mostly because I forgot I had it."

"They will not be disposed to believe that you forgot."

"So what do I do? Should I give it to Monica?"

Antoine steepled his fingers as he thought.

"Do that," he said finally. "And ask her for the details of why the victim hated her so much. But be careful, Madame Dernier."

Maggie took a sip of her drink and frowned.

"Be careful?" she asked.

"This woman is your prime candidate for having killed her friend. If she killed once to protect herself, she will be even more willing to kill a second time if she feels backed into a corner."

18

Maggie felt much better after her meeting with Antoine. She told him that she would be careful in confronting Monica, and she asked him to please not update Laurent with the details of what she was doing.

"He worries needlessly," she said. "I promise I'll tell him everything when it's all over."

Antoine had not been thrilled with the idea of keeping secrets from Laurent, but he seemed to understand the wisdom in doing so and promised her. Now, Maggie felt as if she had more information to help her wade through the complicated machinations of the police with their secrets and dual objectives on the case. Now that she knew *how* Christie had died, she could better navigate the next series of police questioning that she had no doubt was coming.

As she stepped into the Montmartre Hotel, Maggie instantly spotted Beth, Lisa, and Monica huddled together on a couch in a shadowed corner of the lobby. As soon as she saw Monica Maggie was reminded that she needed to have a word with Jason. She looked around the lobby to see if he or Sophie were there, but she didn't see them. She walked over to the three women, noting that their faces were ashen, their eyes wide with dismay.

Instantly, she knew that something had happened.

As Maggie approached, she noticed Beth was cradling an ice pack against her head.

"What in the world happened?" Maggie asked as she joined them.

Lisa and Monica sat on either side of Beth. Lisa's hand rested gently on Beth's shoulder.

"I was just walking down the street, looking around at everything," Beth said, "my mind was totally consumed on what had happened to poor Christie."

She removed the cold pack from her head and winced dramatically as she did.

Maggie frowned. The last time she'd spoken to Beth she had been telling unkind secrets about Christie. Perhaps, like herself, Beth had spent some time thinking about that and felt a belated shame for what had happened to their friend.

"Suddenly—from out of nowhere!" Beth said, loudly, "I felt a terrible pressure on the back of my head. I stumbled, clutching my head, my head exploded in agony. I was lucky I didn't collapse right there!"

"And you saw no one?" Lisa asked.

"By the time I recovered my senses and looked around, there was no sign of anyone."

"Did they grab your purse?" Maggie asked glancing at Beth's handbag on the seat next to her.

"They must have chickened out at the last minute," Beth said.

"So, someone just attacked you and then ran off?" Maggie asked, her voice incredulous.

"You think I'm making this up?" Beth asked her hotly.

She gestured with the icepack and her eyes filled with tears.

"No one thinks that, Beth," Lisa said. "But it is very strange behavior for a mugger. Why would someone just hit you and run away?"

"I have no idea! Why does anyone do anything in this stupid city? Why did we even come here in the first place where everyone hates us? We could've gone any place! We could've stayed in the States!"

"There you only have to worry about someone shooting you," Maggie said and was instantly sorry she did.

Monica turned on her, her face blushing furiously.

"I get that you think France is wonderful, Maggie," she said bitingly. "But the truth is, the French hate Americans."

"Well, they don't," Maggie said with a shrug.

"Explain this then!" Beth said, pointing to her head.

"You can get mugged in any big city," Maggie said. "It's not personal."

"Where did you go this morning?" Monica asked her.

Maggie turned to look at her. The black eye looked even worse this morning although it was clear Monica had tried to hide it with foundation.

"The police wanted to talk to me again," Maggie said.

"Why just you? Do they think you had something to do with Christie's death?" Beth asked.

Maggie turned to her.

"Why would they? You and I discovered the body together."

"It just seems peculiar," Monica said, "that they would want to talk to you and not the rest of us."

Maggie knew Monica was goading her. She was determined not to rise to the bait.

"Can we focus on the main thing, please?" Lisa asked. "The question we need answered is why would someone kill Christie?"

"Who said she was killed?" Beth asked.

"Well, she didn't die of natural causes," Monica said, snorting derisively. "And there's no way she killed herself."

"What makes you say that?" Maggie asked, although she agreed with Monica.

"You saw her! She was full of life! She was always ready to party."

"Or rumble," Maggie said.

"You never liked her, did you?" Beth asked Maggie abruptly.

"Beth, stop it!" Lisa said angrily. "Maggie had no reason to hurt Christie."

"Oh, no?" Beth said. "We weren't exactly nice to her back in school."

Maggie was surprised Beth had that much self-awareness. She thought Beth tended to lean heavily on the fact that, being smart, she didn't have to be nice too. But if Beth knew she'd been a part of the "mean girl" sect back in school, as far as Maggie was concerned that made her behavior now all the more contemptible.

"Speak for yourself!" Monica said to Beth, but she shot Maggie a guilty look.

If anyone had been hateful to Maggie in school, it had been Monica. She'd been the recognized ringleader of the group of high school mean girls. If she didn't lead the attack, she never stopped one from happening. And there was no doubt that Christie and Beth and to a certain extent even Lisa, had often behaved badly in order to win her good opinion.

"May I have a word, Monica?" Maggie asked, glancing at Beth. "Alone."

Monica looked as if she'd prefer to decline but as all eyes were on her she merely shrugged and stood up.

"Fine," she said. "Although I'm not sure what we have to say to each other."

They walked to a vacant section of the lobby and Maggie pulled the envelope out of her purse.

"This was misdelivered to my room yesterday. I believe it was meant for you."

Monica reached for the envelope and then stopped.

"I don't want it," she said suddenly.

"Do you know what it is?" Maggie asked.

"Of course not. How would I?"

"It's addressed to you," Maggie said.

"That means nothing. Your name starts with an M, too."

"She addresses you by your full name in the letter," Maggie said, amazed at Monica's resistance to taking the letter that she must know was from Christie. "There's no question of who the letter is meant for."

Monica snatched the envelope, her lips pursed with annoyance, and opened it. Maggie watched her countenance go from a fiery impatience to a not-so-gradual descent into shock and despair. Her shoulders sagged and her face lost all its color.

"Oh, my God," she whispered. "She really did it."

"Why was she so angry at you?" Maggie asked.

Monica didn't answer for a moment as she re read the note, ending with her shaking her head in despondency.

"It's a very serious attack," Maggie said. "What brought it on?"

A veil dropped over Monica's face.

"That's none of your business. Did you show this to the police?"

Monica's look of indignation and resentment, morphed into one of fear.

"I'll answer that question," Maggie said, "when you tell me what Christie was so angry with you about."

The war of emotions on Monica's face was expressive but brief. She jammed the envelope into her purse.

"Not here," she said looking around the lobby. "I'll meet you tonight upstairs in the rooftop garden."

"Wait a minute, Monica," Maggie said in exasperation. "Why don't you just—"

"I told you! If you want to hear what she had on me, you'll come tonight. But I swear if you try to use this letter against me, I'll make you sorry."

Maggie watched as Monica hurried away and found herself thinking for the first time since she'd read the letter that perhaps Christie had been justified with what she'd written in the letter.

19

M aggie watched Monica stomp away toward the elevators. Then she turned back to where Beth and Lisa and been standing, but they were gone. Sighing, Maggie turned to go back to her room when she spotted Sophie in one of the deep plush armchairs with the baby on her lap. Sophie's eyes appeared glazed with ennui as they idly followed various hotel guests coming and going. Her hair was pulled back into a ponytail with stray wisps framing her face. Her outfit, t-shirt and jeans, seemed out of place in the elegant French hotel lobby.

One hand held her phone while the other held the baby securely, a clear indication Maggie thought of the girl's responsibility despite her obvious boredom.

Maggie walked over to her.

"You look done in," Maggie said.

Sophie looked up from her phone and gave Maggie a half smile.

"Miz W says I'm built cheap," she said. "But Mr. W says it's only the jet lag."

"Speaking of Mr. W," Maggie said as she sat down next to Sophie. "Is everything okay there?"

Sophie looked at her phone.

"What do you mean?" she asked in a small voice.

"I mean, is he making unwanted advances toward you?"

"I don't think so."

But now Sophie wasn't looking at her.

"Or maybe just making you feel uncomfortable?" Maggie pressed. "You know, Sophie, just because they pay you to take care of Emily doesn't mean they can...take advantage of your good nature."

"My mom says I'm everybody's patsy," Sophie said.

"I'm sure that's not true," Maggie said. "But still. Would you like me to have a word with Mr. W?"

Sophie looked at her, horrified.

"Oh, no, ma'am! I need this job."

"I will be circumspect," Maggie said.

"Ma'am?"

Sophie bit her lip and glanced at Maggie in confusion.

"I'll make sure that doesn't happen," Maggie said firmly.

Just then, out of the corner of her eye Maggie caught sight of Lisa hurrying over to where she and Sophie sat. Clearly oblivious to the intimate conversation she was interrupting, Lisa reached for the baby in Sophie's lap.

"Oh, for heaven's sake, Sophie!" Lisa said. "You look dead on your feet. Go take a nap or a walk around the block. You need a break."

Sophie glanced in the direction Monica had gone.

"Are you sure it's okay?" she asked.

Lisa took the baby in her arms.

"Go," she said. "I'll tell Monica I insisted."

Sophie got to her feet and gave the baby and the two women only one quick backward glance before hurrying out the door of the hotel.

"I won't be long!" she called over her shoulder.

Lisa settled the baby in her stroller.

"There's a park across the street from the hotel," Maggie said.

Lisa gave Maggie a grateful look.

"Come with me?" she asked.

"Sure."

They made their way across the cobblestone street to the small pocket park wedged into the intersection of Rue des Trois Frères and rue Yvonne le Tac. The place was deserted and, quiet except for the soft chirping of birds and the rustle of leaves in the afternoon breeze. The sun peeked through the canopy of trees, casting dappled light that danced on the baby's face in the stroller. She closed her eyes and seemed to doze off. Maggie found herself wondering again if she'd been drugged.

They walked to a bench and parked the stroller beside it.

"I'm sorry about those two," Lisa said once she was seated and made sure that Emily wasn't too hot or in too much sun. "Beth is just upset about finding Christie's body like that. Plus, she thinks the cops think *she* killed her and that's freaking her out."

"I'm not taking it personally," Maggie said. "She was always an odd duck back in high school, as I recall."

"You have to remember," Lisa said earnestly, "Beth was oblivious to anything in high school except getting into a good college because of what happened to her dad."

Maggie realized she'd forgotten that there had been a terrible scandal that had forced Beth to miss a lot of school.

"Remind me?" she prompted.

"I don't know if you know," Lisa said, "but Beth's dad had been a high-ranking cop, only it turned out he was crooked. I don't know all what he did but he got caught in a sting. It was devastating for the whole family. Beth was destroyed. Anyway, her dad was so ashamed he killed himself."

"That's terrible," Maggie murmured. "I'd forgotten she'd gone through all that."

"I think he's the reason Beth went to law school," Lisa said. "To prove she was nothing like him."

A siren went off on one of the side streets and Emily screwed up her face but didn't wake.

"On top of that, I have to say—and again I'm not telling tales," Lisa said, "but I thought it was weird that Beth hardly said two words to Christie since we got here."

"Why?" Maggie asked. "Beth isn't close to any of us really."

"She was actually much closer to Christie if you know what I mean."

Maggie frowned and then her eyebrows shot up.

"Seriously?"

Lisa glanced at the baby as if briefly concerned about her overhearing and then turned back to Maggie.

"The way Christie described it," she said in a low voice, "it was just a one-night thing. But she did say that when she told Beth that it was a mistake, Beth got very upset."

"Is Beth gay?" Maggie asked.

"Well, I guess she was that night," Lisa said with a grin. "Anyway, I heard about it from Monica. I guess Beth confided in her."

"Had you picked up on anything between her and Christie this weekend?" Maggie asked.

"Nada. I'm not sure Christie even remembered it happened."

"But you think Beth does."

"Oh, I definitely think she does. Still waters and all that."

Speaking of still waters, Maggie couldn't help but wonder if this might not be a good time to ask Lisa for the details of what had happened on that fateful junior prom night. Lisa leaned over the stroller to straighten the cotton blanket over Emily's lap and to rearrange where the child's stuffed animal was situated in the crook of her arm. Maggie felt a pang of sympathy for Lisa. Clearly life hadn't gone the way she'd planned.

There was no doubt it had started off well—with the publication and blockbuster reception of her bestselling book. But after that, nothing. Maggie knew enough about publishing to know that if Lisa hadn't made her advance back on the next books, regardless of the success she'd had with the first, she'd have trouble getting another publishing contract.

Coming back to Atlanta to work in a corporate communications field—as a single mother—must have been soul-crushing for Lisa, Maggie thought. Still, as a mother, she'd done what she had to. But now that her daughter was grown and gone, it was just Lisa, with no husband or loving partner to curl up with during those chilly Atlanta winters.

Maggie found she didn't have the stomach to ask her about prom night.

We all had such dreams when we left school.

20

M aggie gazed into the sky overhead—a watercolor wash of soft grays and blues—and watched as a glimmer of sunshine tried to break through the cloud cover. To her left, a small playground stood empty, the swings swaying slightly in the breeze, their shadows stretching out on the sandy ground. Nearby, a couple walked their dog, their laughter echoing in the air. Emily was still napping but Lisa continued to rearrange the baby's blanket and smooth out her little sun dress as if she couldn't bear not to touch her.

"I'm working with a retired detective," Maggie said suddenly.

Lisa looked at her with a questioning look on her face. Maggie was just as surprised as she was by her outburst. But once the words were out of her mouth, she knew she was right to bring Lisa into her confidence. Being suspicious of everyone was beginning to seriously wear on her.

"Why?" Lisa asked.

"Well, not to worry you or anything, but there is a possibility that the police will decide that one of us four is their best bet for Christie's killer."

Lisa's face blanched and she put a trembling hand to her mouth.

"I'm not saying they will," Maggie said hurriedly. "But typically, if they don't find someone pretty early on, they start to...improvise."

"You think they'll choose one of us?" Lisa asked, her eyes wide.

"I think they might," Maggie said.

"So you've hired a detective?"

"It's someone my husband knows. This guy has contacts with the Montmartre police and can help us stay ahead of them."

"Maggie, you're scaring me."

"I don't mean to do that, Lisa. I just wanted to let you know what I was doing."

Lisa's eyes popped open.

"I can help," she said. "Right?"

When Maggie hesitated, Lisa turned to face her on the bench. Her jaw was set and her gaze determined.

"I'm serious, Maggie. Let me help. Can I meet this detective, too? I used to write mysteries, you know. I'm not totally useless."

"I know, Lisa," Maggie said. "Well, why not? I mean, your input with Antoine can only help him get a better picture of what happened."

"His name is Antoine? He sounds so exotic!"

Maggie laughed.

"I don't know about that," she said. "But he is very nice and quite sharp."

Lisa shook her head in amazement.

"You know, Maggie, every time I turn around, you're doing something that reminds me of how clever you were back in school."

"I can't imagine that's true," Maggie said, blushing in the face of Lisa's sudden praise.

"I can't believe you constantly deflect the acclaim due you," Lisa said, shaking her head in wonder. "I mean, seriously. It's no wonder Christie and Monica and Beth were acting so jealous of you at dinner the other night."

"I find that hard to believe," Maggie said.

"Seriously? Then let me help recount the ways for you."

Lisa held up one hand and began ticking off her fingers one by one.

"You left the comforts of the US, married a total hunk—trust me, we've seen the social media photos and he's gorgeous —you live on a vineyard, you speak French like a native, you have three great kids—none of whom is addicted to meth and one who actually got married like a normal person. You have a stable and loving marriage and any time you need a little retail therapy you're a two-hour train ride from Paris!"

"But my career fell apart," Maggie said, feeling a mixture of pleasant surprise at Lisa's accolades. "I walked away from advertising, and I never got that job I dreamed of working for one of the major news outlets."

"You published a book."

"A book that never made its advance back," Maggie pointed out. "And which was in the low three figures I might add."

She was surprised she had the nerve to tell Lisa that. But all Lisa did was laugh.

"Do you think that matters? Trust me, Maggie, I'm here to tell you it does not. We're not jealous of you because you're JK Rowling. We're jealous of you because in spite of everything *you* still ended up having it all."

Later that afternoon, after Maggie and Lisa split up to go their separate ways, Maggie realized she felt better about this weekend with her old high school chums. If at some point she really had been hoping to impress them then the last few days had extinguished that notion rather severely. But now Lisa was encouraging her to believe they'd been impressed after all.

What difference does it make? she thought as she peeled off her capri slacks and dropped them on the bed in her hotel room. She certainly didn't need any of these women's good opinion of her to believe the path she'd taken after school had been a good one. But still. It was nice to hear.

She went into the bathroom and ran the bathtub, her mind full of all the different conversations that had happened today. She and Antoine were supposed to meet up again later this evening. She'd texted him to see if he was okay with her bringing Lisa along and he was fine with it. Meanwhile, Maggie had a couple of hours to relax in the tub and try not to worry about all the things there were to worry about. She'd texted Zouzou a couple of times during the day but hadn't heard back. For lack of anything else to do about it, she tried to tell herself that it meant Zouzou was just very busy.

Just as she pulled a stack of fluffy towels out of the room's linen closet, she heard an ominous scratching sound and jumped back. Taking a breath, she got her cellphone flashlight and shot the beam into the interior of her closet.

There she saw a small hole at the back. In front of the hole was a tiny deposit—evidence of the little mouse that must be sharing her room with her. Maggie was aware that most hotels in Paris had mice. It didn't mean the hotel wasn't clean or even regularly fumigated. It was just the natural result of a centuries-old building in an even older neighborhood.

Oh well. It's better than roaches.

Just as she was heading back to the bathroom with the stack of towels in her arms, she heard her phone ring. Thinking it might be Laurent, she picked it up hoping to get in the tub with it while she talked to him. A picture of Zouzou showed up on the screen.

"Zouzou?" Maggie said.

"Oh, Aunt Maggie," Zouzou said, the anxiety and angst pouring out over the phone line. "You've got to help me. I'm desperate!"

Maggie felt her adrenalin spike at Zouzou's words.

"What is it, darling?" she asked. "What's happened?"

"It's Pierre," Zouzou said, gulping past hysterical tears. "He's missing!"

"Call the police," Maggie said as she put down the bath towels and settled on the couch. "Hang up right now and call them."

"I can't!" Zouzou wailed. "The company he works for...the police hate them."

"What does that mean?"

Zouzou gave a gasp of exasperation.

"He works for a publishing house known for its police tell-alls and there was one they did recently about police brutality. They named names and everything. Trust me, if I were to call the police to ask them to find him, they'd laugh me off the phone."

Something pinged in the back of Maggie's brain at Zouzou's words, but she couldn't remember what was setting it off.

"Did you go by his apartment?" Maggie asked.

"I did! His suitcase is gone! Oh, Maggie, if he's run out on me, I think I'll kill myself!"

"Now, Zouzou, don't say that," Maggie said as nausea erupted deep in her gut. "I'm sure he's not run off and we will find him. Do you hear me?"

"I can't imagine why he's not answering my texts!"

"Look, let's meet up, okay? Where are you right now? Are you at your place?"

Maggie was already thinking how she could postpone her meeting with Lisa and Antoine.

"No, I'm at work," Zouzou said. "I only have about five minutes before they come looking for me."

"Are you going to be okay at work?" Maggie asked. "Do you have someone there to talk to?"

"I have Estelle," she said, sniffing. "And once I get working, I'll be okay. Oh, Aunt Maggie, promise me this will all turn out okay!"

Maggie got an instant flash of Zouzou as a small child, always so happy and so eager to please. She had always had a special bond with Laurent, not just because Zouzou's experience with her own father was intermittent, but because they shared the same intense passion for cooking.

"Of course it will, darling," Maggie said, her heart breaking. "Call me when you get off work, okay?"

"It will be two in the morning," Zouzou said, sniffling.

"I don't care. You call me. If I don't hear from you, I'll come looking for you."

Zouzou laughed softly.

"Okay, Aunt Maggie," she said. "I'll call you."

"And don't worry, darling. We will sort this out one way or the other and that I do promise you."

After she hung up, Maggie found that while she could probably use the calming effects of a bath more than ever, she was too wired to take one. She turned the shower on instead. She had things to do and what had happened to Christie was only one of them.

And frankly, not the most important one.

21

That night, Maggie and Lisa stood on a quiet corner of rue Andrè Barsacq and rue Chappe, their faces set with determination as the evening mist swirled around the cobblestone streets. Montmartre, a night-time city, was just waking up, its usually bustling streets momentarily subdued.

Maggie scanned the quaint buildings and narrow alleyways that surrounded them and shivered. Lisa seemed to be brimming with enthusiasm and optimism, confirming to Maggie that it had been a good idea to include her.

"You're sure it's okay if I come?" Lisa asked Maggie for the third time.

"Yes, it's fine. I texted him that you were coming. Oh, there he is now."

Maggie lifted a hand when she spotted Antoine making his way toward them. He looked like he was laboring just a bit and when he joined them. He was definitely out of breath.

"Not as young as I used to be," he said before shaking hands with Lisa as Maggie introduced them.

He turned to Maggie.

"I have news," he said.

Maggie felt a pulse of excitement.

"The autopsy revealed paint under the victim's nails," he said.

Maggie frowned and glanced at Lisa. That was strange. Christie hadn't been doing any painting.

"My contact within the department," Antoine said, "says they identified the paint and Benoit believes it came from a specific art supply store right here in Montmartre. I have the address."

Well, it was at least a lead, Maggie decided, as they made their way toward the address that Antione had.

"So you are the author, yes?" Antoine asked Lisa. *"Death Breeze?"*

"Oh, my goodness, don't tell me you've read it?" Lisa asked, flustered and pleased.

"Not personally, no," Antoine said. "But my wife did, and she quite enjoyed it."

Maggie was surprised. Up until now Antoine hadn't mentioned anything about his personal life. She didn't know why she was shocked to hear he had a wife.

As they walked, she realized that she felt a little more hopeful about their chances of actually finding the person who killed Christie. Action and motion always gave her a sense of optimism. She glanced at Lisa and saw the determination in her face. She'd read somewhere that it was the hallmark of every good writer—that inclination to probe, unearth, research and process.

The address wasn't far. They found the shop wedged in between a laundromat and a cellphone store. With its multicolored painted shutters and ivy winding up the brick façade along with a vintage sign hanging above the entrance that read *Magasin d'Art*, Maggie thought the store represented a tribute to the neighborhood's artistic heritage. Ironically, for a paint supply store, the shop's exterior paint was slightly chipped. But she thought this just added to its charm. The sidewalk display window showcased a collection of canvases, paintbrushes, and shelves of vibrant bottles of paint.

As they stepped inside, a wave of warm, slightly musty air greeted them, carrying with it the comforting scent of oil paints, paper and glue. The interior itself was a labyrinth of narrow aisles lined with shelves reaching up to the ceiling. Canvases of all sizes were stacked against one wall, while bins of brushes, palette knives, and sponges occupied another.

Toward the back, a section of the shop was dedicated to paints, the shelves a riot of different colors, with tubes of oil and acrylic paints arranged in a mesmerizing gradient of hues. Long tables were stacked with sketchbooks, charcoal, pastels, and pencils.

Antoine stepped up to the large counter in the center of the store where a young woman stood in a painter's smock. He spoke to her in very fast French, but Maggie picked up that he was presenting himself as working for the Montmartre police. She felt a twinge of unease when he did that.

The young cashier glanced at the two American women standing behind him as if sizing them up. She turned back to Antoine and spoke sharply to him, telling him that the store did not keep records of which of their patrons bought which paints. Furthermore, she had no idea when the inventory was sold or to whom.

"This is a murder investigation, Madame," Antoine said to the young woman, his voice steely and commanding.

"I cannot help you, Monsieur."

"Show me this paint," he said, handing a piece of paper to the girl.

She glanced at the sheet but didn't touch it, then turned and went to the back of the store.

"What did she say?" Lisa whispered to Maggie.

"She says she doesn't keep records of who buys what," Maggie said.

When the girl came back, she had a tube of paint in her hand and gave it to Antoine. He unscrewed the lid and squirted a dab onto a scrap of paper on the counter. Maggie could see it was a nondescript taupe color. She tried to remember if the painting Christie had bought had that color in it.

"Eleven euros, please," the girl said. "We do not give samples."

As Antoine dug out the money for her, Lisa stepped to the counter and spoke into her phone. Maggie saw the phone was open to a language translation app.

"Have you seen this woman?" Lisa asked.

Then she held the phone out. Maggie saw it now showed a photograph of Christie. The app barked out Lisa's question in robotic French. The girl squinted at the picture. And shook her head. She turned to Antoine.

"I have not seen her," she said.

Even though Lisa's efforts hadn't resulted in a confirmation that Christie had been in the store, Maggie was impressed with her ingenuity. Antoine asked the cashier if she'd been working the day before. She said she had but repeated that she did not see the woman. There didn't seem much to say after that. Antoine dropped the paint tube in a trash can on their way out of the store.

"Well, that was a bust," he said.

"Maybe not," Lisa said, leaning over to dig the tube of paint out of the trash. "Christie bought a painting the day she died. She mailed it home to the States but, maybe there's a connection there."

"She did not mail the painting home, Madame Washington," Antoine said, his eyes beginning to glitter with animation.

"No, I'm sure she did," Lisa said, and Maggie found herself nodding in agreement.

"A painting of a landscape was found in the closet of the victim's room," Antoine said. "Unless she bought more than one painting during her visit to Montmartre?"

Lisa and Maggie stared at him, but Maggie shook her off bewilderment first. She turned to Lisa.

"She didn't mail the painting home," she said holding her hand out for the paint tube and squinting at the color bar on the side. "So maybe she got the paint under her nails from the painting?" She turned to look at Antoine. "What do you think?"

"I don't know, Maggie," he said with a sigh. "It would be very strange, no? To carry a painting in such a way that you get paint under your nails?"

Maggie had to agree that would indeed be very strange.

Insane, almost.

22

A fter their visit to the art store, they decided to stop at a café to debrief and try to make sense of what they'd discovered. The café Antoine led them to wasn't far from the hotel. Maggie kept her phone on the table while the waiter brought their drinks with toast and *paté*. Maggie had somehow managed to skip lunch and was very hungry. She glanced at her phone from time to time. She'd texted Zouzou again when they got to the café and received a thumbs-up emoji back from her. As she continued to check her phone, she reminded herself that Zouzou was at work, and likely texting would be difficult to do until she was off work.

"Have you had a chance to ask your other friend about her relationship with the victim?" Antoine asked as he picked through the nuts from the dish on the table.

Maggie knew he was referring to Monica and the misdelivered note from Christie. For some reason, she decided she wanted to wait until it was just the two of them before relating Monica's behavior when presented with the letter.

"One of our friends was mugged today," Maggie said.

Antoine's eyebrows shot up.

"Assaulted?" he asked, looking truly astonished.

"Hit on the back of the head," Lisa said, nodding.

"How very strange."

"Why do you say that?" Maggie asked.

He looked uncomfortable.

"Well, of course we have pickpockets in Paris. To be sure. They are a plague. But to attack a tourist in broad daylight?" He shook his head as if he couldn't believe it. "Was she draped in diamonds?"

"No, that's what's weird," Maggie said. "Her attacker didn't take her purse."

"That makes no sense at all."

"I know."

"Did she call the police?"

"Presumably."

Lisa turned to Maggie.

"Have you told him about the baby Christie had in high school?"

She turned to Antoine. "It was a big secret then and Christie still wasn't talking about it even now."

"Secrets make good leads," Antoine noted. "And also good motives." He addressed Maggie. "Why not get on the Internet tonight and see where she might have gone to have the baby?"

"She said she went to Switzerland," Lisa said.

Antoine smiled at Lisa. "You would make a good detective, Madame Washington." He glanced back at Maggie. "Then start your search in Switzerland for the appropriate time period."

"I don't know if this is helpful," Lisa said after the waiter replenished their drinks, "but rumor had it that Mr. Beavers wasn't the only man in high school Christie got friendly with."

Maggie frowned. "Another teacher?"

"Monica's husband Jason," Lisa said.

When Maggie's eyes widened in surprise, Lisa added, "I'm just passing on what I heard. I don't have any proof."

"Do you think Monica knew about it?" Maggie asked.

"Can you imagine Christie doing something like this and not telling her?" Lisa said, making a face.

"Do you think Christie's baby could've been Jason's?" Maggie asked.

"Well, the timing's right," Lisa said and then turned to address Antoine.

"Did Maggie tell you that the victim had just inherited a million bucks from a relative?"

"Yes, I heard that. It is a sum definitely worth killing over. If you give me the full names of the other two women, I will do complete financials on them."

"You can do that?" Lisa asked, biting her lip.

Maggie thought she looked a little troubled when she asked the question.

"*Pas de problème,*" he said with a shrug, pulling out a notebook and pen.

"I'll text you Beth and Monica's full names," Maggie said before turning to glance at Lisa.

"Yeah, sure," Lisa said with a blush. "I've got nothing to hide."

"And you already know my details, Antoine," Maggie said. "But listen, I know how the French are about money and if Laurent ever found out—"

"I am the soul of discretion, Madame. Especially where Laurent is concerned."

Twenty minutes later, Lisa excused herself to go to the toilet.

"There is something you do not wish to say in front of your friend?" Antoine asked.

"Wow. You're as good as Laurent for reading people," Maggie said.

He smiled.

"Your face is especially revealing," he said.

"I did give Monica the letter," she said. "And she was very upset when she read it."

"*Naturellement.* Did she say why the victim was threatening her?"

"I asked but she didn't want to tell me. She's worried I might have mentioned the letter to the cops so we're meeting later for an even swap of information."

"Be careful."

"I know. We're meeting in a semi-public place."

"Is that all?"

Maggie started to speak and then stopped. It wasn't that she didn't trust Antoine, but she wasn't sure what he could do to help.

"I do not wish to intrude if it is personal?" he prompted.

"Well, actually," Maggie said. "I do have a separate problem that maybe you can help me with. It has nothing to do with Christie's murder."

"I am happy to help, Maggie, if I can. What do you need?"

"Maybe some information on someone?"

He flipped to a clean sheet in his notebook.

"Name?" he asked.

"His name is Pierre Lambert. He's the father of the child of a special friend of mine. And he seems to have disappeared. I'm not sure he hasn't run off. I don't know him at all."

Antoine finished writing in his notebook and slipped it back into his breast pocket.

"I'll see what I can find out."

Later, as they stood outside the cafe with Lisa, Antoine flagged down a cab and then turned to Maggie and Lisa.

"I have enjoyed my evening with you both," he said warmly.

"But the reason for our acquaintance remains dire. And I worry for you both."

"I'm not afraid," Lisa said. "We just want justice for Christie."

Antoine turned to her with eyes that were suddenly dark and serious.

"Your bravery does you justice," he said. "And yes, we must find the person who killed your friend. But you must trust me on this that if we don't find who killed her, the police will. And they won't be nearly as careful about who they blame."

23

M aggie and Lisa headed back to the hotel as it began to rain lightly, just enough to dampen the streets and fill the air with the fresh scent of wet cobblestones. As they walked, Maggie was aware that the area that had been so alive with energy and tourists just an hour earlier was now nearly vacant in the drizzle. Even so, for Maggie the rain seemed to enhance the charm of the district, casting a magical sheen over the iconic Sacré-Cœur Basilica still visible and looming majestically over them.

Maggie found that she'd appreciated Lisa's contributions to their discussions with Antoine tonight. She'd been right that Lisa's optimism and fresh ideas had added a new perspective to the investigation. Despite that, Maggie was also aware that she was uncomfortable with the memory of how upset Lisa had been on the boat ride when Christie was goading her about the mysterious incident at the junior prom. During high school, Christie had been known for her quick wit, but she also had a cruel streak. Maggie knew she needed to find out the full details of that unfortunate event before she could really trust Lisa.

Once they walked up the wide wet steps to the hotel, they took a moment to stand under the awning and listen to the rain on the overhead awning. Maggie remembered that back in high school Lisa had always been more comfortable holed up in the library than going to parties. Not the most secure one of the group, she was an easy target for Christie and Monica too. Maggie remembered Lisa had always been pretty good-natured about it.

But she would be if she wanted to keep her friends.

"I feel like I'm the only one who doesn't know what happened with you and Christie at the junior prom," Maggie said.

Maggie looked out into the wet street to give Lisa space to answer in her own time. The rain was coming down harder now.

"There was this guy I liked," Lisa finally said with a sigh.

Maggie turned and smiled encouragingly at her.

"It was just your typical high school crush," Lisa said as she wiped a few raindrops from her purse.

"Would I know him?" Maggie asked.

Christie frowned. "Jeff Dixson?"

Maggie shook her head.

"He wasn't a jock or anybody special," Lisa said. "In fact, I think originally I thought he was shy like I was. I don't know why he caught my eye, but you know how that is? You see someone and you build up in your mind this elaborate fantasy about them?" Lisa laughed. "Or maybe that's just me."

"You are an author after all," Maggie said.

"Right. So maybe that's it. But anyway, I liked him. And I was content to watch him from afar, but Christie started ragging me, saying there was something wrong with me if I didn't go after him. She bugged me for weeks until she finally wrote a note signing my name to it and slipped it into his locker —asking him to go to the prom with me."

Maggie was appalled.

"Lisa, that's terrible."

Lisa nodded, her face impassive and restrained as she remembered how she'd felt at the time.

"Yeah, well it would've been," she said, "but miraculously, he agreed to go with me." She looked out over the rainy street scene. "He said yes."

Maggie's stomach tightened painfully. She knew the other shoe was about to drop.

"I had about three weeks of delight and happiness," Lisa said. "Jeff and I talked in the halls and at our lockers. He was very sweet and even teased me for not having the courage to ask him to the prom to his face."

"So what happened?" Maggie asked.

"Basically," Lisa said bitterly, "Christie convinced him to stand me up on prom night."

"Oh, Lisa," Maggie said sadly.

"Yeah, well it's no big deal and I'm way over it. But there I was in a full floor-length dress that cost a fortune, a wrist corsage, the whole nine yards. My mom was taking a million pictures and I'm waiting for my date to show. And finally, I get a call from Christie saying Jeff will meet me at the school auditorium. I knew it sounded strange. I mean, why didn't Jeff call me himself? But I was crazy about him, so my mom drove me there and when I got out Christie took all these pictures of me standing there alone, by now my mascara running down my face, like some loser looking for her date."

Maggie felt a pulse of anger at Christie.

"Did Jeff ever show?" she asked.

"Oh, sure. He danced all evening with anybody and everybody. He even waved to me from across the dance floor. By then I'd already called my mom to come and get me but of course this was pre-cellphone days, so I had to wait for her to get back home and then turn around and drive back to the auditorium.

And in the meantime, Christie was going around telling everyone what happened and having a good laugh."

The two of them turned away from the entrance as the rain began to reach them where they stood. They walked into the lobby. There was no one else there. Maggie would've been happy to talk longer, but Lisa was heading toward the elevators.

"Thank goodness this was before Facebook," Maggie said.

"Yeah, I probably would've blown my brains out. As it was, I just wanted to die."

"Jeff sounds like a jerk, too."

Lisa jabbed the up button on the elevator.

"Yeah, well, I heard he married badly *twice*, and never did succeed in passing the bar so I don't hate him too much. Karma, baby."

"What about Christie? Did you ever talk to her about what she did to you?"

Lisa made a face. "No. Why?"

"All that stuff she was saying to you on the boat tour. She didn't seem too contrite about what she'd done."

"Yeah, can you believe that? She always had the sensitivity of a box of rocks."

"And yet you stayed friends with her."

Lisa shrugged and when the elevator door opened, they both stepped inside.

"Not really," she said as she pushed the button for their floor. "We stayed in touch, but we didn't hang out or anything. She was always more Monica's friend. This Paris trip is the first time I'd seen her in years."

"So you'd forgiven her for prom night?"

"Of course. Gosh, Maggie, I'm not saying it didn't hurt at the time but I'm a big girl now, you know? It was a mean girl thing to do, and Christie was a mean girl. But I am long past all that now."

Maggie nodded at that and wondered if it was true.

24

As soon as her hotel room door clicked shut behind her, Lisa turned and leaned against it, closing her eyes and willing away the last thirty minutes with Maggie. She tried to tell herself that the fact that she'd been able to talk or even laugh about what Christie had done to her was amazing in itself. She should be proud of that. The fact that it had taken everything out of her was a moot point. It was vital that Maggie believe that Lisa had left the incident far behind her in high school.

The incident that killed me in every imaginable way.

She dropped her purse on the bed and kicked off her shoes. Christie was an investigative journalist, known for her hard-hitting exposés. Her work often focused on revealing the hidden truths and dark secrets of high-profile individuals and institutions. Her stories were known for their depth and the stark portrayal of their subjects. She had a knack for uncovering information that most would prefer to keep hidden.

When Lisa thought of how flippantly Christie had suggested writing a "Carrie" book using Lisa's most humiliating moment in life as its centerpiece, Lisa truly believed she could have killed the woman right then.

She felt a surge of emotions—humiliation, anger, and betrayal—wash over her. The room seemed to spin as that terrible night came rushing back, as vivid and raw as if it had happened yesterday.

Lisa sank onto her bed and ran her hand through her hair. In some ways, that night had defined everything she'd done since. Always a mediocre student, she'd dropped out of most of her extracurricular activities to ramp up her grades to reinvent herself. The laughter she'd heard two nights ago when Christie regaled everyone on the boat about the so-called prank was not just the other women on the tour boat—it was the laughter of Lisa's entire high school class. Christie had single-handedly turned what should have been a magical night into a nightmare that had haunted Lisa for years. And now there was Christie, not only unapologetic but reveling in what she had done to Lisa.

The combination of having to relive the trauma and Christie's blatant lack of remorse—combined with the fear that Christie might expose the truth of that night to the world in one of her many lurid investigative stories—had literally kept Lisa awake half the night. That, and thoughts of murder.

Even more problematic than all that was the consideration of the one thing that Lisa still felt she had—her professional reputation. She might have had to eke out a living as a low-level communications drudge, but nobody could take away the fame and success of her first novel—the novel inspired by her painful past. She grimaced as she recalled interviews where she staunchly maintained that the story was purely fictional. If Christie had written an exposé, it would be revealed that the humiliating events in Lisa's book were based on Lisa's own experiences. She felt her cheeks burn, a harsh echo of the blush that had stained her face on prom night. A lump formed in her throat, but she quickly blinked away the tears, refusing to give Christie the satisfaction.

I'm glad you're dead.

At the thought, she felt her body tense as anger pulsed through her. How dare Christie bring up prom night, knowing the pain it had caused Lisa? How dare she laugh, with absolutely no semblance of remorse for her actions?

Lisa felt her resolve harden in her heart. The past had been disturbed and old wounds reopened. But that was Christie all over. Digging and digging until all the bodies were unearthed. Lisa smiled to herself.

Except now Christie was one of those bodies.

25

M aggie felt like it had been days instead of hours since she'd been back in her hotel room.

The heavy hotel room door closing behind her gave a reassuring thud. Her room, bathed in the soft glow of the single lamp she'd left on, felt like a sanctuary amidst the chaos of her day. The bed with its plush pillows and inviting duvet seemed to call her name, promising the rest she so desperately needed.

Yet, despite her exhaustion, she found herself unable to shake off the events and conversations of the day. Her mind was a whirlwind of thoughts, each one a puzzle piece, none fitting together to make sense of anything. She glanced at the night-stand clock. It was well past eleven. She'd already received two text messages from Grace and even one from Laurent. She knew Laurent would be pacified with a brief text response, but Grace needed answers and Maggie had already put her off too long.

She dropped her purse on the desk next to the bed and kicked off her shoes. Across from the bed, a pair of French doors opened onto a small, wrought-iron balcony that overlooked the quiet, cobblestone side street. In the distance, she could just make out the hazy silhouette of Sacré-Cœur.

Zouzou had texted Maggie while she and Lisa were walking home from dinner to say she was home, was feeling better and ready to crash. Maggie knew that meant that Zouzou wasn't up for a phone call. She'd texted her back and they arranged to meet the next day before Zouzou's work shift.

Maggie wanted to text, *Call your mother!* But she knew that sending that message would probably ensure that Zouzou dug in her heels about calling home.

She sat on the edge of the bed and texted Grace begging off until tomorrow.

<exhausted tonight but will call tomorrow. Z alive and well. Love>

Maggie looked at the text before sending it and felt a twinge of guilt. Yes, Zouzou was alive but hardly well. She sent the text and then waited until she saw the emoji thumbs-up from Grace to appear. She nearly groaned with relief at the reprieve. She changed into yoga pants and a sweatshirt before picking up her laptop. She glanced at her wristwatch. She still had a few minutes before she needed to meet Monica. She felt a twinge of misgiving at the rendezvous site—the hotel rooftop garden—but considered it was probably more convenient and safer than anything outside the hotel.

She lay back on the bed and opened her laptop. Antoine had made a good point that Christie had likely searched for her birthing center in Switzerland as the first step in trying find her adopted baby. Maggie took a moment to ruefully reflect that while she had been obsessed with taking AP courses and navigating college entrance applications, poor Christie had been facing one of the most traumatic experiences a young woman could have—hiding a shameful pregnancy and then giving up the baby to strangers. It made Maggie think of Christie in a kinder light. Clearly, she had gone through hell. She had kept her pregnancy secret from even her best friends.

As Maggie googled *Swiss birthing centers* going back as far as 1984, she found herself wondering how Christie's experience had shaped her life going forward. Had she been tormented at having to give up her child? She'd remained childless her whole remaining life. Was that deliberate? As Maggie thought of what Christie's mindset might have been, she inevitably found herself thinking of Lisa and what Maggie could only regard as an above average interest in Emily. Was it all babies Lisa was enamored of, or just this one?

On the other hand, Lisa did seem pretty dotty about her own grandchildren so perhaps she was just a doting grandma. Maggie frowned when she realized that she herself didn't have those yearnings—at least not yet. Although it was entirely possible that raising a strong-willed five-year-old had killed that inclination in her at least for now.

An hour later, she closed her laptop, admitting defeat. She could find nothing in the way of Swiss birthing centers, either now or years ago. While her online search tools were only basic —Google and Bing—she still felt discouraged not to have come up with *anything*.

Had Christie found something?

Just then, Maggie's phone vibrated on the bed next to her. She picked it up and saw from the screen that it was Antoine.

"Hey, Antoine," she said.

"Good evening, Maggie," he said. "I enjoyed meeting your friend tonight."

"I'm glad. I know she enjoyed meeting you too."

"Have you considered why it is that you are not ready to be honest with her?"

As tired as she was, Maggie nearly laughed out loud.

"No," she said. "I'm being very honest with her about what you and I are working on. The other stuff is personal."

"I am honored in that case. I have some news on that front, but first things first."

Maggie felt a shiver of anticipation. At least someone was finding answers tonight!

"It seems that your friend Monica and her husband are in unfortunate financial straits," Antoine said.

That did surprise Maggie. Monica and Jason both came from wealthy families and from what Maggie could tell from social media, that had translated into exotic vacations, expensive cars and purchases of big houses in wealthy Atlanta neighborhoods.

"Really? In what way?" she asked.

"In the way that Monsieur Williams appears to have a bit of a gambling problem."

Maggie felt an instant flood of sympathy.

Poor Monica.

If Monica was aware of her husband's problem, it would be mortifying for her—on top of being financially debilitating. And of course it was a great motive for someone hoping to get their hands on that million-dollar inheritance—especially Jason. Maggie's mind began to race as all the possibilities stemming from this new information began to open up.

Jason had direct access to Christie's room.

"I can hear your mind whirling," Antoine said. "But even if Monsieur Williams wanted Christie dead, the question remains: how did he do it?"

"Maybe he tried to seduce her?" Maggie said. "Maybe he opened the diet soda as if he would drink it and then passed it on to Christie?"

She knew even as she said it that it was weak. She wondered if the autopsy had revealed that Christie had recently had sexual relations. Although it was possible that Jason might have seduced her without actually having sex with her.

"Well, at least it makes him a strong suspect," Antoine said. "And now on to the personal matter."

"Did you find Pierre?" Maggie asked.

It would make everything so much easier for Zouzou if Pierre could come clean about why he'd disappeared.

"I am sorry to disappoint you," Antoine said. "I didn't find him. But I did discover he has a criminal record."

ntoine's words hit Maggie like a punch to the stomach. She put a hand to her head and felt heat flush through her body.

"It is not so terrible," Antoine said on the phone.

How do I tell Grace? Does Zouzou know?

"It is only a juvenile record," Antoine said. "And it is sealed."

"So you don't know what the crime he was arrested for?"

"Not yet. I'm sorry, Maggie. I know this was not what you wanted to hear."

A few moments later, after she'd hung up from Antoine, Maggie was still reeling from the news. She tried to imagine if Pierre's criminal record had anything to do with his disappearance. The person she'd met two nights ago with Zouzou did not seem like the kind of man who would run off when he found out he was going to be a father. He'd struck her as being in love and fully engaged. Not the kind of person who would cut and run.

But what do I know? I've been surprised before.

After that, Maggie needed to hurry to make her appointment with Monica. She made her way up the stairs, her heart pounding in anticipation as she pushed open the door to the garden. When she did, a cool late-night breeze greeted her, carrying with it the faint scent of blooming flowers and damp earth. A colorful oasis during the day, the garden took on a whole different character at night. Bathed under the silvery glow of the moon the garden was a sprawling canvas of shadow and light. The quiet hum of the city below seemed to fade into the background.

Monica was already there, a solitary figure standing by the edge of the rooftop railing overlooking the sprawling cityscape below. She turned as she heard Maggie approach, her face partially illuminated in the moonlight. She held herself stiffly with an air of dignity, yet Maggie detected something cold in her eyes. She was reminded of Antoine's warning. If Monica was responsible for Christie's death, she wouldn't hesitate to try to stop Maggie from revealing her crime. Maggie walked toward her, careful to keep her back to the door that led back to the hotel. She stayed well away from the waist high railing that separated her from the five story drop below.

"You always were pathetically prompt," Monica said with a slight curl of her lip. "Always wanting to please."

"Knock it off, Monica," Maggie said. "I've had about enough of memory lane walks with you. Why did Christie want to destroy you?"

"My. So dramatic."

"Fine. So I guess the police will figure it out for themselves with the copy I made of Christie's letter."

Maggie turned to leave.

"Wait!"

Monica ran across the distance separating them, and Maggie instantly turned and put her hands up to defend herself. Monica laughed.

"Seriously, Maggie? What do you think I'm going to do? Toss you over the side? You outweigh me by at least thirty pounds. I guess those French pastries are every bit as good as people say they are."

Maggie was astounded that Monica thought attacking her weight would wound her. It was clear that Monica thought being overweight was the worst thing that could happen to anyone. Maggie took a step closer.

"My husband likes me whatever weight I am," she said. "Can you say the same about Jason? Or are those constant trips to Pilates and Jazzercize just for your own pleasure? Don't you ever wonder what would happen to your marriage if you just stopped? Or do you already know?"

"Shut up!" Monica said. Veins were visible in her neck as she clenched her jaw. "You don't know anything about my life."

"I guess you think you still look twenty," Maggie said with a laugh before realizing that Monica's venom was contagious. Realizing it made her even angrier—at herself.

"Just tell me why Christie was so mad at you," Maggie said. "That's all I want to know."

"Why? So you can decide if I had good reason to kill her? Forget it."

"Whatever it is, it must be pretty bad if you won't tell me," Maggie said. "Let's see. What might it be? Let me guess. Does it have anything to do with the baby she gave up in Switzerland?"

Maggie did not expect the reaction she got. She only threw it out to let Monica know that she was in on Christie's secret. She never for a moment thought she'd hit center mass. Monica's mouth fell open and she took a step back as if she could walk away from what she was hearing.

"That letter she sent me was personal," Monica said. "It has nothing to do with any baby or you or why Christie died."

"How about I make up my own mind about that?"

"Because it's none of your business! Did you tell the police about the letter?"

Monica looked nearly to the point of hysteria. She covered

her mouth as she waited for Maggie's answer, dread and fear warring in her eyes. Maggie didn't have the heart to lie to her.

"No," she said.

The look on Monica's face was a mixture of relief and disdain. Her expression hardened and she turned on her heel and walked away without another word. Maggie watched her go and realized that just because she'd told her she hadn't told the police didn't mean that Monica would feel safe with only Maggie knowing.

27

M aggie made her way back downstairs to her hotel room. Her movements were slow and laborious. She felt defeated. Once back in her room, her gaze lingered on the desk strewn with notes and her laptop. Every piece of information she'd discovered, each potential lead, seemed to weigh heavily on her mind. Whatever story they had to tell, she wasn't any nearer to understanding it yet.

With a sigh, she slipped off her shoes, the relief immediate as her feet sank into the soft carpet. Quickly she changed into her nightgown, washed off her makeup and brushed her teeth. By the time she finally collapsed into bed, her body surrendering to the exhaustion—her mind refused to quieten. The events of the day kept replaying in her head like a silent movie that had no end. She thought about texting Antoine to tell him about her rooftop meeting with Monica but since it had been basically fruitless, she decided to wait and update him when he called with the details of Pierre's juvenile record.

The news about Pierre's record was unfortunate but until Antoine was able to tell her *why* he'd been arrested, Maggie was only spinning her wheels worrying about that. Besides, she owed it to Zouzou to give Pierre the benefit of the doubt. At least for now.

She lay in the darkness of her hotel room, the soft hum of the city filtering in through the closed window. The bed, although perfectly comfortable, somehow felt too vast and too quiet, echoing the turmoil in her mind.

The day's events—and more specifically her encounter with Monica on the rooftop—rolled on and on in her mind with each scene, each conversation, each clue adding to the growing knot of anxiety in her stomach. Her eyes, although heavy with fatigue, stared blankly at the shadows dancing on the ceiling, the dim glow of the streetlights seeping in through the curtains painting an abstract pattern of light and dark.

She turned restlessly, her mind yearning for the oblivion of sleep. Yet, every time she closed her eyes, the unsolved mysteries and unanswered questions of both Pierre and Christie would resurface.

A glance at the bedside clock revealed the late hour, the glowing numbers a stark reminder of the time slipping away, the new day drawing closer with each passing minute. But the promise of that new day also brought with it the promise of new challenges, and an unsettling feeling of dread crept over her. She would have to talk to Grace tomorrow and if Zouzou hadn't told her the truth by then, Maggie would have to.

Finally, she got out of bed. She couldn't sleep and there was no sense trying. She went to her laptop in an attempt to put thoughts of Monica and Grace and Pierre out of her mind. To do that, she would switch gears and focus on another member of the group—the one she hadn't given much time or thought to up to now.

She opened up a browser window on her laptop and typed in: *William Jefferson Atlanta police chief 1984.*

Instantly she was presented with a long list of links covering Beth's father's suicide as well as the crimes he'd been indicted for that had landed him in prison. Maggie felt a twinge of guilt as she clicked on each link, drilling down deeper and deeper into the shame of Beth's family, a shame that just like Lisa's junior prom debacle, Maggie had somehow managed to have had little to no inkling of at the time.

After an hour, she found an article published in the Atlanta Journal-Constitution that spring of her senior year. The headline read:

Buckhead Ex-Police Chief Commits Suicide in Prison Following Indictment.

In a shocking turn of events, the former Buckhead Police Chief, William Jefferson, ended his life yesterday at Reidsville prison in Savannah where he was serving a twenty-two-year sentence. The tragic incident comes in the wake of Jefferson's recent indictment on multiple charges, casting a somber shadow on a community still grappling with the revelations of his crimes.

Maggie sat back and tried to imagine how horrific this time must have been for Beth. Her father killed himself in the summer after they graduated from high school. But Maggie remembered that Beth had left school a couple of months before graduation, citing illness, and because Maggie had been so intent on her own plans after high school, she had not given it much thought.

She continued finding and reading stories about Beth's father's tragedy, even running her finger down a line of those friends or relatives who came to visit him when he was incarcerated. There were very few. Maggie noted that Beth's mother had visited him the day before he killed himself. Maggie found a list of various relatives—Hendersons, Jeffersons, Lopezes,

Daniels—but never found Beth's name on any of the visitors' lists.

As she sat back and stared at the decade's old online articles, Maggie wondered if Beth's mother had said something to him in that last visit that led him to give up all hope? She rubbed a weary hand over her face and glanced at the clock on her laptop. It was nearly three in the morning now and she was beginning to finally tire. Besides, what did any of this have to do with Christie? At least with Lisa, it was easy to see where Christie fit in, although killing Christie over what she'd done at the prom was almost as far-fetched.

Maggie turned back to her laptop. She and Lisa had plans to meet up with Antoine again tomorrow, but they had no leads. If she could just find *some* clue to point them in a direction! This time, she turned her attention to Christie's social media pages and was surprised to see that they hadn't been taken down. She wasn't sure if disabling a deceased family member's social media account was something the police could do or whether it had to be a family member. In any case, she scrolled to the Facebook post that Christie had made a couple of days before she filmed the last one in the hotel room with the unopened soda can behind her.

Although the post wasn't geotagged, Maggie instantly recognized the photo Christie posted as having been taken in front of *Le mur des je t'aime*, just a short walk from Sacré-Cœur. It was a popular spot where tourists could be photographed in front of the wall on which "I love you" was written in 250 languages. The picture Christie had put up was of herself, alone, standing in front of the wall with a caption that read: *It's true what they say about the first cut being the deepest. #Carrie #juniorpromatlantahighschool #lisawashington #newbookcoming #watchforit*

Maggie was astonished when she saw the post, even more so because the police seemed to have completely missed it.

This was a definite reference to the embarrassing book she'd threatened to write about Lisa. Maggie read and reread the post, noting specifically that Lisa had been tagged. Was Christie trying to bait Lisa? Or was she just doing a little pre-book promotion?

The more Maggie stared at the Facebook post and Christie's grinning face, the more she thought she'd finally found the smoking gun she'd been looking for.

28

T he next morning, Maggie and Lisa met up in the lobby of the hotel. Beth and Monica were visible through the breakfast area and both of them looked up from their juice and croissants to glower at Maggie and Lisa as they passed.

"What's with them?" Lisa asked Maggie as they stepped out onto the front steps of the hotel.

"Who knows?" Maggie said, dismissively.

She hadn't told Lisa about her meeting with Monica the night before because she wanted to wait until they met up with Antoine before getting into it. She honestly wasn't sure that anything important had come from that meeting aside from rancor and defensiveness on Monica's part. In any case, the bigger revelation for Maggie was the public threat that Christie had made to Lisa by way of the Facebook post.

It was one thing to rub Lisa's nose in the shame of what had happened thirty years ago.

It was another thing altogether to threaten to tell the world.

As soon as they were on the street, Maggie and Lisa stopped at the same *pâtisserie* they'd gone to two days earlier for pastries. Maggie ordered two Americanos and another two *pain au chocolat*. She knew what the French thought of people—usually Americans—who walked and ate at the same time. She'd actually heard Laurent bluster about it more than a few times over the years, one of the few times he came near to ranting. But Montmartre was crammed with tourists of every stripe, and Maggie couldn't help but think it didn't matter what the people dispensing the coffee and sweeping the streets thought of her as she and Lisa walked to their meeting with Antoine.

Maggie had asked Antoine to meet them at Square Jean Rictus by the Wall of Love. She didn't expect to find any physical clues beyond the post that Christie had made, but she was just desperate enough for leads to take a chance on wasting the morning. She and Lisa walked to the Mountain of the Martyr where Montmartre's famous over three hundred steps began. Maggie glanced up them. Each step was steeped in history, the worn stones echoing stories of artists and lovers who once walked these paths as well as Christian saints from 250 AD and Nazis during their occupation.

Turning a corner, they passed the famous Bateau-Lavoir, a place that once served as a melting pot for artists, including Picasso and Modigliani. Now a historic site, its façade was adorned with plaques proudly commemorating its rich artistic history. As they neared their rendezvous point, Maggie finished her pastry and tossed her half-drunk coffee in the nearest trash bin. Random Parisians she would never see again were one thing, but she cared what Antoine thought of her.

"Bonjour, Antoine," she called as they joined him on the corner of rue Ravignan and rue d'Orchampt.

When he turned and smiled, Maggie was shocked to see he held a Starbucks cup in one hand.

"Bonjour Maggie," he said. "Madame Washington."

"Please call me Lisa," Lisa said.

"Okay," Maggie said. "We're here because Christie came

here with Monica and Beth that day that you and I got separated from them." She turned to Lisa. "Remember?"

"I remember they didn't wait for us," Lisa said archly.

"Right, so I was going over Christie's Facebook timeline last night," Maggie said, "and I saw a post she made in front of the Wall of Love."

Lisa laughed. "Wall of Love?"

"You sound very cynical, Lisa," Antoine said, wagging a finger at her. "Love is not something you can dismiss."

"Okay, if you say so," Lisa said with a grin. "Lead on, Maggie."

They turned down the rue d'Orchampt and followed the crowd. Even at nine in the morning, a large group had already gathered to stand in front of the impressive mural of dark blue tiles that covered four hundred square meters. Maggie had only ever heard of *Le Mur des je t'aime* but never seen it, and she found the outdoor presentation breathtaking. All around the square, interspersed among the tourists with their cameras and cellphone cameras, artists were at their easels eager to capture the crowds, the picturesque streets and the wall itself.

"Wow," Lisa said. "Paris is really hammering away at its reputation as the City of Lovers, isn't it?"

Maggie opened up her cellphone and scrolled to Christie's Facebook page. She had already sent the link to Antoine last night. Now she turned it around for Lisa to see. Lisa squinted at the post and blushed darkly.

"Ugh," she said. "Okay. What of it?"

"So you didn't see this post before now?" Maggie asked.

"I don't think Christie and I are Facebook friends," Lisa said.

"You don't know if you are Facebook friends?" Maggie gave her a dubious look.

"Well, I might have accepted a Friend request from her at

some point. I can't remember. But I'm hardly ever on Facebook."

"You'd be pretty unusual if you weren't on it," Maggie said. "It's addictive."

"That's the reason I try to resist it."

"So you're saying you *didn't* see this post?"

"You already asked me that, Maggie. Don't you believe me?"

Maggie put her phone back in her purse.

"Of course I believe you," she said.

She turned to go to the wall and began to scour it for any clue, any detail that might open up another lead. She found the exact spot where she thought Christie had taken the photo from and looked around from every sightline. She rejoined Lisa and Antoine who were standing back watching her.

"Why did she make that post specifically in front of the Wall of Love?" Maggie asked them.

Antoine turned to look at the wall and shrugged. Lisa said nothing at all. From the stiff set of her neck and the way she held her shoulders, Maggie realized that Lisa was angry with her. Maggie had probably been too forceful about why Christie might have included Lisa in her Facebook post. She had a tendency of doing that. Laurent said it was the American in her, the brash inclination to bulldoze her way through any situation. She was sorry if she hurt Lisa's feelings.

That is, assuming Lisa hadn't killed Christie.

29

Maggie was vaguely uncomfortable at her startling thought that Lisa might be Christie's killer. Did she really suspect her? Why had she agreed to team up with her if she didn't trust her? But one way or the other, Maggie was aware she was holding back debriefing with Antoine because Lisa was present. It was probably better to admit it than simply wish it weren't so.

"What next?" Lisa asked, glancing at her watch. "Or are you not done here?"

"I'm done," Maggie said.

The three of them walked in silence toward the center of Montmartre until they reached the rue Lepic and *Le Moulin de la Galette*, Montmartre's historic windmill.

"Oh, I recognize this place!" Lisa said. "We ate lunch here Saturday!"

Antoine snorted. "Surely not."

It was then that Maggie remembered that they had in fact eaten in the restaurant after Maggie had suggested there were much better, less touristy options in the same area, and was ignored. She reminded herself that the whole so-called reunion had been one constant display of disrespect. That thought triggered a flash of fury at Lisa and whatever snit she was in, but also at herself for having ever been interested in seeing these women just to show them how good her French was and how comfortable she was navigating a foreign country. Thinking about it now made her cheeks burn with humiliation. It hadn't even occurred to Maggie that with the easy availability of Google Translate, nowadays nobody felt on the back foot in any country where they didn't speak the language.

Whatever edge Maggie thought she'd had on everybody had been erased by the advancing technology and AI. As she stared up at the garishly iconic windmill, she thought back to her conversation with Lisa yesterday when Lisa related that Maggie's happy marriage and well-balanced kids were the points of envy for the rest of them. Maggie's children had problems and challenges like anyone else. But on the whole it was true—she'd been blessed. But then, they'd all finished college, found mates and were relatively settled.

Now if I really wanted to make them jealous, I should've let Laurent come to Paris this weekend.

She smiled at the thought of what the other women would've thought when they laid eyes on him. At six foot five, Laurent was memorable even if he wasn't also darkly handsome, which he was. Taciturn and towering, he commanded attention—especially the female variety—in every room he entered.

Once they reached the Place du Tertre Maggie realized that Antoine was leading them to the famous Renoir Gardens. Renowned for its tranquility and beauty, the park was a place to take a breath, do a reset, to stop and reflect in the heart of the metropolis. As they stepped onto the gravel paths that wove through the garden, Maggie marveled at the wide beds of colorful roses lining.

It didn't surprise her that Antoine had moved them to a

place known for peace and reconciliation. He'd no doubt picked up on the tension between her and Lisa. As they moved further into the garden, the famous swing, immortalized in Renoir's painting "The Swing" came into view. Its simple structure, nestled under the shade of a large chestnut tree, seemed to invite the visitor to relive a piece of history, a moment captured in time by the renowned artist.

They came to a long bench where they all sat down. Maggie was starting to feel the tension leave her shoulders for the first time all morning. Unfortunately, just when she was about to truly relax, Antoine spoiled it all.

"My contact says the police are close to making an arrest," he said.

"Really?" Lisa gasped, the fear radiating off her in waves. "Who?"

"That I do not know," he said. "It is almost certainly one of you four."

Lisa began to rub her hands against her slacks.

"They can't suspect me," she said looking from Maggie to Antoine. "I mean, can they? My room didn't connect with Christie's. I wasn't even in touch with her over the years."

It occurred to Maggie that a natural defense would be to look at whoever's rooms were connected to the victim's. It didn't surprise her that Lisa would be aware of that. But it did surprise her that she seemed to be counting on it.

"*Whoever* they arrest," she said to Lisa, "they'll scour that person's Internet history on any laptop or cellphone you have."

"Why are you telling me that?" Lisa asked, indignant. "I have nothing to hide."

"Then you have nothing to worry about."

Maggie turned away and tried to focus on the garden again. She tried to get back some of the peace she'd been experiencing just moments before. A part of her was glad the police were about to make an arrest. That meant one way or the other, this cat and mouse game would be over.

Assuming of course that they didn't just grab the first person who looked good to them.

Maggie glanced at Antoine, but he seemed content on taking in the garden, oblivious to his companions and their now bubbling anxiety. Maggie was grateful that Antoine hadn't made any references to Pierre. If he had any news for her, he'd give it to her confidentially.

"I already told Maggie," Antoine said, turning to Lisa, "that Jason and Monica Williams are in a serious financial predicament."

"Really?" Lisa blinked in surprise at the news.

"It would be helpful if you were to lean on Monica Williams," he said to both Lisa and Maggie. "Get her to admit the cause for his financial troubles. It would be even better if you could record her saying it."

"Monica would never admit she and Jason were having money problems," Lisa said.

"If you confront her with it, she will either lie or defend herself," Antoine said with a shrug. "Either way, I promise you she will say more than she intended."

"You're pretty devious, Antoine," Maggie said with an involuntary grin.

I can see why you and Laurent get on.

He turned to her.

"What did you find out about the Swiss birthing clinics?" he asked.

"I found several ," she said, "but none that were operational in the seventies."

"Even the religious ones? They're more likely to still be standing."

She hadn't thought of that.

"I'll try again," she said.

"But along those lines," Antoine said, watching a nuthatch in the towering maple tree overhead, "a contact of mine looked for documentation connecting any form of the name Williams in Atlanta with any off-the-books adoptions and found something that showed a baby was adopted by a Robert Williams in 1988."

Lisa sucked in a breath. A hand went to her throat in surprise.

"Robert Williams is Jason's father," she said with a gasp. "So the baby *was* Jason's?"

"Monica and Jason adopted Christie's baby?" Maggie asked, feeling the astonishment welling up inside her. *What had made Antoine decide to search for Williams? Had he suspected all along?*

"Very possibly," Antoine said. "And if it can be shown that she was the baby given up by the victim, and if the victim died without a will, it might be possible for her to inherit."

"Adele is a meth addict. I'm sure Monica and Jason must have power of attorney."

"We only have Monica's word that she's a meth addict," Maggie said. "Adele might be a perfectly normal woman."

"In that case, why did she give up Emily?" Lisa shot back.

"How do we know she did?" Maggie retorted.

"The point is," Antoine interrupted, "*if* the mother was found to be impaired in any way, her adopted parents would likely have control of her money."

"Monica adopted Christie's baby," Lisa said, shaking her head in disbelief. "And she kept it a secret from her all these years?"

Maggie turned back to Antoine.

"So you're saying Monica and Jason might be able to inherit the money from Christie?" Maggie asked.

"I don't know how inheritance laws work in the US. They are very different here."

"Trust me," Lisa said. "If there's money involved, Jason and his father will move heaven and earth to get their hands on it."

"Whether they're able to or not," Maggie said, "it's at least motive. So did your contact find the name of the clinic in Switzerland?" she asked him.

"Sadly, no," he said. "They are attempting to trace the adoption papers back to its source, but Robert Williams was careful to cover his tracks."

Lisa turned to Antoine as if appraising him.

"In any case, you're right about us needing to question Monica," Lisa said. "We need to do something to get the cops pointed in her direction."

"And Jason's," Maggie added. "That way, if the cops do swoop in to make an arrest, they'll at least be looking in the right direction."

"Right," Lisa said with a humorless laugh directed at Maggie. "Assuming of course, that you or I didn't do it."

30

The rest of Maggie's afternoon with Lisa and Antoine was progressively less productive. Because Lisa was present the whole time, Maggie hadn't been able to talk about Pierre with Antoine—or to even analyze in more detail the fact of Christie's Facebook page where she blatantly threatened Lisa with publication of her high school humiliation. Because Maggie was meeting up with Zouzou in front of her workplace in Pigalle, she left Antoine and Lisa in Montmartre and took the Metro to Clichy.

Maggie wasn't sure precisely what she was going to say to Zouzou beyond encouraging her again to please come clean to her mother—and then to give whatever comfort and support she could about Pierre's disappearance. As she rode on the train to Clichy, she found herself more and more concerned that Pierre was not who he said he was—given his secrecy about his criminal record. Antoine had yet to track down what crime Pierre had been arrested for.

Once back on the street, Maggie saw Zouzou striding toward her on the sidewalk in the iconic chef's clogs and jacket. They both raised a hand in greeting. Maggie couldn't stop the inevitable thought from forming that perhaps Zouzou had dodged a bullet with Pierre running out on her. Except that now she had a baby and no father.

The closer she got to Zouzou she noticed that Zouzou was smoking a cigarette. Maggie pressed her lips tightly together. She knew Zouzou used to smoke but hadn't realized she still did.

"Hey, Aunt Maggie," Zouzou said.

Zouzou's clothes, usually a vibrant testament to her lively personality, now mirrored her subdued mood. She wore a simple, loose-fitting blouse, and baggy jeans under her white chef's jacket. Her eyes seemed to reflect the anxiety gnawing at her every moment Pierre did not reappear.

"How are you doing?" Maggie asked.

"I'm managing. I called Mom a few minutes ago and told her what was going on."

Thank the Lord.

"She wanted to come up, but I told her not to. I told her I had you here."

Maggie reached out and squeezed the girl's arm reassuringly.

"We'll find him, Zouzou," she said.

Zouzou tossed her cigarette in the gutter and turned to dig something out of her bag.

"To that end," she said, "I went back to his apartment and found this."

She handed Maggie a crumpled note.

"I found it in his trash can," Zouzou said.

Maggie read the note.

Back off or people you love will die.

"Goodness," Maggie said. She felt a constriction in her chest as she reread the message.

"What do you think it means?" Zouzou asked. "Who do you think sent it? Don't you think that's the reason he left?"

Maggie turned the note over but there were no other words or clues as to who had written it.

"It's definitely a threat," Maggie said slowly.

"Well, duh!" Zouzou said, impatiently. "That's why he left!"

"Okay," Maggie asked. "That makes sense but who would threaten him like this?"

"What do you mean?"

Zouzou's face was pinched with dread as if she didn't want to hear whatever Maggie was about to say. Maggie took in a breath and chose her words carefully. She was well aware that Zouzou was very defensive. It wouldn't help to lie to her but she would try not to upset her unduly either.

"How does an acquisitions editor know the kind of people who might threaten him with his life?" Maggie asked.

Zouzou blushed in anger.

"Well, first of all, it wasn't his life they're threatening," she said, jabbing at the note with her finger. "It's his *loved ones*. And secondly, what are you implying? Are you saying he hangs out with thugs?"

"Zouzou, just think about it for a moment. You know him better than anyone. Does he gamble? Does he know people who do drugs?"

"Are you saying he's a drug dealer?" Zouzou said, her voice shrill.

"Calm down," Maggie said. "I'm not saying that. I'm trying to find out who might have left this message because yes, it's clearly tied to him disappearing. Stop being so defensive. We're on the same side."

Zouzou dug out another cigarette and lit it up.

"Sorry," she muttered.

Maggie looked again at the note which was written in English.

"I thought you said Pierre didn't speak English," she said.

"He doesn't. I'm sure he just ran it through a translator app.

Although it's not very complicated, Aunt Maggie. He could probably figure it out on his own."

"But it might mean that whoever wrote the note is English speaking."

"So?"

"I don't know. But it's something. It means something."

Maggie looked at the note again. Suddenly a strange connection jumped into her brain.

Pierre is a publisher. Christie was looking for a publisher for her book. Could the two be connected?

Or was Maggie spending so much time thinking about Christie's murder she couldn't see the world except through that lens?

"I have to go," Zouzou said.

"Can I keep this?" Maggie asked, holding up the note.

"Are you going to give it to the police?"

"Probably."

She turned with Zouzou to walk down the boulevard de Clichy toward Zouzou's restaurant.

"I'm glad you talked to your mother," Maggie said.

"Yeah, I knew you would be. She said she'd call you later."

"Zouzou, try not to worry. I know you're concerned about Pierre—"

"Of course I am," Zouzou said sharply. "He's been threatened? And then he disappears? Maybe whoever wrote that note came after him and...and..."

Maggie stopped her with a hand on her arm.

"Don't go there," she said. She held up the note. "This is actually a good lead and it'll help us find him. Think of it that way."

"I'll try."

"Otherwise, how are you doing?" Maggie asked.

"I'm better," Zouzou said. "It helped talking to Mom. I'm sorry I snapped at you, Aunt Maggie."

"Don't worry about that."

"Oh. One more thing."

She dug into her purse and pulled out a slim leather book.

"I found it on his desk," Zouzou said, handing it to Maggie. "It's Pierre's work diary. I haven't had time to look through it."

Maggie slipped it into her purse.

"Can you find him?" Zouzou asked, suddenly sounding and looking like the five-year-old that Maggie had known so well.

"We'll find him," Maggie said as she hugged her goodbye. She watched Zouzou disappear into the restaurant before turning to walk back down the famous Pigalle promenade. Her mind was buzzing ferociously, so much so that she passed the Clichy Metro without realizing it and then decided to walk the rest of the way back to the hotel.

The weather was overcast again and because of the heat of the day the air felt muggy and uncomfortable. Maggie walked ten blocks down the boulevard de Clichy before heading east on rue Caulaincourt. She'd missed a shortcut that would've taken her straight to rue Lepic, the historic shopping area near the hotel. Caulaincourt would get her there eventually but first it would wind past the *Cimetière de Montmartre*.

When Maggie came to the gates of the cemetery, she hesitated for one brief moment, then went inside. She very much wanted a moment alone with Pierre's diary without any chance of interruption. As she entered the cemetery grounds, the sounds of the bustling Montmartre shopping district behind her seemed to fade, replaced by the soft rustle of leaves and the cooing of pigeons. The air was cooler somehow within the gates and carried with it a faint scent of damp earth and age-old stone.

Once inside, the cemetery unfolded before her like a city within a city. Cobblestone paths wound through a labyrinth of elaborate tombs and simple gravestones. Towering trees lined the gravel and pebble paths, their branches casting a dappled shade on the graves below. Here and there, patches of green broke up the monotony of stone. Monumental sculptures and intricate carvings caught Maggie's eye, their details weathered by time but still exuding a sense of grandeur.

As she ventured deeper into the cemetery, she felt a sense of solemnity wash over her. The silent rows of gravestones, the eerie whispers of the wind, came together to create an atmosphere of reverence of unsettling tranquility. She found a bench under a large linden tree and sat down.

She briefly considered calling Grace but decided that could wait. If what Antoine said was true—that the police were close to making an arrest—she needed to follow any and every lead she had and the sooner the better. She couldn't shake the notion that Pierre's disappearance and Christie's murder were somehow connected. She opened his diary and glanced at the week before. Every day he'd written the letter Z and then encircled it with a heart. That reassured Maggie. She already believed that his show of affection for Zouzou hadn't been fake, but it was gratifying to see in the privacy of his work diary that his regard for her was real.

A photograph fell out of the pages as she held the book and she saw it was a picture of Zouzou in her chef whites, looking at the camera with a grin on her face, She looked relaxed and happy. Except for that first night, Maggie hadn't seen her looking so happy. She tucked the photo back within the diary's pages.

Going back two weeks she found entries as she would've expected from a junior acquisition's editor. Having been on the other end of the publishing process, Maggie found it fascinating to see it from Pierre's point of view.

Reviewed 3 manuscript subs today. One showed promise, a unique spin on the fantasy genre. Talk to Marie.

Editorial meeting: presented my thoughts on 2 promising mss. Marie seemed impressed.

Met with Longieux to discuss market trends in YA fiction. Fantasy and dystopian still popular. Longieux believes fading interest.

Reviewed contract for new author book deal. Sent queries to legal re: royalty rates and rights.

Lunch mtg at Café Coucher de Soleil with C. McCoy—American —on new book idea. Another tell all? Too soon? Hatchet job? Viable? Talk to Marie.

Maggie stared at the entry and felt her breath catch in her throat. Her heart thundered in her chest as she read the entry over and over again.

So it was true.

Pierre had lunch with Christie McCoy the day she died.

31

L

unch mtg at Café Coucher de Soleil with C. McCoy—
American—on new book idea. Another tell all? Too soon?
Hatchet job? Viable? Talk to Marie.

Maggie stared at the words. She felt her body temperature rising as she realized Pierre had met with Christie!

And then he disappeared!

Her mind whirling, Maggie thought back to the weekend. Christie must have met with Pierre the day the rest of them had gone to lunch after their Montmartre walking tour. Christie had begged off, saying she wanted to mail her painting home. The very painting that Maggie now knew Christie had never intended to mail home. Instead, she'd gone to a lunch appointment with the young acquisitions editor of *Lumière* to talk about the two book projects she was looking to shop.

Why had she turned to a French publisher? Surely Pierre wasn't senior enough to make a deal with her? Was his disappearance connected to the lunch? If so, why would a lunch with Christie prompt Pierre to disappear? Maggie searched on her phone for *Lumière*'s website. She scanned the list of editors in its online directory until she found a senior editor named

Marie Durand. That had to be the same Marie Pierre had referenced in his diary. She called the number to make an appointment, but it was after hours, and she only got the answering service.

Her questions would have to wait. Just then she noticed she'd received a text from Antoine telling her to check her email. When she did, she saw he'd sent her two emails, one detailing Christie's internet history and one listing her phone records.

Maggie had never had this kind of inside track for information before. It was like working with the police for a common goal. She glanced at both emails but decided they were too cumbersome to access through her phone. She'd wait to look at them on her laptop when she got back to the hotel. Meanwhile, she called Antoine.

"Good stuff," she said. "What am I looking at?"

"In a nutshell," he said, "after looking through the victim's internet history, I believe Christie succeeded in finding the name of the clinic in Switzerland where she gave birth. And attempted to contact them."

"Attempted?"

"It is hard to tell from the phone records but none of the calls appear long enough for her to have asked many questions or gotten any answers. My source says the clinic closed down decades ago."

Maggie felt a wave of discouragement. One step forward, two steps back.

"Well, that sucks," she said.

"Anything on your end?"

"Since you ask, I just found out that Pierre had a meeting with Christie the day she died."

"Now that is interesting," Antoine said.

"And my young friend went through his apartment and found what looks to be a threatening note addressed to him.

I'm photographing it and sending it to you now." Maggie pulled out the note and photographed it and sent it to Antoine as a text message.

"I'm a little surprised you're so tech-savvy," she said. "I don't want to imply that you wouldn't be at your age, but you do seem to be able to use all the latest tools pretty easily."

"Thank you, Madame," he said with a smile in his voice. "It is all part of a lifelong aim of mine to try to stay ahead of the younger ones. Until now, I was sure I was failing terribly."

"Not at all. Half the time Laurent doesn't even carry his phone and the only texts he's ever sent are two-word requests for me to pick up bread when I'm out."

Antoine laughed.

"He does sound thoroughly domesticated," he said. "It is hard to imagine. Ah, yes. I see what you mean about the threatening note."

"Do you think it's connected to Pierre's disappearance?"

"Don't you?"

"I was afraid you'd say that," she said. "Now I'm worried."

"Remind me again why he might be meeting with the victim?"

"She had two tell-all books she wanted to shop," Maggie said. "Zouzou told me that Pierre's company *Lumière* made a name for itself with those sorts of books."

"I see."

"They're closed for the day, but I'll get in tomorrow to talk to his supervisor."

"I have a call coming in," he said. "Let me call you back in a few minutes."

Maggie disconnected and sat on the bench staring into space trying to make sense of what she had discovered so far. If the clinic didn't exist anymore, she was sure Christie would try to track down the employees who worked there. Would her phone records show that? Were some of those calls to the clinic's former employees?

Frustrated, Maggie got up and began to walk toward the cemetery exit. As she did, she tried to imagine Christie's frame of mind when she was trying to track down the Switzerland clinic. Christie had never married and had no children. Her career was everything to her. Maggie imagined that when Christie came to the age when it was no longer a possibility of having children, she probably threw herself into her career.

What would her mindset have been when she came to the dead end on finding the baby she'd given up for adoption? Or had she given up? Did she suspect that Monica and Jason had adopted her baby? Why would she? Well, Antoine had found documentation proving it. And Christie *was* an investigative journalist. So did she know that Monica had raised her baby?

Her phone rang and she saw it was Antoine.

"Sorry about that," he said. "I thought it was my contact on the force checking on Pierre's record, but he is still looking into it."

"That's okay, listen," Maggie said. "If the birthing clinic that Christie went to is closed, I'm sure she would've tried to track down its employees. Can you get me a list of everyone who worked there before it closed?"

Antoine laughed.

"You do not give up, do you?" he said.

Maggie grinned as she watched a flock of pigeons leave the ground in a flurry and sail into the air.

"I have a hard time seeing that as an option," she said.

"So very American. I can see why Laurent married you."

32

Maggie was one block from her hotel when her phone rang and she saw it was Grace. She spotted a sidewalk bench and made her way there while she took the call.

"Hey," she said.

"Hey, yourself," Grace said. "So I guess I'm finally on the same page with everyone?"

"I'm sorry about that," Maggie said. "I would've told you if she had waited much longer. How are you doing?"

"I'm in a state, if you want to know," Grace said with a sigh. "Zouzou insists she doesn't want me to come to Paris and I think I have to respect that."

Maggie agreed that treating their adult children as adults was the hardest part of letting them out of the nest.

"I'm going to be here a few more days," Maggie said. "I'll look out for her until I go."

"Thanks, darling. I wish we were still in the days when a big hug and a bowl of ice cream could fix this. I feel pretty helpless."

Right then a domestic situation on Grace's end involving

Philippe and a broken bowl in the kitchen forced them to cut their conversation short. After they hung up, Maggie made her way back to the hotel. The weather had turned again by the time she trudged up the broad marble steps of the hotel. The lobby was vacant except for one person.

Jason stood at the reception desk idly scrolling through his cellphone. Maggie didn't know why he couldn't do this in his hotel room but imagined it had something to do with the fact that Monica was up there—perhaps with the baby. Maggie strode over to where he stood. He looked up, surprised to see her. Maggie knew he knew who she was. Although they probably hadn't spoken two words to each other in high school, they were at least aware of the other.

"I need a word," Maggie said.

Jason frowned and made a bit of a production of turning his head to look around as if to suggest that surely she wasn't interested in talking with *him*. He smiled in that disarming way of his and Maggie had a sudden image of him smiling his way through all kinds of trouble in his life. Much of it of his own making.

"What can I do you for?" he asked easily.

"I think you're making Sophie uncomfortable," Maggie said.

His smile stayed firmly tacked in place, but she saw his eyes dart about without turning his head.

"Excuse me?"

"Sophie? Your sitter?"

"I know who Sophie is," he said with a trace of irritation in his voice.

"I am suggesting your behavior with her might be perceived as being inappropriate."

"Perceived by whom?"

"Does Sophie count?" Maggie asked archly.

He blushed darkly. His eyes, normally so direct and

assured, flicked away from Maggie's piercing gaze. He rubbed the back of his neck, a telltale sign of unease.

"She said something to you?" he asked, not looking at her.

"She did," Maggie said. "It's not a problem. Not yet."

"I would never do anything to make Sophie uncomfortable," he said, jamming his phone into his pants pocket as if he didn't know what to do with it or his hands.

Maggie knew that was not the truth, but she wasn't going to call him on it. She'd delivered the message she'd intended and he'd received it loud and clear.

"I...we value Sophie highly," he said. "She's a...lifesaver."

"She's afraid she'll lose her job if she asks you to back off."

A dark flush crept up the side of his face.

"That would never happen," he said.

"Good." Maggie turned toward the elevator.

Once back in her room, Maggie kicked off her shoes and called downstairs to order an omelet and a small demi-bottle of Bordeaux. She curled up on the bed with her laptop and felt the trials of the day ripple through her. On the one hand, she was glad Grace was no longer being kept in the dark, but a tragedy shared didn't always lessen the load for all the people enduring it. Sometimes it just meant more people suffered.

Maggie couldn't stop thinking that whoever killed Christie was sophisticated and savvy enough to also threaten Pierre. Did that mean Pierre was in danger? If he ran away because of the note, then clearly *he* thought so. Maggie couldn't imagine Monica being able to track down Christie at her lunch with Pierre and then follow Pierre back to his office to slip a threatening note under his door. Before then killing Christie? It was preposterous. If for no other reason than the fact that Monica was always at the hotel. When would she have had time to run around Montmartre tracking Christie and Pierre?

Maggie was glad to have at last spoken to Jason about Sophie. That was one thing hanging over her that was done and dusted. At least Sophie would no longer be the target of his advances—regardless of how benign they were. She still believed what she'd told Antoine about Jason being basically a passive kind of guy. But that didn't mean he couldn't take advantage of a situation. In fact, that was exactly the sort of passive-aggressive opportunistic behavior that Maggie could imagine Jason doing.

She got up and retrieved a Perrier from the small mini-fridge in the room while she waited for her food to arrive, then came back to bed. It had been a hot day and she'd not hydrated nearly enough. After that, she did some basic research on *Lumière*. Thirty minutes later, she now knew that it was a progressive company but smaller than she'd thought. She wondered if Christie had known that it was so small when she approached them. She wouldn't likely have gotten much of an advance from them. But of course, Christie had other motives for the things she did. Perhaps with a million dollars inheritance, she could dismiss the need for a big advance from her publisher.

Maggie was about to open up another browser window to explore Catholic birthing centers in the mid-eighties when there was a knock at her door. Assuming it was room service, she hopped up and opened the door to see it *was* room service but also Lisa, holding Emily.

"Evening, Maggie," Lisa said, her eyes bright. "Mind if we come in?"

Maggie opened the door and took the tray of food from the hotel staff and set it on the desk. She tipped the girl at the door and then turned to see Lisa sitting on the bed with Emily.

"Is everything okay?" Maggie asked.

"Yes, of course," Lisa said. "It's only...well, no. Look, Maggie, I'm sorry about today. I feel like we weren't communicating very well."

Lisa patted Emily on the back and watched Maggie with troubled eyes.

"I'm sorry about that," Maggie said, coming to sit next to her. "I've actually got some other things going on."

"Anything you want to talk about?"

"It's not that big a deal. So what are you two doing wandering around?" Maggie took Emily's hand. The baby giggled.

"Monica was having trouble getting this one to settle and I said I'd help," Lisa said, kissing the child's head.

"Where's Sophie?"

"Asleep, I think. That girl's in a constant state of exhaustion. I don't mind."

"You miss your grandkids," Maggie said.

"My daughter thinks I overexcite them," Lisa said, gazing at Emily.

Her eyes welled up with unshed tears as she continued to stare at Emily. Maggie didn't know why she hadn't seen it before. Lisa's unhappiness was a palpable, unavoidable thing, like a tangible cloud that surrounded her. Her cheerfulness was just a mask for the deep sadness that lurked beneath.

"Oh," Maggie said. "Surely not."

"It's true. She said it's what Bill thinks—that's her husband. But I know it's her. She always has an excuse for why the kids aren't available."

"Oh, Lisa," Maggie said. "I'm sure they're just really busy. You know young families these days."

"I know. I'm sure you're right." Then she laughed. "If I'd known that my only kid was going to screen my calls, I would've had more kids, you know?"

Maggie smiled ruefully but just then her laptop dinged. She

went to the bed and saw that an email had come in from Antoine.

"Important?" Lisa asked, standing up.

"Probably not," Maggie said as she sat down and opened the email. "Are you hungry? I've got an omelet getting cold that I'm happy to share."

"No, I've eaten. What does it say?" Lisa leaned over Maggie's shoulder to look at the computer.

"It's from Antoine," Maggie said. "I asked him to get me a list of the employees at the birthing clinic where Christie had her baby."

"Seriously?" Lisa said. "That's really smart, Maggie."

"Oh! This is interesting," Maggie said, still reading the email. "He says that one of the contacts on the list matches a phone number that showed up in Christie's cellphone records!"

Maggie felt her pulse quicken as she saw the next connection Antoine pointed out.

"And even better, it's a Montmartre address! Can you believe our luck?"

This was proof that Christie had had the same idea Maggie did about contacting the birthing center employees.

"Antoine says her name is Marie-Thérèse Remey. She's a retired nun living right here in Montmartre," Maggie said. Her eyes widened as the next thought came to her.

"Is it possible Christie knew about her even before coming to Paris?" she wondered out loud.

"Maybe she's the real reason Christie came," Lisa suggested.

Maggie chewed a lip as she thought about that.

"Possibly," she said. "Except in the three days Christie was here before she was killed there wasn't a single hour we haven't all been together—except for that one lunch."

"That's not true," Lisa said, earnestly, patting the baby's back. "Christie bailed on dinner that first night in Paris."

Maggie turned to look at her in surprise, tilting her head as if to hear her better.

"She did?"

That was the night Maggie had eaten dinner with Zouzou and Pierre.

Did Christie meet up with the ex-employee of the clinic where she'd had her baby that night?

"What do you say, Lisa?" Maggie asked, closing her laptop with a grin. "Want to come with me to meet a ninety-five-year-old nun tomorrow?"

Lisa smiled back at Maggie.

"Absolutely definitely," she said. "Trust me, I'm vested."

33

The next morning, Maggie got out of the shower to find a missed call from Laurent and a text message from Lisa.

<sorry. fighting a migraine>

Maggie texted back that she hoped Lisa felt better and then called Laurent.

"Everything okay?" she asked. "I'm just heading out."

"All is good here. Have the police made an arrest?"

"No, but Antoine thinks they're about to. I got a lead last night that I'm following up on this morning."

"Is not dangerous?"

"It's a ninety-five-year-old nun."

"Hmmph."

Maggie laughed at his response.

"I'm serious, Laurent," she said. "She was one of the nurses at the Swiss birthing clinic thirty years ago."

"You are going alone?"

"It's broad daylight. I'll be fine. How's Amèlie?"

"She is alive. I am hoping not to strangle her today."

"Hashtag Grandkid goals," Maggie said with a laugh, but

she found herself wishing she was heading home. Amèlie was devoted to Laurent, but Maggie knew the child tended to be a little off balance when Maggie wasn't around.

It takes a village for sure. That, and an inviolate, unmovable routine.

After dressing for the day, Maggie called *Lumière* and made an appointment with Marie Durand for later in the afternoon. She decided to keep the purpose of her appointment deliberately vague when scheduling with Durand's assistant. Instead, she promised the young woman that she was not an author or a sales rep and would keep her visit brief.

Once she left the hotel, Maggie plotted a route to the address of the clinic's ex-employee using the GPS on her phone until the sounds of tourists and street performers gradually faded away. When they did, she found herself in a quiet, residential neighborhood.

A single lane cobblestone street wound its way up and around a steep hill, flanked by townhouses, each one unique in design and color. As Maggie passed them, she thought that some of them must date back centuries. All were covered in climbing ivy and the ubiquitous window boxes of geraniums.

Winded and red in the face from her climb, she finally arrived at a small, blue-shuttered house tucked away at the end of a narrow lane. A wrought-iron gate led to a tiny garden which Maggie made her way through to a small slate stoop where she knocked on the front door. Within moments, the door opened to reveal a petite elderly woman with stark white hair and blue eyes who regarded her with vague suspicion.

"Excuse me, *Ma Soeur*," Maggie said. "My name is Maggie Dernier. I'm hoping you are Marie-Thérèse Remey."

The woman smiled and then beckoned Maggie inside.

"So you have found me," she said stepping aside to allow Maggie inside. "How much do I owe you?"

"I'm not selling anything," Maggie said. "And I'm not a debt collector."

"Then you are most welcome," Marie-Thérèse said. "Come and I will make us some tea."

Maggie made herself comfortable in the old nun's small sitting room. The place seemed to exude a sense of peace and simplicity that was somehow both humbling and comforting. The walls, painted a soothing cream color, were covered with framed portraits of saints and family members surrounding a small, well-worn wooden cross. Maggie decided that the cozy little apartment not only showed the elderly nun's faith but her love for a simple life.

When Maggie estimated that the tea was nearly ready, she went into the kitchen to bring the tray into the sitting room while Marie-Thérèse directed her.

"Now," Marie-Thérèse said as she sat opposite Maggie in the sitting room, "tell me why I am talking to the second American who has come to my house in a week."

So Christie did track her down.

Maggie felt a pulse of excitement as she poured their tea.

"I'm here to talk about Christie McCoy," Maggie said. "I heard she wanted to see you."

Marie-Thérèse snorted.

"What she wanted was information," she corrected. "Visiting with me was the necessary step to achieving that."

"Did you remember her from before?" Maggie asked.

"From the clinic? Of course. I remember all my mothers."

The old woman's hands were clasped tightly in her lap, her cup of tea untouched on the coffee table in front of her. It was clear that while the passing years may have worn her physically, they'd done nothing to her spirit. The aura of peace and wisdom around her was almost palpable. Maggie found herself feeling an indelible sense of reverence for the life this woman had lived. She found herself wondering what Christie had made of her.

"Do all the girls come looking for you?" Maggie asked.

"Looking for their babies?"

Marie-Thérèse smiled sadly.

"Many," she said. "If not in person, then in spirit. The loss of a child you have carried within you is not something one survives without scars."

Maggie wondered if Marie-Thérèse had ever had a child herself.

"The clinic was called *Le Paradis des Anges*," Marie-Thérèse said. "It was nearly hidden in the Alps in the village of Huémoz in Switzerland."

"You make it sound like a fairytale," Maggie said.

Marie-Thérèse seemed to seriously consider the comment.

"In many ways it was. Especially for a young American girl with no experience feeling afraid and helpless." She finally reached for her tea. "They were all afraid."

"Did Christie want to give up her baby?"

Marie-Thérèse shrugged. "That I don't recall. In any case, her feelings were irrelevant. You have to remember, this was thirty years ago. I believe it is different today although perhaps not."

"Christie came to you to find out who adopted her child," Maggie pressed. "Right?"

"Americans are always in such a hurry," Marie-Thérèse said with a sigh.

"I'm sorry," Maggie said.

She'd already decided she would not tell Marie-Thérèse that Christie had been killed. There was no point. But that meant she could not imbue the visit with the kind of urgency she felt it needed either.

"No matter," Marie-Thérèse said getting up from her chair. "But I am glad you came."

She walked over to a table and pulled open a drawer. "I didn't mention this to Christie when she visited last weekend because I thought I'd lost it but after she left, I went looking for it."

She returned with two notebooks in her hands, a large one and a smaller one.

"Christie's diary," Marie-Thérèse said. "She gave it to me to give to whoever adopted her baby. She wanted the child to know that she'd not happily given her up."

Marie-Thérèse, her hands spotted with age and trembling slightly, passed the smaller worn, leather-bound diary to Maggie. Maggie cradled the book in her hands, feeling the weight of its history and also the secrets within its pages.

"Unfortunately," Marie-Thérèse said, "the adopted parents refused to take it, so I have kept it safe all these years. I think it will hurt Christie to know her daughter never got it but perhaps she would want it back. May I leave it with you to decide?"

"Yes," Maggie said, tucking the diary away in her purse. "Do I take it then, that you were not able to tell Christie who adopted her daughter?"

Now Marie-Thérèse sat back down and opened the larger notebook. Maggie's heart beat quickly as she realized what this book must be—the ledger of all the mothers and the adoptive parents from Marie-Thérèse's time at the clinic. Marie-Thérèse opened the book and ran her finger down the line of names.

"Of course the child would be a grown woman by now likely with children of her own," Marie-Thérèse said. "But Christie might still want to know her."

Maggie held her breath as Marie-Thérèse's finger stopped.

"Ah, yes," she said. "Here it is." She frowned and looked at Maggie. "Normally, of course, the clinic only allowed married couples to adopt. But we were a private clinic, and the rules were whatever Monseigneur said they were."

Maggie detected a faint hint of judgement in the woman's voice.

"Why would the rules be different for this baby?" Maggie asked.

"Money," the nun said. "The child was essentially bought."

Maggie tried to imagine how Christie had taken this news when Marie-Thérèse told her.

"The babe was given to a man named Robert Williams," the nun said closing the ledger. "And that's what I told Christie."

Although Maggie had already learned this from Antoine, she still felt a queasy heaviness fill her chest as her shoulders lowered in sadness.

So that was that.

Before she was killed, Christie had found out that her baby had been adopted by Jason and Monica. Maggie could only imagine the betrayal Christie would've felt—after years spent looking for the child—knowing that Monica had known all along and never said a word.

The image of Monica's black eye came vividly to mind.

The threatening letter made sense now. Christie would have been determined to get her revenge for what she believed Monica had done to her.

Unless she was stopped somehow.

As she had been.

34

M onica sat in the waiting room of the Montmartre police station. Her muscles felt jumpy as she smoothed out her skirt. She reminded herself that she needed to keep her cool and stay calm when she talked to the detective. Failing that, she needed to at least *look* calm.

The station was a hive of activity, filled with the low murmur of conversations.

Is this where Maggie had sat when they asked her to come in? she wondered. Do they do things differently if you volunteer to come in for questioning? She felt a bead of perspiration form on her forehead and discreetly wiped it away.

Surely, they look more favorably on you if you come in with helpful information?

A policewoman came into the waiting room and scanned the occupants. Monica knew she was looking for her. They locked eyes and Monica felt her stomach twist even as she felt an involuntary twitch of pique.

Can the French not even ask you to come with them without being hateful about it?

She got to her feet and followed the policewoman through a

door that led down a narrow hall to a small room. Inside the room were the two French detectives she'd seen at the hotel. Detective Benoit was a tall, handsome man, Monica noted as she stepped into the room.

A handsome man with a gaze like a hawk and probably the predatory tendencies of one, too.

The other detective in the room was a petite woman with sharp, intelligent eyes and a sneer on her face. Her cold demeanor did little to ease Monica's growing anxiety. She took a seat at the table opposite them. A single, harsh overhead light bore down from above casting a shadow on the table.

"You asked to speak with us, Madame Williams?" Detective Benoit said.

Monica was slightly unnerved that he didn't bother introducing his partner. Nor did either of them look suitably grateful for the information she was about to give them.

"You said if any of us remembered anything no matter how trivial, to tell you," she said.

"What did you remember?"

She was surprised that he was so direct. She thought he might at least thank her for taking the time to come in. It was more than slightly disconcerting that he wasn't doing that.

"The night that Christie died—" she began.

"We have not revealed the time of death," the woman said to her.

Monica looked at her, her heart pounding. Was the woman trying to trip her up?

"Go on, Madame Williams," Benoit said, a definite flicker of annoyance in his voice that Monica felt sure was directed at his partner.

"You were referring to the night the victim died," he prompted.

"Yes," Monica said.

She had to get it out in one breath. She thought she might

hyperventilate in the process but it was how she'd rehearsed it in front of the mirror, looking as totally honest and earnest as she could manage.

"After we all said goodnight that night and went to our rooms," she said in a rush, "I stepped out into the hallway around eleven o'clock to get some ice and I saw Maggie Dernier standing outside Christie's room."

The lie was out. It was on the table between them. Her heart was literally thundering in her chest. Would they believe her?

"You saw Maggie Dernier in front of the victim's door," Benoit stated, as if to clarify. "Doing what?"

Monica took in another breath. "Honestly? She was in the process of closing the door behind her."

"Going in or leaving?" The other detective asked, now not looking quite so suspicious, Monica thought.

"Leaving," Monica said.

The female detective pulled out a notebook and jotted something down in it. Monica needed to believe that was proof that she believed her. She felt her hands getting clammy and she pushed them under the table into her lap.

"And you did not remember seeing this until just now?" Benoit asked, his eyes narrowing as he regarded her.

"I was upset," Monica said. "Everything was a blur until this morning when the memory popped into my head."

"Are you sure it didn't pop into your head because it was a different night?" he asked.

"No." She shook her head. "Maggie wasn't friends with Christie. Not really. She wouldn't have been in her room."

"But you just said she was."

"Yes. That night she was. But I mean, she wouldn't normally have been in there."

"And why do you think she was there this time? This abnormal time?" Benoit asked.

Monica opened her eyes wide in as close an approximation to innocence as she could imagine. This too, she'd practiced in the mirror.

"Well, I don't know," she said. "But I remember it was the night Christie died."

"Are you suggesting Madame Dernier could have killed the victim?" the female detective asked, her pen poised over the notebook.

"Well, I guess so," Monica said. "I mean, I haven't seen Maggie in decades. I really don't know the kind of person she is any more."

Suddenly from out of nowhere a voice penetrated her brain with the single word.

Monica. The word was uttered in a disappointed tone in a voice Monica knew very well. She swallowed hard. It was her mother's voice. Her mother would be horrified for what she was doing to Maggie. But if she knew all that Monica had to lose, she'd understand.

Monica was sure she would.

"Do you need a glass of water, Madame Williams?" Benoit asked, his eyes still drilling into her. "You look pale."

"No, thank you. It's just...this is all very upsetting."

She dug her fingernails into the palms of her hands to remind her to stop speaking. Saying any more now would just make her look suspicious—or worse, guilty. She'd said what she'd come to say, and they could do with it what they would. Except for the ticking of a clock on the wall, the room fell completely silent.

Monica felt a strange mix of relief when she realized that the hardest part was over. All she had to do now was keep her mouth shut. Any anxiety they detected on her part would be the natural demeanor of a woman who had regretfully seen something that might hurt a friend. As she tried to meet

Benoit's eyes, she suddenly saw in her mind an image of herself flinging a poisonous copperhead away from her.

She dug her nails deeper into her palms. She'd done what she could to protect what she had.

All that was left to do now was pray the snake would slither away to find other prey.

35

The *Lumière* waiting room seemed to Maggie to be less a testament to the publishing company's rich literary heritage than a conscientious place in the center of artsy Montmartre. Maggie sat deep in a plush, velvet sofa, with matching armchairs flanking a glass-topped coffee table upon which lay the latest editions of various literary magazines.

The walls of the room were lined with paintings depicting Sacré-Cœur as well as the stairs leading up to it from every possible angle and the famous Abbsesses metro station with its iconic art deco styling. To one side of the room was a polished oak bookcase, its shelves lined with a selection of the house's most distinguished publications. The books, neatly displayed, were a physical indication of the publishing house's rich contribution to the literary world.

A modern crystal chandelier hung in the center of the room, but the rafters, molding and pillars all looked like they'd been there since the Reformation. All in all, Maggie decided it was quite a magical presentation.

She imagined hopeful authors sitting where she was sitting while hoping to talk to one of the editors about their manuscripts. To that end, she thought the room was a harmonious blend of elegance and comfort, designed to put writers at ease while subtly alluding to the esteemed reputation of the house.

"Madame Dernier?"

A young woman stepped silently into the room and smiled at Maggie.

"If you will follow me," she said.

Maggie was surprised the young woman spoke English but then, if they were open to buying manuscripts in English perhaps that wasn't unusual. She followed the woman down a long, thickly carpeted hall to a set of double doors. The woman opened the doors and ushered her into the room.

Inside, large French windows flooded the room with natural light and offered a picturesque view of the bustling streets of Montmartre. Maggie was momentarily distracted by the sight before quickly turning to focus on the middle-aged woman coming from around the desk to shake her hand.

"I am Marie Durand," the woman said. "How can I help you, Madame Dernier?"

Marie Durand was dressed in a beautiful Chanel suit paired with a crisp, white blouse. Her blonde hair was styled in a chic bob, framing her probing eyes.

"I am here," Maggie said evenly as she sat down in the chair opposite the desk, "because a client of yours was murdered two days ago."

She watched Marie's eyes reflect surprise at this information, and then wariness. The woman sat back in her chair behind the desk.

"I guess I should say *potential* client," Maggie said.

"I see," Marie said, frowning and watching Maggie closely.

Maggie was a little surprised that Marie wasn't immediately asking *which* potential client Maggie was referring to.

"I believe that there is a possible connection between one of the two books she was pitching to you and the reason she was murdered," Maggie said.

Marie simply watched her but said nothing.

"And I guess I find it curious that since then," Maggie said, "your assistant editor Pierre Lambert has gone missing."

Silence throbbed in the room like a threat.

"Remind me again of your role in this murder investigation?" Marie asked. "Are you connected to the police?"

"Not at such."

Marie tilted her head, her eyes suddenly cold as if to convey that that answer was not sufficient.

"I am very close to the young woman who is dating Pierre," Maggie said.

Maggie got up and showed Marie the photograph on her cellphone of the note that had been left in Pierre's apartment. She watched Marie's face blanch.

Marie read the note over and over, her expression a mixture of shock and concern.

"Pierre called in sick," she said. "When I called him to say it would be worth his job if he did not come in, I got only his voicemail." She looked at Maggie. "Do you think he is in trouble?"

Maggie gestured to her phone.

"You know as much as I do," she said.

Marie handed Maggie her phone and then stood up and walked to the window overlooking the bustling square of boulevard de Clichy. Then she turned back to Maggie.

"This potential client of ours," she said. "It is the American woman?"

"Christie McCoy. That's right."

"Why do the police think she was killed?"

"They're not saying," Maggie said. "But Christie bragged to anyone who would listen that she was writing a book about an event that happened to one of the women I'm traveling with. An event that was humiliating for her."

"The *Carrie* book."

When Maggie frowned at her words, Marie waved her hand dismissively.

"That is just what we call it in-house. It was described to us as a coming-of-age story that was a combination of *Mean Girls* and *Carrie*."

"So you *were* considering buying it?"

"Most definitely. There was another project she pitched to us, but it dealt with police corruption and even though it was based in the US, we decided it was not right for us." She looked ruefully at Maggie. "We are in constant hot water with the police. We are not afraid of them but if we don't have to poke the bear, we won't. The police suicide book was not a big enough scandal to make the inevitable blowback worth it."

The police suicide book.

So, Christie was also writing about Beth's father's disgrace.

Did Beth know about this?

"Did you tell Pierre to tell Christie that you would buy the *Carrie* project?" Maggie asked.

"No. We hadn't gotten that far. She had wonderful credentials. It is a shame this happened. Her book would've sold well."

Maggie felt a sick twinge in her gut at the woman's words.

But first it would've destroyed someone's life.

36

E specially in late summer. Square Louise Michel at the base of Sacré-Cœur was a vibrant oasis of lush greenery, flowering plants, and winding paths. Because it ascended the hill with its terraced gardens, the park also provided a great view of Paris. Plus, it was situated midway from the offices of *Lumière* and Maggie's hotel on rue Gabrielle. Maggie knew the walk back to the hotel wasn't going to give her anywhere near enough time to process all the ramifications of what she'd learned at *Lumière*. She always thought there was something about wandering through a park that was extremely helpful in being able to sort out her thoughts.

Inside the park, she sat down on a bench in front of a duck pond where she could hear the excited squeals of the nearby children playing on the lawn.

What Maggie now knew was that Christie had been in the process of selling two ruinous books. Books that gave both Beth and Lisa motives for killing Christie—if they'd known what she was doing. Lisa definitely knew about the possibility of the so-called *Carrie* book because Christie had practically rubbed her nose in it during the boat tour. Suddenly Maggie's phone rang. She saw it was Grace and immediately accepted the call.

"Hey," she said.

"Hey yourself. Where are you?"

"Sitting in a park."

"Uh oh. Does that mean you've broken the case?"

"It means the opposite of that," Maggie said with a laugh. "It means my head is about to explode with all the stuff I've learned—most of which I can't make sense of."

"Talk to me. What's going on?"

"Well, I went to talk to someone who worked at the clinic when Christie had her baby twenty-six years ago. She remembered her. Christie had tracked her down, too."

"What did she tell you?"

"For one thing, she told me that she told Christie who it was who adopted her baby."

"Is that legal?"

"It was a religious-oriented clinic. I think they answer to a higher power."

"Yeah, okay. Go on."

"Not only did Christie find out where the baby went to after she gave it up, but she found out it was adopted by the biological father of the baby."

"You're kidding me."

"No."

"And Christie never knew this?"

"Not a clue. In fact, it was *his* father who gave a big enough donation to the clinic to get past all the inconvenient paperwork that most adoptions require."

"So her baby was essentially bought."

"Basically. I mean, I'm not positive Christie put it together that it was Monica and Jason who bought her baby—"

"Didn't you say Christie was an investigative journalist?"

"Yes."

"Well, no offense, darling, but if you figured it out, she probably did too."

"You're right," Maggie said with a sigh. "In fact, Monica got a letter from Christie the day she was killed saying she was going to ruin Monica's life."

"Which gives Monica motive for killing her."

"Not only that, but I just came back from a visit to the publishing house where Christie was trying to pedal two books that would blacken the reputations of the other two women in our group."

"Good Lord, this Christie was a piece of work. Are you sure the hotel maid or the bell hop didn't have motives to kill her, too?"

"Honestly, the real problem," Maggie said as she watched a group of toddlers with their minders skipping down the wide park pathways toward the playground, "is that all motives aside, there doesn't seem to be any way anyone could've gotten the poison that killed her into her."

"Why couldn't they just poison her drink?"

"There's no evidence that anyone but Christie touched the can the poison was found in."

"Maybe they wiped their prints off the can?"

"But just imagine someone popping the top of a diet cola and handing it to you."

"That would be weird."

"Right? It wouldn't happen. And Christie was a prickly sort. There's no way she'd drink out of a can someone else opened. Even *I* wouldn't."

"So she opened it herself."

"That's what forensics insists happened."

"But it isn't suicide?"

"The ME says not. And if you knew Christie, you wouldn't believe it either. Plus, there was no suicide note. And she had her clothes all laid out for the next day. On top of that, she was in the process of meeting with publishing houses to pitch her books. No. She didn't kill herself."

"It's definitely a puzzle."

"How are you doing?" Maggie asked. "Have you talked to Zouzou recently?"

"Not yet, but we've exchanged texts. She's pretty upset about Pierre being missing. I don't suppose you've found out anything?"

A twinge of concern pinged inside Maggie's head as it suddenly occurred to her that Zouzou might have left out the part about being pregnant when she talked to her mother yesterday. In fact, now that Maggie thought of it, the idea that Grace wouldn't mention the pregnancy to Maggie if she knew about it was pretty nearly impossible. Maggie felt her heart sink. Grace still didn't know.

"No," Maggie said. "I went to his place of business and they're just as perplexed as we are. He got this strange threatening note and then disappeared."

"Are you sure that's all?"

"Well, Zouzou didn't think the apartment looked as if there had been a struggle. And his suitcase is missing."

"Any possibility that *he* killed Christie?" Grace asked.

"And then went on the lam? What would his motive be?"

"I don't know."

"Listen, Grace. When I met Pierre, I really liked him. Please don't make up your mind before you meet him."

"*If* I meet him."

After they talked for a few minutes more, Maggie disconnected and sat in the park with her eyes closed. She tried to find some kind of assimilation or distillation of all the facts she'd garnered today. She found herself eager to tell Antoine what she'd learned to see what he could make of it all.

Although she was now convinced that Zouzou hadn't told Grace she was pregnant, Maggie was glad that Zouzou was at least in communication with her mother. It made Maggie want to connect with her own daughter. She picked up her phone and checked the time and saw that it was eleven in the morning in Atlanta where Mila was. Laurent had said Mila had decided to come home for the harvest this summer for which Maggie was grateful. She was also grateful that Mila always seemed so level-headed, although Maggie missed her. She sent her a text.

<just checking in. All good?>

Then she turned to her purse and pulled out the diary that *Soeur* Marie-Thérèse had given her. She ran her hand over the leather and imagined seventeen-year-old Christie pouring her heart and soul and tears into this little book, not knowing what the future would bring her or her little daughter. It made Maggie sad to think that Christie had written these passages in order that the child might someday know who her mother was. Maggie was glad Christie never knew that her baby's adopted parents refused to take the diary.

Just then Maggie's phone dinged heralding an incoming text message.

<Yep! Just heading out to lunch with Anna. Heart emoji.*>*

Maggie smiled at the text and put a thumbs up emoji on Mila's text. She was careful not to be too needy or oppressive with all her children, but she was grateful to have the easy technology to unobtrusively connect with them.

She opened the diary to a random section in the middle. Christie had used a fountain pen and Maggie was surprised to find her handwriting flowery and almost childlike.

Diary Entry - March 8, 1988

Today the snow falls gently outside, each flake unique, just like the life growing inside me. I feel you stir, my little one, a tiny flutter that's both alien and beautiful. I want you to know, even now, that every heartbeat of yours echoes within me, a testament to a love I didn't know I was capable of.

Maggie swallowed hard with emotion and surprise. This was a Christie she had no idea existed.

Diary Entry - March 25, 1988

I saw you today, a blurry image on a screen, but unmistakably you. And in that moment, every fear, every doubt, felt insignificant against the overwhelming love I felt. I am alone here, in this foreign place, but with you, I feel a strange sense of companionship. I want you to know that, my darling.

Diary Entry - April 10, 1988

I dream of you often. I dream of holding you, of seeing your face, of hearing your laughter. I dream of a future that I wish we could share. But I want more for you, my sweet child. More than what a scared, seventeen-year-old can provide. I hope you understand one day.

37

It was with a much heavier heart that Maggie walked the short route back to the hotel that afternoon. Christie's words swam in her head the whole way. All Christie's hopes and dreams for the baby she was carrying were described in the diary, captured in Christie's neat hand. The writer of that diary was not the girl that Maggie had ever known. And certainly not the woman she'd become.

That girl was afraid. She knew that the future was not her friend. In spite of that, she was facing it bravely. She and her baby.

Maggie texted Lisa as she stepped into the lobby.

<how are you feeling? Call me if you feel up to it>

She watched the text until a caption appeared reading: *message not delivered.* That didn't worry Maggie since she assumed that if Lisa was battling a migraine, she probably had turned her phone off. She walked across the lobby and heard sounds coming from the hotel bar and rerouted there out of curiosity.

She peeked into the bar and saw Beth and Monica sitting at

a table. With them was Sophie and the omnipresent stroller with Emily inside.

Maggie walked over to their table and as she did, she seemed to feel the whole room go cold.

"What's up?" she asked, smiling briefly at Sophie who quickly looked at the floor.

"I don't think we're supposed to talk to you," Beth said, looking at Monica as if for guidance.

"What are you talking about?" Maggie asked.

"You should tell her," Beth said to Monica.

Monica sighed.

"I went to the police this afternoon with something I remembered," she said.

Maggie was instantly on guard. She glanced at Beth who wasn't meeting her gaze.

"Something about the night Christie was killed?" Maggie asked.

"You might say that," Monica said, "No, you're right, Beth. I shouldn't say anything."

"Whatever," Maggie said in annoyance, on the verge of turning away just as Detective Benoit and a woman in plain-clothes filled the doorway of the bar.

The way they were looking at her, there was no doubt in Maggie's mind that they were here for her.

38

The holding cell at the Montmartre police station was a stark contrast to the cozy hotel bar she had just left. Maggie sat on a metal bench bolted to the white-washed floor that held an institutional chill. The cell was a small, austere space, intentionally devoid of any warmth or comfort. The harsh fluorescent lighting overhead did little to dispel the gloom.

Opposite the bench, a small, barred door made of heavy steel marked the only entrance and exit.

Instead of questioning her or giving her a chance to ask questions or clear herself or tell them what she'd discovered about Christie, Maggie was brusquely escorted from the hotel to a police van and then to the holding cell where she was simply left. She hadn't even been processed. She was allowed to keep her purse—further baffling her as to what their possible intentions could be—but they'd taken her cellphone. If they wanted to make her feel alone and helpless, they'd succeeded. She couldn't reach Laurent or Antoine. And the only people who knew where she was—Beth and Monica—were likely the ones who'd helped her get here.

Maggie's mind was a whirlwind of conflicting thoughts and emotions. Mostly, she felt a sense of disbelief, as the events of the day played out in her mind repeatedly like a surreal, disjointed movie. How could this be happening?

She had started this weekend full of hope and excitement, only to find herself sitting in this bleak cell. When she thought of how foolish she'd been to anticipate seeing these women again, she was flooded with recriminations. Now that she thought back to that time in high school, she remembered she had always been an outsider to the group. Her family was wealthy, so she'd had the guise of acceptance by the other girls, but she knew that they talked about her behind her back.

The way Monica and Beth looked at her today in the bar was a look she remembered very well from so many times in the high school cafeteria.

They were toxic, both of them. Caring only about themselves.

How could I have been so naive?

She leaned up against the cold wall and turned to look inside her purse. She found a mint that she ate and then Christie's diary. She pulled it out and flipped to a later section in the book, closer to when it would be time for her to deliver.

Maggie wanted to remember Christie as someone human and real. And vulnerable. These passages showed a girl about to become a mother. And about to have her heart broken like few teenagers ever have to experience.

Diary Entry - May 3, 1988

The nurses are kind. They give me books about babies, about what to expect when you arrive. Each word I read, each picture I see, makes you more real to me. And with every passing day, the decision I have to make grows heavier. But I want you to have the world, my love, even if it means not having me.

Diary Entry - May 20, 1978

Your kicks are stronger now, a constant reminder of the life within me. Sometimes, I lay awake at night, my hand on my belly, feeling you move. I talk to you then, about my hopes and dreams, for me, for you. I want you to know them all.

Maggie closed the diary and felt her eyes fill with tears. She'd never gotten to know *that* Christie. Probably nobody had except maybe *Soeur* Marie-Thérèse. Fear began to creep into her as she sat there in the cell and considered the potential consequences of her situation. Her mind raced with worst case scenarios, each one more terrifying than the last.

How long could they keep her here? Would she at least be allowed a phone call? It was evening now. Would there be someone at the American embassy to help her?

Just as she felt her despair beginning to infuse her entire body, she heard footsteps coming down the hall. She got to her feet. She was expecting to see the jailer, but it was Detective Benoit. He unlocked the door.

"You should have mentioned that you knew Antoine Berger," he said.

"In my country," Maggie said, trying to keep her voice from shaking, "we don't rely on favors and personal connections when we're innocent."

He smiled at her, and Maggie was astonished to see it wasn't a mean smile.

"If you say so, Madame Dernier," he said.

Calling her by her last name like that reminded Maggie that Benoit was aware of Laurent's reputation. She still didn't know if that was a good or bad thing. Benoit stepped aside to let her out.

"You may leave, Madame Dernier," he said, handing over her cellphone.

"You...you're not going to question me?"

"Not tonight," he said, motioning for her to go in front of him.

Maggie walked down the hall, enjoying the feeling of the relative warmth that contrasted so starkly with the cold room she'd just left. When they reached the door leading to the waiting room, Maggie saw Antoine Berger standing in the doorway waiting for her. She flushed with gratitude and met him in the middle of the room where they shook hands. Her first impulse was to hug him but that was the American in her and she knew it would probably make Antoine uncomfortable. As she turned to glance back at Benoit, she saw he still had that same enigmatic smile on his face. He gave her a casual salute and disappeared back into the interior of the station.

Before Maggie could find out how Antoine knew she had been brought into custody, she turned her phone back on and saw that Zouzou had called her five times. While her first inclination had been to call Laurent, she put a call in to Zouzou instead as she and Antoine walked out of the building.

When Zouzou answered, she didn't give Maggie a chance to speak. She said just a few bitter words and then hung up, leaving Maggie standing on the sidewalk staring at her phone, the world having suddenly ground to a screeching halt.

"Maggie?" Antoine asked, his voice laced with concern. "What has happened?"

Maggie looked at him sadly.

"She lost the baby," she said.

39

B eth sat alone in the dimly lit corner of the hotel bar, the usual cacophony of clinking glasses and hushed conversations a muted hum in her ears. She held a half-full glass of whiskey, the amber liquid reflecting the soft lighting above her table. She glanced in the antique mirror over the bar and saw a glowering middle-aged woman staring back at her. The lines around her eyes seemed more pronounced than usual. She looked away.

Small wonder after what I've done.

She took a slow sip of her drink, the burn of the alcohol a welcome distraction from the whirlpool of flashbacks and what-ifs churning inside her. Her past actions rose up in her mind like specters in the dark.

What was I thinking? How could I have even considered it?

The questions were relentless, seeming to gnaw at her from her very insides. She glanced in the direction that Monica had gone with Sophie and the baby. The thought of Monica as a mother physically tortured Beth. Beth would have given everything to have had a child. But that was not God's will.

Cruel, heartless God. After everything He put me through.

And yet Monica had been blessed with a child. Beth shook her head violently as if to shake loose the offending images. It didn't matter *how* the child had turned out. Meth addict or Rhodes Scholar. That wasn't important. Monica had taken her child to carpool and made her lunches and bought her school uniforms and read to her at night. None of that could be taken away from her. She'd had it all while Beth had worked nights to get ahead in the law firm before coming home to frozen dinners and an empty house. She clenched her hands into fists. And now Monica was being blessed again with little Emily. Only Monica didn't care.

Beth held her fists tightly in her lap, her fingernails biting into her palms. The regret of not having tried harder—even without a husband, although granted there had been two—tortured her.

If I'd been born a generation later, I'd have just gotten a sperm donor. Why did I think I needed a husband to have children?

But now it was too late. And then came all the other missteps, miscalculations, and missed opportunities since they were all in school together—a virtual mountain of failures. Her career, her relationships, her self-worth—everything seemed to be tangled up in a web of regret.

The guilt alone felt as if it would crush her. And who did she have to blame but herself for how it was all turning out? She glanced at her phone on the bar top. Like the true masochist she was, she kept waking up her screen to see the last text her husband had sent her an hour earlier.

<im sorry please lets be amicable about this>

Who was it David thought he had married all those years ago? Who was it he thought she was now? She lifted a finger to the bartender for another whisky. She wasn't driving. She could just go upstairs and collapse.

Who was she kidding? None of that mattered. Being drunk, not being drunk, getting behind the wheel of a car. Or not.

None of it mattered.

She missed the woman she used to be—confident, in control, unapologetic, ready for life, ready to change things for the better—the world, her own family. She closed her eyes and for a moment saw her mother—and her father. Smiling, happy. Had they ever really been happy? Or had what Dad done spoiled even the pre-history?

Or was that spoiled by what I did to him?

40

Antoine led Maggie down two long circuitous streets and up the famous stairs to where the imposing presence of Sacré-Cœur dominated the horizon. At first Maggie thought they would stop outside. Even now at nearly eleven in the evening, the square in front was filled with tourists milling about. But Antoine walked to the massive front door and pushed inside, startling Maggie that the church was open at this time of night.

She followed him in and was immediately struck by the quiet, interrupted only by the sounds of their footsteps on the slate floor as Antoine led her to the back row of pews. Maggie stared everywhere at once, her own problems momentarily forgotten.

While Sacré-Cœur was a popular tourist attraction, it was first and foremost a place of worship. Antoine sat and motioned for Maggie to do the same. She stared at the grand mosaic of Christ in Majesty located in the apse. She knew it to be one of the largest mosaics of its kind in the world, depicting Jesus with outstretched arms against a golden background, surrounded by various biblical figures. Just looking at it filled her with a quiet peace and awe. The vibrant colors and intricate details of the mosaic seemed to glow with an ethereal light. The smell of burning candles and incense was everywhere. Here, where Maggie sat at the back of the basilica, the air was rich with the scent of old stone and wax, a unique aroma that seemed to carry the weight of centuries of prayer and contemplation. The coolness that prickled her skin was from the icy reflection of the stones all around and above her. The beautifully carved statues of saints looked upon her with serene expressions, their stone eyes seeming to hold a comforting promise of sanctuary.

It took Maggie a good twenty minutes of just sitting and staring, of being in this historic, healing place of worship and respite before she was able to focus on what had happened to her.

"Ready?" Antoine asked in a soft voice.

"Almost," Maggie said.

She got up and went to the votive candle station, where she dropped five euros into the collection box and picked up a long match to light one of the candles. Then she knelt and said a prayer for the soul of Zouzou's lost baby. She bowed her head.

Heavenly Father, I pray You welcome this little innocent soul into Your kingdom, where there is no pain or sorrow. Please bring healing and comfort to Zouzou. Remind her she is not alone, that You are with her in her time of sorrow, and that it's okay to grieve.

Just as Maggie was about to get to her feet she hesitated.

And Lord, please welcome Christie too into your embrace. Amen.

As they stepped outside, evening was descending on the square in front of Sacré-Cœur, the moon settling into the sky heavy with dark low-hanging grey clouds. The air was cool, carrying the scent of impending rain. The looming silhouette of Sacré-Cœur, behind them, stood solemn and imposing, somehow adding to the profound silence around them.

Antoine spoke softly to Maggie as they walked, explaining

that when she hadn't shown up for her rendezvous with him, he went to the hotel where he was told by the staff that she'd been arrested. From there he went to the station where he spoke with Benoit.

"So you just showed up and he handed you the keys to my jail cell?" Maggie asked.

"I still have some measure of respect in reserve with the young ones," he said with a smile.

Maggie let the comment pass since she was sure Benoit was easily in his mid-forties.

"They really let me out just on your say so?" she pressed.

"That surprises you?"

"A little."

"Benoit never believed you had anything to tell him."

"Then why—?"

"He was obliged to follow up on the allegation made against you by your fellow countrywoman."

"I'm guessing that was Monica," Maggie said. "Do you know who he's looking at as a suspect?"

"He didn't share that information with me. Nostalgic esteem only goes so far. I am retired so I am out of the loop as they say."

"Well, you were in the loop good enough to rescue me tonight. Thank you, Antoine. I owe you."

"You don't. If anyone owes anyone it was me to Laurent and I fear I'll never even that score."

"That sounds very mysterious."

"I fear it must remain so."

Just then Maggie's phone dinged signaling the receipt of a text message. It was from Zouzou.

<*ur prob thrilled the babys gone*>

Maggie felt her jaw tighten painfully. She texted her back.

<*call your mother. Tell her about the baby. Talk to her. We love you*>

"Your young friend?"

Maggie nodded.

"I'm sorry, Maggie," he said.

Maggie turned to him and realized that he was genuine. Despite the brevity of their acquaintance, she felt as if their friendship was one of many years, not days. She knew that phenomenon was partially due to Laurent. He'd vouched for Antoine and Antoine had naturally assumed that any woman Laurent married must be special.

"Thank you, Antoine."

She looked at him with misty eyes which quickly resulted in him clearing his throat and looking away. She remembered how often the French were uncomfortable with strong emotion, considering it strictly an American tendency, or worse —Russian.

"I know a place that is open late," Antoine said. "Unless you are weary from your ordeal?"

"Lead on," Maggie said.

It was a small bar tucked away in the heart of Place du Tertre which, at this late hour, was nearly deserted of its usual crush of tourists. Maggie was surprised there were so many people inside. They took a table in the back and Antoine ordered sherry for both of them.

Once they were settled, Maggie told him about her visit with *Soeur* Marie-Thérèse and then with Pierre's boss Marie Durant.

"So both women have motives for wanting Christie dead," Antoine observed.

"Well, in so much as Christie was planning tell-all books on each of them, yes," Maggie said. "But don't forget that Christie knew about Monica getting her baby and never telling her."

"Ergo the threatening note."

"Right. So make that three motives."

"I notice Lisa has dropped out of our coterie?" he said lightly.

"That's another thing," Maggie said as she sipped her drink, enjoying the feel of it as it raced down her throat in a heated line. "She bailed on my interview with the nun this morning and I haven't been able to get in touch with her since. I'm actually a little worried."

"In what way?"

"Well, in the way that Pierre disappeared and now I can't find Lisa."

"Your friend has not been abducted."

Maggie narrowed her eyes at him.

"What do you know?"

He shrugged.

"I know that the police searched her room this morning and found her clothes and suitcase gone."

41

M aggie's mouth fell open in shock.
"She...she just left? She checked out?"
She felt a dizziness come over her at this unfathomable news. She rubbed her temples with both hands.

Lisa ran off?

"That I do not know," Antoine said. "But it does not look like an abduction."

Maggie pulled out her phone and called Lisa's number, but it went instantly to voicemail as it would if the phone were turned off.

"I can't believe this," she said. "She lied to me."

"It does sound like it."

Maggie looked at him in bewilderment.

"The police don't care that she just left?"

"They have her passport. And they're keeping an eye on trains and planes and rental cars."

Suddenly Maggie got a memory of Lisa watching Emily intently. Fear coiled in her gut as her mind backtracked to the bar where she'd seen Sophie with the baby.

But that was hours ago.

"What is it, Maggie?" Antoine asked.

Maggie held up a finger to him asking him to wait and then called Monica.

"What do you want?" Monica answered coldly.

"Is Emily there?" Maggie blurted. "Do you see her?"

"Is this some kind of joke? Emily's fine."

"Are you sure? Did you—"

"I'm looking at her right now," Monica said before disconnecting.

Maggie laid her phone on the table and felt a flutter of relief.

"You thought your friend might have taken the baby?" Antoine asked.

"I don't know," Maggie said. "I guess. Maybe."

"She is an unhappy woman."

Maggie glanced at him.

"You saw that?"

Honestly, Maggie hadn't been sure she could make that determination before this minute. When she looked at Lisa— or any of them—she always saw who they were in high school first. It was hard to separate the women they'd become with the dreams and hopes they'd started out with.

"It was clear to anyone with eyes," Antoine said with a shrug.

"I just don't understand," Maggie said. "Lisa left after three days of acting like she couldn't keep her hands off the baby. That's so..."

"Schizophrenic?"

"It's mystifying. Behaving very passionately one way and then just not?"

Maggie chewed a nail and stared around the bar. Why would Lisa leave without a word? They had built a bond of friendship Maggie had thought. She felt a sting of betrayal that Lisa would just walk away. As the bewilderment started to fade, it was replaced by a growing suspicion. Maggie found herself returning to their last conversations, turning over Lisa's words, her expressions, looking for any sign, any hint that she might be planning to run off.

Did Lisa know about Christie's meeting with Pierre? All she'd have had to do was follow Christie to her lunch meeting and then follow Pierre back to his office to discover the connection.

Maggie remembered Lisa's growing restlessness, the way her eyes would dart to the door, the fidgeting, the tight smiles that didn't quite reach her eyes. At the time, Maggie had brushed it off as stress, the pressure of their attempt to find out who had killed Christie. But now, she couldn't help but wonder if there was more to it. She felt a knot of worry tighten in her stomach.

If Lisa's disappearance was related to Christie's murder—and how could it not be?—then the whole case had taken a very unexpected turn. Had Maggie gotten too close to something Lisa needed kept hidden?

"Is she a suspect?" Maggie asked Antoine. "I mean, by the police?"

"I don't know. But leaving like that won't help her case."

42

After making plans with Antoine to meet up again in the morning, Maggie went back to the hotel, determined to have it out with Monica. Not only did she lie to the police to try to implicate Maggie—without any evidence—in Christie's murder, but now that Maggie knew the reason for the threatening letter from Christie, she intended to see how Monica could possibly defend herself. The fact was, when Maggie added Monica's attempt to throw Maggie under the bus with the fact that she and Jason had clear-cut motives —and opportunity—for wanting Christie dead, it seemed pretty clear that it was Monica who had the most to lose.

Even though she was exhausted from her ordeal at the police lockup, Maggie was determined to confront Monica before she did anything else. She went straight to her room and knocked. When Monica opened the door, Maggie charged inside.

"Surprised to see me?" Maggie said as she looked around the room, satisfied that they were alone.

"How dare you—"

Maggie turned on her.

"You don't have any lines in this scene, Monica," she said. "I know you went to the police to try to implicate me in Christie's death."

Monica recoiled dramatically.

"That's not true!" she said unconvincingly.

"But more than that," Maggie said, "the police know you lied and right now they're asking themselves why. My bet is they'll come to the conclusion that you were attempting to distract them from the truth—that you and Jason killed Christie."

Monica shook her head vehemently.

"That's not true!"

"What difference does truth make?" Maggie asked. "The cops have their prime suspect—you—and Christie will get justice. Personally, I think you killed her so I'm fine with it. Are you going to tell me it was all Jason's idea? Because nobody who knows you two as a couple will believe that."

Monica wrung her hands.

"Look, you've got this all wrong! The police don't suspect me. They haven't even asked me to come in to give a statement."

"Trust me, they will."

"Trust you?" Monica said with a snort. "Like I can trust you not to interfere with my family?"

"What are you talking about?"

"How dare you insinuate my husband was inappropriate with Sophie! You and your liberal cancel culture! You make me sick."

"What you're doing right now is called displaced aggression," Maggie said crossing her arms, "and it won't work on me. Besides, I never implied he was inappropriate. I suggested that if he didn't want there to be a question of impropriety, he should reconsider his behavior with her."

"You've been spying on us!"

Maggie nearly shot back that *Sophie* had asked her to talk to Jason, but she couldn't be sure she wouldn't lose her job if she did.

"I've simply seen certain behavior that might be innocent, or it might not be," Maggie said firmly.

"You've got a lot of nerve."

"And you've got a lot of explaining to do," Maggie said. "Why not start with the night Christie was killed? You said you were talking to her that night. Does that mean Sophie and Jason were alone?"

"No, they weren't! Jason was out most of that night and I'll testify to that!"

Maggie stared at her.

"Did you just say that Jason wasn't in your room that night?" Maggie asked.

Monica's gaze darted around the room as if looking for an escape route.

"You're confusing me!" she said.

"Didn't you tell the police that Jason was with you all night?"

"He *was* with me all night! You're twisting my words!"

Maggie knew that Monica might have just said Jason was gone to respond to Maggie's claim that he was alone with Sophie. But what if he really hadn't been there?

There went both Jason and Monica's alibis.

"Did Christie ever find out that the baby in that stroller was her granddaughter?" Maggie asked.

Maggie knew the answer to this, but she wanted to see if Monica would come clean. She could see the internal struggle in Monica's face of wanting to play the wounded party and justifying herself. Finally, she opted for the truth.

Monica's eyes tightened with bitterness, and she clenched her hands into fists.

"She's an investigative reporter! Of course she found out."

"And then she confronted you?" Maggie asked.

"She wanted to be a part of the baby's life, if you can believe it. But how was that going to work?"

"Is that what you told her? You said no?"

"She made threats. She said she'd write a story that would ruin us—ruin Jason. Well, you saw what she wrote in that letter."

"Sounds like motive to me."

"I knew that's what you'd think. If you tell the police, it's what they'll think, too."

"So it made more sense to make up a bunch of lies about me? You've got a lot of nerve, Monica." Maggie pointed to her black eye. "You saw her that night, didn't you?"

Monica burst into tears.

"I didn't hurt her! I swear it! We just...we just talked."

"Is that how you got that shiner? Just *talking*?"

"You don't understand! Christie was crazy! She wouldn't listen to reason! Jason and I have taken care of her child! Just the cost of Adele's rehab alone nearly bankrupted us! But do we get credit for that?"

"Why did Christie want to ruin you?"

"Besides being a malicious bitch?"

Monica sat down on the bed, her shoulders sagging, her eyes glistening with tears. She shook her head as if trying to push away the whole conversation.

"She said I turned her child into a drug addict," she said. "She said I hadn't loved it enough."

It.

"That must have been hard to hear," Maggie said.

"I guess that's what everyone believes. I guess that what all my neighbors, the ladies in my women's club, my tennis club all think. They all think it was me who turned Adele into the disappointment she is."

"Getting back to Christie?" Maggie prompted her.

"Christie said she'd tell everyone that Jason was Adele's bio father. She said she'd prove we got her illegally—except she couldn't! We have the papers!"

"Bought and paid-for papers," Maggie said. "Falsified papers."

"You sound just like Christie!" Monica clenched her hands into fists in her frustration. "We paid twenty thousand francs for that baby! Does that sound *falsified* to you?! But Christie didn't care about that. All she wanted was revenge. She just wanted to hurt us for what she thought I'd done to her child."

As Monica continued to justify herself, Maggie couldn't help but hear the sound of Christie's voice coming to her through her diary, all the hopes and dreams she'd had for her baby. And now she was seeing how Monica had never really wanted the baby and had treated her accordingly. She felt exhausted and sickened listening to Monica. It was clear that Christie was probably demented with the need for revenge when she confronted Monica.

"You lied to the police when you said you didn't see Christie that night," Maggie said.

"Of course, I lied. What else could I do?"

"Maybe you killed Christie to keep her from upsetting your life. It's as good a reason as any."

"I didn't. I swear I didn't," Monica said, shaking her head.

"You've got a double motive," Maggie insisted. "Christie was threatening to disrupt your life, plus by killing her you could collect the inheritance."

"Why would I care about that? In case you're blind, Maggie, Jason and I are very well off."

"You can quit posturing for me, Monica. I know about Jason's gambling debts."

Monica shot her chin up defiantly.

"Okay, fine! So *of course* I didn't tell anyone I saw her that night."

Maggie handed her the phone.

"You'll tell the police right now. If you didn't kill her, you have nothing to worry about..."

"Like anyone would believe that!"

"It doesn't matter what anyone believes. You'll tell them the truth, or I will."

"Will I get in trouble for saying I saw you come out of her room?"

Maggie felt a flash of fury at the question.

"Yes, probably," she said. "Does the world not work for you like it works for everyone else? You lied to the police, Monica. Repeatedly."

"Surely, they'll understand."

"Do you seriously believe that? What a charmed life you must lead."

"Does it *look* like I'm leading a charmed life?!"

"It looks like you've made a couple of big mistakes. Here's your chance to correct them."

"I'm sorry, Maggie. I haven't come this far to be arrested and thrown into a foreign prison cell."

"What about Lisa?" Maggie asked suddenly.

"What about her?"

"Where does she come into this? Where is she?"

Monica looked at her, blinking rapidly in disbelief.

"What are you insinuating? I have no idea where she is! I didn't do anything to her! Are you mad?"

"You lied about seeing me outside Christie's door. You lied about how you got your black eye. You lied about where Jason was that night—"

"I had to!"

"That does not justify lying! Covering your ass does not make the lies okay! How is it you are not understanding this?"

Just then there was a knock at the door and Monica jumped up at the interruption. She ran to the door and pulled it open. Lisa stood there staring at both of them. She was dressed for travel, and she carried a suitcase. She looked past Monica to where Maggie stood.

"Please," she said, desperately. "Let me explain."

43

———————

The atmosphere of the hotel bar seemed muted tonight, Maggie thought as she and Lisa made their way into it. Maggie ordered wine for both of them and sat at one of the many small tables set in the back of the bar. Lisa's eyes were downcast and she wrung her hands nervously.

"I'm so sorry, Maggie. I can't imagine what you must think of me."

"I'm not sure what to think."

Lisa's chin trembled as she struggled to get control of her emotions. She took in a breath but didn't look at Maggie directly.

"I've had problems with panic attacks in the past, and I was getting to the point where I just needed to walk away and decompress."

"You had a panic attack?"

Maggie frowned. She wasn't really familiar with all the typical symptoms of a panic attack. She wondered if methodically packing your suitcase and slipping out of your hotel room by the fire escape was really a symptom.

"I went to a clinic that I found online that accepted walk-ins for an over-night consultation," Lisa said.

When Maggie didn't immediately respond, Lisa continued.

"Being here with everyone, having to relive what Christie did to me that night—it brought it all back is all I can say."

"So, unlike what you told me two days ago, you're not over what happened on prom night."

Lisa's eyes turned hard and flinty as she finally looked at Maggie.

"No, I'm not. Okay? I know that sounds pathetic, but I'll probably never be over it. My therapist takes an annual vacation to Maui because I can't get past it."

"Sounds like you were basically fine with Christie dying," Maggie said.

Maggie knew that was severe, but she wasn't at all sure she wasn't being played. Lisa had lied to her before. How was she to know she wasn't lying to her now?

"I didn't kill her, Maggie," Lisa said firmly, her face flushed with the intensity of her emotion. "And her dying hasn't stopped my panic attacks, okay? It hasn't stopped the feeling of insecurity I get that comes over me. Or the urge to want to hide myself away. Or die."

Maggie looked at her without blinking. She steeled herself to the pain she saw in Lisa's face.

"Still," Maggie said. "Revenge. Be hard to turn that down."

"I'm not a killer. I can hate her. I did hate her. But I couldn't do that."

Maggie wasn't going to push her further on this. Lisa had motive, means and opportunity. But if she really wasn't a killer, none of that mattered.

"I just had to get away," Lisa insisted. "I'm sorry. I know what it looks like."

"The police think you're a missing person," Maggie said.

"No, they don't. I went to them as soon as I got myself sorted out and cleared that up. I told them I have a disability."

She reached over to where Maggie's hand was next to her drink on the table and picked it up.

"Look, I wouldn't blame you if you don't trust me," Lisa said, "but I knew I needed to come back and do what I could to help. I need to be a part of the solution. That's what's going to get me through this. Please, Maggie."

"Are you asking me to let you know what I found out?" Maggie asked, removing her hand from Lisa's grip. "And what if it turns out you are the one who killed Christie?"

"You don't really think that."

"What I think is that what Christie did to you was so excruciating that thirty-three years later you had to run away and check into a foreign walk-in clinic just to process the memory of it."

Lisa reached for her drink and Maggie saw her hand was shaking. But she didn't deny the accusation.

"I don't mean to be harsh," Maggie said. "I'd say this whole group has had way more of that kind of thing than anyone needs in a lifetime. But you're still not telling me the whole truth."

Lisa stared at her shaking hand as it held the glass and then nodded.

"I was afraid the police were going to arrest me for Christie's murder," she said.

Maggie felt the hardness inside her begin to soften.

Lisa tipped her head back to look at the ceiling and then let it flop forward, her hair hanging in her face. She moaned softly.

"I wish I could explain what it feels like," she said. "When I feel an attack coming on, I feel an overpowering urge to run away."

"You came back awfully fast."

"Because the counselors at the clinic told me I needed to!"

Lisa said, snapping her head around to look at Maggie as if filled with new energy. "And it's not rocket science! They said I'm feeling guilty, even though I didn't kill her! They told me I need to be a part of the solution!" She reached out and grabbed Maggie's hand. "Please, Maggie. Let me help."

"I'll think about it," Maggie said. "But first, I need you to tell me what really happened that night."

Lisa looked at her, horrified.

"That...you mean my junior prom?"

"Yes. And don't tell me you already told me. Publishers don't agree to buy books about someone getting stood up on prom night. What really happened?"

Lisa stared at her hands. When she finally lifted her head to look into Maggie's eyes, it was as if a rod of steel had rammed into her spine. Gone was the apologetic, whimpering affect. In its place was a mask of hard determination.

"Yeah, you're right," she said. "What happened was a little worse than that."

Lisa began to speak calmly of the excitement she'd felt in the days leading up to the prom—just as she described to Maggie before—dreaming of her perfect night. She'd chosen her dress carefully—a beautiful lavender gown that made her feel like a princess. Her date, the cute boy she'd had her eye on for months, had seemed genuinely excited about the night as well.

"I can't believe you didn't hear about this," Lisa said shaking her head. "It went viral. Or as much as something could back in 1987."

"What happened?"

"Like I told you before. Jeff didn't pick me up at the house, so my mom drove me to the school. Once I got there..."

Lisa stopped, the expression on her face fighting between tears and fury. Maggie held her tongue. She would allow her to tell it in her own time.

"Once I got there, Christie grabbed me and pushed me toward the girls' restroom. I was looking everywhere for Jeff and didn't see him, and she said he had a surprise for me. And that was the reason he wasn't able to pick me up at my house."

Lisa took in a long breath.

"In the rest room, Christie locked the door so no one else could get in and then pulled this outfit out of a bag I didn't realize she had."

Maggie frowned. "Like a costume?"

"Yeah," Lisa said with a sneer. "Like a costume. A skimpy maid's outfit with...with cut outs. Christie said Jeff was waiting for me in the hall, but he was hoping I'd put on the outfit for him."

Maggie grimaced. Lisa glanced at her.

"Yeah, you've never met anyone as stupid or as pathetic."

"Don't say that. That's not what I was thinking. You were young."

"Christie kept saying Jeff was waiting. I don't know what was going through my head. I stripped out of my beautiful lavender dress and put on the...the thing."

Maggie could guess what happened next.

"Christie took my dress and walked out of the restroom with it," Lisa said. "Just like that. I stood there in this thing, my boobs hanging out. My everything hanging out."

"What happened then?"

"I opened the restroom door and peeked out, looking for Jeff, and there was Christie and half the student body. I tried to cover myself. I turned around and tried to get back into the bathroom."

Maggie felt nausea roiling in her gut.

"But one of the boys held the door closed. Everyone was pointing and jeering. And yeah, Jeff was there, too. It felt like it went on forever. Eventually someone took pity on me and gave me my dress back but not before Christie had taken pictures."

"I can't believe she would do something so cruel." Maggie said.

"You didn't really know her," Lisa said bitterly. "The shock and humiliation of that night went on forever. The pictures of it were passed around school. After that, I sort of retreated into myself, skipping school and eventually transferring to a different one."

Maggie suddenly remembered that Lisa *had* transferred. She'd been so focused this weekend on their high school years together that she completely forgot that not only had Beth and Christie vanished for half their senior year, but Lisa herself had moved to a different school.

What in the world made me think we were a group needing a reunion?

"It took a lot of therapy and support from my family to help me recover," Lisa said, reaching for her drink, her hand still shaking. "I had to fight every step of the way to reclaim my self-worth. And as evidenced by my running away yesterday, I guess I'm still not there."

After all that, Maggie found herself stunned that Lisa would agree to go on a trip to Paris with Christie.

Unless she came because she was plotting her revenge.

44

Maggie stood in the front door of the hotel, armed with one of the hotel umbrellas and looking out at the weather. Rain was pounding all of Montmartre this morning, casting a fresh, dewy glow on the cobblestones and turning them into a shimmering mosaic.

She watched as droplets fell from the awning over the hotel entrance. She didn't mind walking in the rain. This kind of weather tended to discourage the throngs of tourists and made for a more pleasurable walking experience.

After she and Lisa had parted company last night—hugging so that Lisa knew that Maggie understood and had forgiven her disappearance—Maggie had found it difficult to fall asleep. She'd been tempted to call Laurent but decided he had his hands full at home with Amèlie and didn't need any more problems added to his plate.

In spite of the sympathy she'd felt for Lisa, she hadn't even briefly considered inviting her along to her meeting with Antoine this morning, even though she'd agreed to allow her to help in some way. The unfortunate fact was, she just didn't trust Lisa. She didn't trust the excuse she'd given for why she'd disappeared, or the fact that she couldn't recognize the immense motive that Christie's cruel prank had given her.

Maggie stepped out into the drizzle and put a call in to Laurent. She should have called him earlier from the warmth and dryness of her hotel room, but she knew that Amèlie was an early riser and Laurent would have his hands full just getting her breakfast into her without a battle.

"Where are you?" Laurent asked when he answered the call.

Maggie laughed.

"I'm on my way to meet Antoine," she said.

She hadn't yet mentioned to Laurent that she'd spent three hours in police custody and was determined not to until she could tell him face to face.

"He is being a help to you?" he asked.

In the background, Maggie heard the dogs barking. They were barking as they did when Amèlie was teasing them more than was good.

"Very much so," Maggie said. "He thinks there's going to be an arrest soon."

"Not you, I hope?"

"No, my darling. Not me."

"I still think I should come up there. I do not like you being asked not to leave town."

"It's almost over," Maggie said as she approached the corner of the cafe where she was meeting Antoine. "Besides, what could you do?" she asked. "I've got Antoine. Just sit tight."

Just then she heard Amèlie scream and a crash in the background.

"*Merde*," Laurent muttered.

"What was that?" Maggie asked.

"Nothing. I have it under control."

"Okay, well, call me if you want to talk but do *not* come up here. I'm fine."

After disconnecting, Maggie hurried to the table where she

could see Antoine slowly getting up from his chair to greet her. For the first time, they cheek kissed in greeting. Maggie saw by the carafe of French pressed coffee on the table and two cups that he'd already ordered for both of them.

"I have a lot to tell you," Maggie said.

"Ah, yes?"

"I talked to Monica and also Lisa last night."

"Ah, so the wandering friend has returned? Did she say why she left?"

"She did. But I'm not sure it's terribly believable."

Antoine nodded sagely.

"And Monica?" he asked. "Was she repentant for attempting to put you under the bus?"

Maggie snorted.

"Hardly. But she did reveal that Jason might not have been in the room with her the night Christie was killed."

"That is significant."

"Why did Benoit just accept his alibi?" Maggie asked as she sipped her coffee. There was already a cube of sugar in it. Just the way she liked it.

"Are you sure he has?"

"Well, you said he was leaning toward arresting Lisa for the murder."

"I did?"

"Didn't you? Did I imagine that?"

"I am afraid we must all wait to see what Detective Benoit has in mind. Frankly, I'm surprised he hasn't made a move yet."

"I think he should know that Jason might not have been in Monica's hotel room that night."

"Why don't we wait to see how things play out? Meanwhile, how is your young friend?"

"Zouzou?" Maggie frowned. "She's upset and not currently talking to me."

She picked up her phone and texted Zouzou.

<just checking in. BTW can you get me into P's appt?>
<seriously?>

Maggie was delighted that Zouzou had at least responded to her which was more than she'd done all last night or this morning.

<I can meet you there. Thnx, A. Maggie>

Maggie felt a shudder of relief. Not only did Zouzou sound less angry but the meeting would give her a chance to see for herself how she was doing. Plus, she and Antoine might actually find something in Pierre's apartment that would point in the direction of a lead.

"Up for a visit to Pigalle?" she asked Antoine.

His eyebrows raised. "But of course."

"I'm not sure it'll tell us anything," she said. "But there might be something in Pierre's apartment."

"It is worth a look."

Just then Maggie noticed Sophie walk onto the terrace of the cafe. She looked unsure of herself, in fact nearly afraid as she glanced around before apprehensively taking a seat at an empty table.

"Someone you know?" Antoine asked.

"Monica's babysitter," Maggie said. "It's weird seeing her without the baby. I didn't know Monica gave her any time off."

She raised her hand and caught Sophie's eye. The girl looked at her with relief and waved back.

"I'm kind of impressed she's here on her own," Maggie said.

"It is better than with her nose in a video game on her phone," Antoine commented.

Seeing Sophie here without the baby made Maggie wonder if Lisa was babysitting Emily. She watched Sophie leave her purse at her table and walk over to where she and Antoine sat, her eyes darting nervously at Antoine.

"Hey, Maggie, can you order a Coke for me?" she asked. "I can't get the waiter to under—"

Before Sophie could finish her request, her elbow connected with the coffee carafe on the table. Maggie reached for it, but it was just out of her grasp as the glass carafe toppled, spilling a river of dark coffee across the pristine white tablecloth. Sophie stood frozen, her eyes wide with shock, her cheeks flaming.

"Omigosh, I'm so sorry!" she said, her eyes filling with tears. "I...I..."

Maggie snatched up a napkin, her mind recalling Monica's words about Sophie's clumsiness and began mopping up the tablecloth. She had brushed off Monica's criticism at the time, but it seemed there was some justification for it.

"It's fine, sweetie," Maggie said to the girl before glancing at Antoine who was busy dabbing at his sweater vest.

Sophie's eyes, filled with embarrassment, met Maggie's. And in that moment, Maggie felt a pang of sympathy.

"Forget it, okay?" Maggie said. She raised a hand to call the waiter over. "Meanwhile, how are you? I see you're out without the baby."

"Yeah, Miz W gave me the afternoon off," Sophie said. "She told me to get out of the room. But I wasn't sure where to go."

"Well, café sitting is the first and last bastion of French culture and society," Maggie said. "Especially in Paris."

The waiter showed up and Maggie quickly ordered Sophie's drink. Then she turned back to Sophie.

"Would you like to join us?" Maggie asked.

"No thanks," Sophie said holding up her cellphone. "I'm good." Then she stopped abruptly on her walk back to her table and turned around again, dropping her voice.

"Thanks for talking to Mr. W," she said. "He's backed off."

"No problem," Maggie said. "But I'm sure you could've gone to Monica too."

Sophie just shrugged and gave a weak smile before returning to her table.

"There would not have been a Resistance if this generation of young people had been alive during the war," Antoine commented as he watched her go.

Maggie laughed.

"I'm sure they'd have stood up when the time came," Maggie said. "Most people don't know what they're capable of until they have to do it."

"If you say so," he said, finishing the dregs of his coffee. "How is Laurent? It is hard to imagine him a husband and a father."

"And a grandfather," Maggie said. "He's good. He owns a vineyard, you know."

"Ah, yes, Laurent the farmer. It is all a puzzle. The man I knew..."

He's still that man, Maggie wanted to say, because it was true. Laurent wasn't fleecing tourists on the *Avenue des Anglais* anymore but the heart of the man he was then still beat in his chest today. He was brave and stubborn and intuitive and opportunistic. And yes, he was a family man. As if he'd been born to the role.

"So is Monica watching her grandchild?" Antoine asked, his eyes on Maggie.

Maggie laughed.

"Am I that transparent?"

"In some things."

"I was just wondering if Lisa was watching the baby because I can't imagine Monica letting Sophie off the hook if it meant *she* had to mind the child."

"You do not trust Lisa," Antoine said.

"I want to."

"That is not an affirmative answer."

Maggie sighed. She watched the waiter show up at Sophie's table and set down a tall glass of cola. Sophia turned to Maggie and gave her a big thumbs up and Maggie smiled at her.

"It's just that she has a big motive for wanting Christie dead," Maggie said, turning back to Antoine. "Christie was threatening to write a book on the biggest humiliation of Lisa's life. Plus, I can't make sense of her disappearance this week."

A few minutes later, Maggie and Antoine paid their bill and got up from the table. Maggie turned to wave goodbye to Sophie but saw she was engrossed in her cellphone.

Oh well, she thought. She is a part of that generation after all.

Pigalle was only a short walk from where they were, so she and Antoine decided they would skip the Metro. As soon as they stood out on the sidewalk in front of the café looking at their phones for directions, Maggie looked up and saw Jason and Monica coming down the sidewalk. Jason's face was flushed and he was staggering unevenly towards them. Maggie was surprised to see he was inebriated so early in the day. His eyes, clouded by alcohol, flickered menacingly from Antoine and then back to Maggie.

"Look who it is," Jason slurred, with a sneer. He took a step towards Maggie, his intentions unclear but threatening. "The lady who wants to get me cancelled in my own home."

Before he could get any closer, Antoine stepped in front of Maggie, his stance firm and unyielding. His eyes were hard, a clear sign for Jason to back away.

"You are drunk, Monsieur," Antoine said, his voice steady but laced with warning.

Ignoring him, Jason tried to take another step toward Maggie, but Antoine held his ground. He put a hand up, not touching Jason's chest but nearly.

"You can't tell me what to do," Jason said cracking his knuckles and glaring at the elderly Frenchman.

"Jason, come on," Monica said. "Leave them alone."

"Don't tell me what to do," he snarled at Monica before

suddenly turning and lunging at Antoine, knocking his hand away and pushing him on his chest.

Maggie watched in horror as Antoine rocked back on his heels and then staggered, his arms windmilling for balance, his eyes wide with surprise. One hand clawed briefly at his chest before he crumpled to the ground.

45

M aggie felt as if time were standing still as the controlled chaos of the hospital waiting room swirled around her. Rows of uncomfortable plastic chairs, bolted to the floor, were filled with people. Each carried their own story, their own worry etched into the lines of their faces.

The air was thick with a blend of antiseptic smells and anxiety, a scent as synonymous with hospitals as it was unsettling. The only sounds were the cold, impersonal announcements over the PA system, the occasional ringing phone at the reception desk, and the soft murmur of hushed conversations.

Jason and Monica had stayed until the ambulance came to take Antoine—still alive—to the hospital. Jason had quickly sobered but was still unsteady on his feet. Monica was silent, knowing that one phone call from Maggie would likely have both of them in police custody before the day was done.

There were plenty of witnesses to say what had happened. Even if nobody actually saw Jason shove Antoine. They saw him charge. And they saw Antoine go down. It would be enough for the police to justify an arrest. But Maggie resisted the impulse.

When the ambulance came, she rode with Antoine while Jason and Monica disappeared into the crowd. Now sitting in the waiting room, waiting and wondering, Maggie felt wrapped in a miasma of worry, her hands clasped in her lap. Her eyes darted from the reception desk to the automatic doors, waiting for any sign of a medical person who might update her on Antoine's condition. Each time the doors swished open, her heart leapt, only to sink again as another gurney rushed in and another family was ushered into the waiting room.

She kept checking her phone for messages from Zouzou and left long voice mails when she didn't find any.

"Zouzou, call me. There's been an accident and I wasn't able to meet you."

Maggie felt the pressure of the ticking clock on the wall, each second stretching into an eternity. Around her, life continued — a nurse calling out names, a child's soft sobbing, the vending machine dispensing its goods with a mechanical clunk. Yet for Maggie, time was marked only by her racing heartbeats and the agonizing wait for news of Antoine.

The image of Antoine collapsing on the street replayed on a loop in her head. How had it happened? The push hadn't seemed that hard. Was it his heart? Maggie wasn't a relative. She had no legal right to be told anything about his condition. She knew they'd contacted Antoine's wife although she hadn't yet shown up. A dozen times Maggie had been tempted to call Laurent, but he could do nothing at this point but worry. She couldn't take him away from Amèlie and there was nothing for him to do here anyway. She would tell him later and pray the story she told didn't end with Maggie being the reason his old friend Antoine didn't pull through.

As the afternoon wore on, the hospital's harsh lights seemed to grow dimmer, the shadows stretching longer. The waiting room, once a hub of activity, started to empty out, leaving behind only the ones with the heaviest of hearts. Lisa arrived, her footsteps echoing in the sterile corridor. She found Maggie in the waiting room, and without saying a word, came to sit beside her, offering a comforting presence in the tense silence.

"How is he?" Lisa asked finally.

"Nobody's telling me," Maggie said. "I'm not family. Every now and then a nurse will throw me a bone but not much."

"Where's his wife?"

"She hasn't shown up yet. I think she was out of the country visiting relatives."

"Was it a heart attack?"

"Jason pushed him," Maggie said. "But there was no blood when he fell. He just sort of drooped to the ground."

"Are you saying the push might not have been the reason he fell?"

"I don't know."

"Maggie," Lisa said, her voice steady as she gripped her hands in her lap. "Especially now that Antoine is out of the picture, you need to let me help you find Christie's killer."

Maggie looked at her, her eyes searching Lisa's face. She was concerned about Lisa's nerves—as evidenced by her disappearing yesterday. But right now, there seemed to be a steely determination in her affect. Especially with Antoine out of commission—possibly for good—it *would* help to have someone to bounce ideas and theories off of.

"Are you sure?" Maggie asked.

Lisa reached over and squeezed her hand.

"Positive. Now. Tell me what you know."

Maggie took in a breath and tried to center herself. The sounds of the hospital public address system were disconcerting. Being in a hospital always was.

"Okay," she said. "I think Jason might have killed Christie."

She watched Lisa's eyes widen.

"I'm also suspicious of the fact that we ran into him just before he attacked Antoine."

Lisa gasped. "Wow. Jason?" She frowned. "No way! Why? How? Start with Christie. Her drink was opened by her. Right? So how did Jason get the poison in the soda can?"

"I'm still working that out," Maggie said.

"And doesn't he have an alibi?" Lisa asked. "I mean, he's gone all day and comes in late and sleeps right next to Monica. Wouldn't she know if he got up in the middle of the night and left? And Sophie's in their suite too. That's *two* people he'd have to get past."

"Monica said he wasn't there that night after all. And even if she retracts *that* statement, he only had to slip out of bed and be gone for five minutes," Maggie said. "About the time it would take to go to the toilet."

"But how would he do it?"

"All he'd have to do would be to go through the connecting door and poison the can of diet soda on her bedside table."

Lisa frowned.

"Yeah, but first he'd have to hope that she'd already opened it before he got there and hadn't drunk it all, and then, why would she drink more in the middle of the night?"

"As I said, I'm still working out some of the puzzle pieces," Maggie said with a sigh.

A flashing blue light beamed out over the waiting room, but Maggie didn't see any nurses or medical staff race around as a result of it.

"I admit I don't know much about forensic stuff," Lisa said, "but honestly, if Jason planned on killing her, wouldn't it make more sense to just smother her with a pillow?"

Actually, that was a good point. If Christie was poisoned— and forensically Maggie knew she was—then it had to have been planned. It couldn't be a spontaneous act by a midnight visitor. Maggie felt a wave of discouragement. Did that mean Jason *didn't* do it?

"Look, I don't know the details of how he did it," Maggie said. "That will all come out in the confession. Right now, we just need to trap him."

"Okay, good," Lisa said, rubbing her hands together. "How?"

"I'm going to write a note to Monica—who I believe is one hundred percent an accomplice with Jason in the murder and get her to meet me."

Lisa leaned forward, her eyes focused intently on Maggie, her brows furrowed.

"I'm going to make it sound as if I want money," Maggie said, "so they won't think there's a danger of me going to the police."

"You're going to blackmail them?" Lisa asked with surprise.

"No. I'm going to make them *think* I am. Then I'm going to meet up and record our conversation. I'll get them to admit they killed Christie."

Lisa frowned.

"Where were you thinking of meeting them?" she asked.

"I thought maybe Montmartre Cemetery."

"I don't know, Maggie," Lisa said with a pained look. "That sounds dangerous. Can't you confront them someplace more public? Or in broad daylight?"

"They won't feel safe spilling the beans in broad daylight," Maggie said. "Look, I already gave Monica a chance to come clean today and she just dug in her heels. I don't have proof of any of this. I need her to admit what she did."

"Okay. How can I help?"

"Well, honestly, there's comfort in numbers. Just be with me when I go to confront them."

Lisa took in a big breath.

"I let you down once before," she said firmly. "Trust me. I'll be there."

46

An hour later, a nurse came over to where Maggie and Lisa sat to say that Antoine was asleep, and the doctors were cautiously optimistic. Maggie was welcome to come back in the morning when Antoine's wife would be present. Relieved and weary, Maggie called for an Uber and she and Lisa rode back to the hotel together.

"It's been a long day," Maggie said when they walked into the hotel lobby. "I'm hoping to get an hour's nap before tonight."

"Are you sure I can't talk you out of going? I really don't like the sound of it."

"You don't have to come, Lisa. I'll be fine."

"I'm definitely coming if you insist on doing it. Meet up in the lobby?"

"Let's meet at the north gate of the cemetery, okay?"

"I'll be there," Lisa said as she leaned over to give Maggie a hug. "It's the least I can do after disappearing on you."

After that, Maggie bypassed the elevator, to her room floor. The stairwell opened up just past where Monica and Jason's room was located, and Maggie did not want to chance bumping into them if at all possible.

Once in her room, she knew she wouldn't have time for the nap, regardless of what she'd told Lisa. She went to the writing desk, pulled out stationery and sat down. As she looked at the stationery, she was sharply aware that this was the same paper Christie had used to pen her threatening note to Monica.

She picked up a ballpoint pen with the name of the hotel on the side. She knew exactly what she was going to write. She'd composed it in her head the whole ride from the hospital. She said a quick prayer for Antoine and immediately squelched the guilt she felt for what had happened to him. Whether his collapse was caused by Jason or by a coincidental health issue was irrelevant to what she had to do tonight.

She wrote in a careful hand:

I know who killed Christie and I have video proof that I have not yet turned over to the police. Meet me at Edgar Degas's grave in Montmartre Cemetery at two tomorrow morning or I will take my evidence to the police.

Then Maggie signed her name, photographed the note with her cellphone, folded it and slipped it into an envelope. She wrote *Monica/Jason* on the envelope and sealed it. Her hands were shaking as she tiptoed down the hallway and slipped the envelope under Monica's door.

Her nervousness seemed to ramp up as she crept back to her room. Regardless of how Monica had sometimes acted friendly toward her, Maggie knew that she was in fact a dangerous person willing to do anything to keep her secrets safe. Antoine was right about that—and so was Lisa. Her mind buzzed with the fact that she hadn't told Laurent what she was doing. And she remembered the vow she'd made to Danielle last year about not putting herself in danger—if for no other reason than she knew that Amélie needed her. She pushed both unsettling thoughts from her mind.

By the time she was back in her room she found herself wondering if she really needed to confront Monica or Jason when they showed up at the cemetery. Wasn't it enough to simply videotape them showing up at two in the morning? The video would be timestamped, and she could take the footage from behind any of a dozen hiding place among the gravestones. The video, combined with a photocopy of the letter that had brought them there, would be enough to point the police in the direction of Monica and Jason's guilt.

This new plan calmed Maggie somewhat. She checked the time. It was nearly midnight. That meant there was a good chance Laurent was asleep. By the time she talked to him tomorrow she might even be on her way home with all of this wrapped up and done. She was hesitant to text and wake up Lisa if she was trying to catch a few winks before meeting Maggie at the cemetery. With her new strategy, Maggie didn't believe there was a need for Lisa to come with her. She decided she'd wait until closer to the meeting time to call Lisa to tell her not to bother coming after all.

She looked around her room, thought briefly about turning on the television set before deciding it would just make her edgier, then got up to get a bottle of water from the minifridge. She drank from it thirstily, but her nerves were still getting the better of her. As she tightened the lid on the bottle before setting it down on the desk, she missed the desk and the bottle fell to the floor with a loud thump. She jumped at the sound and her eye caught movement as the tail end of a startled mouse dove for its bolt hole in the base of the wall. Maggie blinked when she saw it. It had been there and gone in a blink of an eye.

She glanced at her watch to see the temperature gauge indicated it would be much cooler tonight. She went to her closet and selected a dark sweater and pulled it on over her cotton sleeveless top, her mind racing as she did. A few things were suddenly niggling at her that she didn't know how to make sense of.

She found herself reflecting how Monica had plenty of motive for wanting Christie dead—and the opportunity for killing her. And Maggie believed she was just cold blooded and spiteful enough to do it. But the problem with that scenario was that Monica wasn't a clever woman. Her focus spun around her vanity and her perceived needs—usually involving rank and privilege.

Christie had been killed in a manner that was confounding all the detectives of the Paris Homicide—as well as Maggie and Antoine too. Yes, Monica could've killed Christie. But Maggie found it hard to believe she had the necessary finesse or ingenuity to kill her in the nearly impossible way she had been killed.

She glanced at her watch. She still had an hour before it made sense for her to leave the hotel. She took in another long breath and ran through the events of the murder starting at the beginning. Starting with how she and Beth had found the body. When she closed her eyes and really concentrated—something she'd instinctively avoided doing before now because it was so unpleasant—she remembered two things—two seemingly unimportant and unconnected things—that she'd forgotten until just this moment.

First was the smell when she and Beth entered Christie's room. Maggie concentrated hard in an effort to bring back the memory of the scent which was delicate but unusual. It was why Maggie hadn't remembered it. Nothing in her experience allowed her to readily identify the smell, so she'd dismissed it. It wasn't floral or musk. Now that Maggie thought about it, it was almost medicinal. And so faint that with everything else that was happening Maggie was really only cognizant of it in a remote part of her brain. She hadn't brought it to the foreground of her memory since she'd experienced it.

And the second thing she'd forgotten until this moment was the mouse.

She glanced at the tiny hole where the little mouse in her room had scurried into. Maggie's room was next to Christie's although there was no connecting door. But mice don't need connecting doors to come and go. She realized she'd either dismissed the memory of having seen the mouse in Christie's room that day or discounted it since she knew most places in Paris—Airbnb's included—had mice. Like with the odd smell, she'd forgotten having seen it in Christie's room. But now that she *did* think of it, she realized that the mouse she'd seen in Christie's room hadn't been dead at all, but only sleeping.

She blinked as the thought came to her and she ran an agitated hand over her face as she realized that the creature had *stayed* asleep even though Beth had flung open Christie's door and she and Maggie had rushed stomping into the room. They'd both spoken loudly. In fact, they'd shouted at Christie and moved around the room, knocking magazines to the floor and pushing aside chairs and luggage.

In spite of all that, the mouse had slept.

And Maggie knew it was sleeping and not dead because just before it disappeared into her wall a few moments ago, she'd seen the same notch in its little shoestring tail whip around behind it.

It was the same mouse.

She picked up her phone and turned off all audible notifications and slipped it into her crossbody bag.

What was the connection between the smell in Christie's room and a sleeping mouse?

When the answer came to Maggie, she stood up in horror of its gut-wrenching implication.

What if, like the mouse, Christie had only been in a deep sleep?

What if Christie wasn't dead when we went into her room?

Maggie's heart began to pound. She turned to pull her phone out of her purse with the thought of texting Antoine to ask him if there had been any aerosol substance detected in Christie's room when the forensics team had swept it. But of course, Antoine was unreachable. She sat back down on the bed and tried to slow her breathing and her heart rate. The pieces that were fitting together now had less to do with who killed Christie than how they'd done it.

And *how* had always been the key to *who* all along.

47

A s Maggie walked down the now familiar streets of this part of Montmartre, she saw them take on a different persona in her mind. The moon hung low in the sky, a lone sentinel casting long, spectral shadows across the cobblestone streets. The stars that usually dotted the Parisian sky were hidden behind a thin veil of wispy clouds, their light diffused into a soft, ethereal glow. Spooky. Creepy. Eerie.

The air was still, the usual hum of the city reduced to a faint echo in the distance. Every now and then, a gust of wind would rustle through the nearby trees, their leaves whispering secrets to the night. It was cold enough to make Maggie's breath fog up in the air. The vibrancy of the day had been replaced by an uncomfortable eeriness that slithered along the cobblestones, casting long, ominous shadows that danced with the flickering glow of the streetlamps.

The quaint cafés and vibrant galleries were shuttered for the night. Above her, the iconic Sacré-Cœur Basilica loomed, its white façade ghostly under the pale moonlight.

Maggie felt a chill creep up her spine, not entirely due to

the crisp night air, but from the anticipation of her destination. Montmartre Cemetery lay ahead, its ominous presence a stark reminder of the gravity of her situation. Every so often, the silence of the streets was punctuated by the distant tolling of a church bell, the sound reverberating through the quiet streets, a solemn reminder of the late hour.

The cemetery gates appeared before her, wrought iron and formidable, standing guard to the tales of the past. Beyond them, a sea of stone and marble stretched into the darkness, an eternal resting place for the souls of Montmartre, famous and commoner alike. Despite the eerie atmosphere, Maggie felt a sense of calm. The cemetery, with its quiet dignity and timeless stories, was a constant amidst the chaos of life.

She stood in the shadows at the gate before realizing she'd forgotten to text Lisa not to come. She pulled her phone out to text her and saw she had received a text five minutes ago. From Lisa.

< can't do it; forgive me >

A wave of disappointment washed over Maggie, followed by a surge of anger. Even though she'd planned on doing this alone any way, it felt like a slap in the face for Lisa to bail on her again.

Maggie jammed her phone back in her bag and turned her gaze to the cemetery gates. With Lisa backing out, the quiet of the night seemed even more profound to Maggie. She took in a breath and moved stealthily through the massive cemetery gates. Moonlight bathed the tombstones in a macabre glow, creating elongated shadows that stretched like dark fingers reaching out from the graves.

She felt a chill deep in her bones that had nothing to do with the weather.

Crumbling tombstones jutted out of the ground, their weathered fronts etched with the names of the souls they sheltered. Elegant mausoleums, some with grandiose sculptures and ornate ironwork, stood tall amid the sea of graves, their regal façades softened by the tendrils of ivy that clung to their stone surfaces. Marble busts of the cemetery's famous inhabitants, their features weather-worn with time, gazed out over the necropolis, their expressions frozen in an everlasting vigil.

As Maggie walked, she was aware that none of her senses were picking up anything out of place, no sounds or smells or movements other than those made by herself; still, somehow, something wasn't right. From the souvenir map she'd found in her hotel room, she was aware that Edgar Degas's grave was near to the center of the cemetery off the main entrance path. It was not difficult to find. She moved deeper into the interior, scanning both sides of the pathway in case Monica decided to come early intending to ambush her rather than meet. She scanned the area for a likely spot to hide so she could safely film the pair when they showed up.

Suddenly, her heart stuttered in her chest as her eyes landed on a shape on the pavement ahead. At first, it was just a darker shadow among all the rest, but as she moved closer, the shadow took a terrible form.

It was a body, sprawled lifelessly on the cold, hard ground.

Maggie's pulse quickened. The moonlight illuminated the body starkly. Maggie's mind was instantly swamped with panic. She took her eyes off the body long enough to scan the perimeter of the walkway again. She couldn't afford to panic. Now more than ever, she had to stay focused.

Were they hurt? Were they dead?

Taking a deep, shaky breath, she moved slowly forward. Every shadow seemed ominous, now, every sound a precursor to a threat. She stepped within two feet of the body and gasped, the sound discordant and sharp in the night air.

It was Monica.

48

Maggie ran to where Monica lay and knelt beside her, her mind whirring with confusion and disbelief. The moonlight washed over Monica, giving her pale face an almost ethereal glow. Maggie's mind raced with chaotic thoughts.

Lisa cancelled tonight. Lisa knew I was coming here.

Lisa knew I was hoping to catch Jason. Or Monica.

Maggie put a hand on Monica's neck and felt her heartbeat steady and strong. Monica's eyes fluttered as if she was trying to bring herself to consciousness. Maggie looked around. Whoever had done this might still be around. Were they watching? Waiting for her?

"Monica?" Maggie said in a soft voice. "It's Maggie."

Monica moaned but didn't open her eyes. Maggie felt her own heartbeat racing as if threatening to explode in her chest. Her hands, now trembling, hovered over Monica, unsure of what to do. Cold air filled her lungs, and she looked around the cemetery, its tombstones standing like silent witnesses to her fear and confusion. The crypts and mausoleums, once just structural elements of the scenery, were now ominous in the dim light. She was holding her breath while her thoughts brain ricocheted off the walls of her skull. She couldn't make sense of what she was seeing.

Jason wouldn't have done this. If he'd wanted to hurt Monica, he didn't have to go to Montmartre Cemetery to do it.

If Monica wasn't the killer, then who was? And where were they? The process of elimination began to spin diabolically in Maggie's head as the obvious answer came to her over and over again.

It had to be.

When Maggie got to that point, the rest of the answers tumbled through her brain like an avalanche of evidence, each more obvious than the last. *Beth*, asking her to accompany her to Christie's room the day they found the body. *Beth*—who hadn't spoken an unprompted word to Maggie all weekend—nor, as far as Maggie could remember, even back in high school. Why was she all of a sudden asking for Maggie's company? Why?

Because she needed her for her alibi.

Maggie remembered the detective asking her why she'd gone to the other room to call the police after seeing Christie's body. She'd done it because Beth, seemingly on the verge of hysteria, had insisted she do so.

Beth had needed Maggie to step out of the room for a few seconds.

Just long enough so she could finish the job.

Maggie stood up and pulled out her phone. She held it up and saw she had no signal here.

Idiot! Why didn't you think of that before you chose this as a place to meet?

"You need to put the phone down, Maggie."

Beth's voice came out in the silent night air among the gravestones shaky but clear. Maggie turned in the direction of the voice. A shadow near one of the higher statues moved. She flashed the beam of her cellphone flashlight and Beth's face was illuminated from where she stood beside the tombstone. Maggie continued scanning with the flashlight until she found Sophie, ten yards away.

"I told you I didn't hit her hard enough," Sophie said in disgust.

Maggie turned her attention back to Monica, her mind shifting from confusion to concern. She needed to get them both out of this graveyard. On the tail end of this nauseating revelation, Maggie got a lightning mental snapshot of the article she'd read about Beth's father and groaned when she recollected something she should have remembered. The list of family and friends had included a sister, Jacqueline Lopez. Lopez was her married name. And it was also Sophie's last name.

Beth and Sophie were related.

"Beth," Maggie said in a clear voice. "Monica needs to go to the hospital."

"Yeah, that ain't happening," Sophie said as she walked over to Maggie.

Everything about the girl was changed. The teen's face, once so shy and naïve, was now hard and ugly. The transformation was complete. Sophia looked down at Monica with a sneer on her lips and tapped the woman's hip with her boot.

"How's it feel, Missus W?" Sophie taunted. "Need me to run get you an orange juice? How about I run a bath for you? Huh?"

"Hush, Sophie," Beth said as she made her way to the clearing.

"Don't tell me to hush, Aunt Beth," Sophie snapped. "If it wasn't for me, her and Maggie would've had a good ol' chin wag about things and then where would you be?"

"How did you know to come to the cemetery?" Maggie asked.

"You mean your little note-under-the-door gambit?" Sophie

scoffed. "Trust me, Monica doesn't look at the floor. But I saw it. I couldn't believe my luck."

Maggie nodded grimly. At least Lisa hadn't betrayed her. But if Monica hadn't seen the note, why was she here? As if reading her mind, Beth spoke.

"Monica must have heard Sophie leave," she said, wringing her hands in distress. "That's all we can figure."

"Jason could sleep through an air raid," Sophie said. "Ask me how I know." She laughed. "And oh, yeah, thanks by the way for going to bat for me with him. That tickled the stew out of me."

"Sophie came by my room to get me," Beth said sadly, "and Monica must have followed us here."

"She lit into us a few minutes ago," Sophie said with a laugh, "saying she knew we'd killed Christie."

"So you assaulted her," Maggie said.

"It wasn't me!" Beth said.

"Yeah, it couldn't be her," Sophie said derisively, "since Aunt Beth has the backbone of a noodle. Like anything else, if it had to be done, I have to do it."

"But why kill Christie? What did she ever do to you?" Maggie asked, knowing she was stalling for time even though nobody but Lisa knew where she was, and Lisa had signed off. Stalling was useless. Help was not coming.

"Christie told me she was researching my dad's suicide," Beth said bitterly. "She said she was going to write a book about it."

When Maggie said nothing, Sophie grew angry.

"Tell her the rest, Aunt Beth."

Beth took a long breath as if to fortify herself.

"It turns out Christie managed to track down one of the retired investigators on the original corruption case against my dad. He let slip that the original informant had been a family member."

Maggie realized then what must have happened. When Christie discovered the truth–that *Beth* had been the secret informant, she figured she had an even more sensational book project.

"She bragged to me about it," Beth said bitterly. "Like I'd be impressed. Like I hadn't been tormented by that fact for the last thirty-three years."

"But she didn't have a name," Maggie said. "She didn't know for sure it was you."

"She did after she confronted me directly," Beth said bitterly, wiping the tears from her eyes. "I tried to deny it, but she saw the truth on my face."

"Your generation are all basket cases," Sophie said derisively. "I would've punched her in the face."

"Yes, and I'm sure she wouldn't have found *that* at all revealing," Beth snarled at her.

"So Christie told you she was going to write a book about it?" Maggie asked. "Regardless of the personal ramifications to your family?"

"Yes, can you believe it?" Beth said earnestly.

"And you?" Maggie asked Sophie. "How do you figure into all this? I'm pretty sure you weren't even born when your great uncle killed himself."

"Doesn't matter," Sophie said. "It's still all the family talks about. It almost killed my mom and my grandmother. I wasn't going to let Christie dredge it all up again."

"And what about Pierre Lambert?" Maggie asked.

"Who?" Sophie asked, looking at her watch impatiently.

"The young man who worked for *Lumière* publishing," Maggie said.

"Oh, him," Sophie said. She turned to look at the confusion on Beth's face. "I followed Christie to some lunch she had with this dude and when it was over, I followed him back to work.

She was pitching your book, Aunt Beth. It wasn't an idle threat. She was really doing it."

Maggie felt a ripple of dread as she formed her next question.

"Did you kill him too?" she asked.

Sophie laughed.

"Oh, Sophie," Beth said. "Please tell me you didn't."

Sophie's laughter stopped abruptly.

"Stop talking about me like I'm a psychopath," she said, her lips curled in fury. "I sent him a note telling him to back off, that's all."

"Did you think you were going to send threatening notes to all the publishers in the world where Christie might shop her book?" Maggie asked.

Sophie looked at her, her face a mask of chilling resolution.

"No, because I knew I wouldn't have to worry about it after that night."

49

The moon cast a pallid glow over everything in the cemetery. The soft light filtered through the black, gnarled trees as Maggie stared down the young woman whose face was as cold and aloof as the stone angels that watched from atop the surrounding graves.

"So you went to Christie's hotel room and killed her," Maggie said.

Sophie looked at Maggie in mock innocence.

"How could I have done that? Everyone knows the soda can with the poison in it hadn't been opened until Christie opened it."

"You think you're so clever," Maggie said.

"I do," Sophie said. "I think I'm really clever. The cops didn't figure it out. *You* didn't figure it out."

Maggie turned to Beth. She wanted to know the details of how she did it, but she couldn't bear to hear Sophie crow about it.

"You killed her when we discovered the body," Maggie said to Beth. "She was alive when we found her."

Beth blanched and looked away.

"Oh, congratulations!" Sophie said, slow clapping in Maggie's direction. "Gold star for you."

With a sinking heart Maggie saw how it all how must have happened. When she and Beth entered Christie's room, Christie *had* still been alive. Beth told Maggie to go get help and had pointed to the other room. Maggie hadn't even questioned it. Believing Christie was dead, she had responded to Beth's urgency and rushed to the other room to call for the ambulance.

And Beth had finished Christie off.

"You drugged her first," Maggie said. "I smelled it."

"You're smarter than I gave you credit for," Sophie said. "You're right, I planted a slow-release aerosol can of valerian in her room earlier that day. Then when she went to bed that night over the next several hours, the aerosol put her into a deep sleep. The next morning, when you saw her, she probably looked dead. All Aunt Beth had to do was act hysterical—not a very challenging role for her—and scream for you to get help. Which you did. After that, all Aunt Beth had to do was slip the aerosol can into her pocket, add two drops of cyanide into Christie's mouth and another two in the open can of soda on the bedside to make everyone think that's where the poison had come from. Bada bing."

With mounting nausea Maggie reflected on the question Detective Benoit had asked her more than once: *Why had Maggie gone to the adjoining bedroom to make the call for help?*

She'd done it because Beth told her to. It was as simple as that. She'd done it without thinking.

And because of me, Christie is dead.

"What would you have done if the can of soda hadn't already been opened?" Maggie asked.

"Are you kidding? Christie was addicted to the stuff," Sophie said. "*That* was something I never had the slightest worry about."

The bile rose in Maggie's throat as she asked herself why she hadn't examined the body herself.

"The whole thing was timed perfectly," Sophie said. "By the time everyone showed up: me, Monica, Lisa, Jason and the hotel medical staff, Christie was dead. And voila!—We all had built-in alibis. When you guys went to lunch that day, Aunt Beth dropped the aerosol can in the nearest trash can. Ta-da!"

Maggie glanced at Beth who was sitting now, hugging her knees, her face hidden. A thought came to her and she turned to Sophie.

"The elderly gentleman I was with at the café today," Maggie said. "You slipped something in his coffee cup."

Sophie grinned. "Pretty clever, huh?"

Antoine's collapse wasn't the result of Jason's push. Or a heart attack. He had been poisoned.

"Why would you do that?" Maggie felt helpless fury strumming through her.

"I had to do something," Sophie said with a shrug. "On your own you might not put it all together. But I overheard you talking to Lisa. That old French dude was asking all the right questions. He had to go."

"You're a monster. You both are," Maggie said, looking at Beth.

"We only wanted to stop Christie from destroying our family," Beth said fretfully as she lifted her head from her knees. "We didn't mean for anyone else to get hurt."

"And of course there was the matter of the inheritance," Maggie said with a look of disgust on her face.

"No," Beth said. "The money was never a reason."

Sophie snorted loudly.

"Yeah, sure, Aunt Beth."

Maggie turned to Sophie.

"You really think you have a chance in hell of inheriting any of that money?"

"Well, it ain't going to her kid. I googled it. As soon as the kid got adopted, the ties that led back to the mother were cut. Legally, she can't inherit."

"But somehow you think *you* can?" Maggie asked in disbelief.

Sophie pulled a piece of paper out of her back pocket.

"Turns out, I can," she said. "Christie and I had a few heart-to-hearts in the last few days and when I said I'd love to grow up to be just like her, she said she'd mentor me."

"Mentoring and money are two different things," Maggie said.

"Yeah, but Christie had no one to pass the money on to. She said she'd love to set me up in life."

"And you believed her?" Maggie asked, her voice incredulous.

Sophie flushed angrily and waved the piece of paper at her.

"Stop saying it like that! This right here is her written vow to pay for my education. She said I reminded her of her. She said she'd take care of me."

"Well, you're either a fool," Maggie said. "Or just plain stupid. That piece of paper won't supersede a written will. Was it even witnessed? Is that the only copy?"

Maggie shook her head in disgust.

"You might have gotten to her during a sentimental moment," Maggie said. "Or maybe she was drunk, but that won't stand up in court."

"Well, we'll see about that, won't we?" Sophie said angrily. But Maggie could tell she had lost some of her confidence.

Maggie turned to Beth who had become very quiet.

"You won't get away with this, Beth," Maggie said. "There are people who know what I know. Lisa knows I've come here tonight. My husband knows, too. If you kill me and Monica, how will you explain our deaths? How will you explain why Monica and I were out here in the middle of the night?"

"Good thing we have your handwritten note," Sophie said. "The one you wrote to Monica, to explain that. It's obvious that Monica came to meet with you, and you killed each other."

"I'm pretty sure you're not big enough to hold me down and force poison down my throat," Maggie said.

"Not a problem," Sophie said, pulling out latex gloves from her jacket and then a slim knife.

"You are a cold-blooded little thing, aren't you?" Maggie said. But her heart was beating faster at the sight of the knife.

"I am so sorry, Maggie," Beth said, now weeping softly. "I didn't want any of this to happen."

"And yet, here we are," Maggie said grimly before pulling out her cellphone. "In case you're interested, I have both your confessions on tape."

"Thanks for letting us know," Sophie said. "I'll be sure and dispose of your phone before we leave."

Maggie turned to Beth.

"Can you really do this? This isn't putting drops into someone's unconscious mouth. You'll have to kill me and then finish off Monica. Are you really up for that?"

"Don't listen to her," Sophie said, her voice menacing. "I'll do all the work."

"Why are you making this so hard?" Beth wailed to Maggie. "We don't want to hurt you!"

"And I'm still recording you," Maggie said. Then she held up another device. "Know what this is?"

Sophie frowned.

"I know it's not a gun," she said, "which is the only thing that can beat a knife."

"No, cherub. It's an air horn."

Maggie switched the device on and instantly a thunderously loud noise blasted the surrounding area. Both Beth and Sophie jumped at the sound and Maggie flung the device into the bushes where it continued to blare. She turned her phone around to show to them.

"Not just recording," she shouted over the blaring horn. "But videotaping you. Because juries like pictures."

Sophie charged her at the same time Maggie turned and threw her phone onto a stone ledge that jutted out overhead. Sophie stopped to stare at where the phone had landed. Maggie saw the girl's mind racing to figure out how to climb up and get the phone.

"It's over," Maggie said. "You can't get it before the police get here."

Maggie could tell Sophie wasn't ready to give up but just then the air horn died, making it easier to hear the sounds of the police sirens in the distance, coming ever closer.

Sophie looked bewildered. She took a few quick steps in the direction of the sirens before whirling around to glare at Maggie, the expression on her face shuffling between fury and fear.

"It's over," Maggie said to her again.

Beth's sobs seemed to fill the space between them. Beth was slumped on the ground, her face in her hands. Sophie looked at her aunt in disgust and then turned to Maggie, the knife still gripped in her hand. Maggie snatched up the airhorn from the ground and threw it at her and missed. The horn broke against a tombstone, the sound of it seeming to echo all around them in the night air.

Sophie turned back to Maggie, when all of a sudden, they heard the sounds of heavy footsteps coming down the path in their direction—and coming fast.

Cursing, Sophie finally made up her mind. She threw the knife at Maggie in frustration then turned and ran. The knife hit Maggie and then fell to the ground. Maggie lunged for it. But Sophie was already tearing through the bushes and leaping over gravestones as she fled. Maggie rubbed her hip where the knife had hit but hadn't penetrated through her slacks.

"Maggie?" Monica called weakly.

Maggie started toward her, before remembering the heavy footsteps heading their way. She turned to face whatever was coming, the knife in her hand and listened as the police sirens came closer and closer, but knowing they couldn't arrive in time. She saw a shadow morph out of the darkness on the path. She held the knife out in front of her, knowing she couldn't leave Monica. But when she saw who materialized on the path before her, she did run—straight to him.

Laurent caught her up in his arms.

"*Chérie*," he murmured into her hair as he held her. "You are all right?"

"I can't believe you're here," she gasped.

The fact of him suddenly there in her arms ignited a powerful surge of joy inside Maggie.

"What has happened?" he asked, disengaging himself and moving to where Monica lay on the ground.

"I think she's concussed," Maggie said as Laurent knelt and pulled his jacket off, tucking it around Monica.

He handed Maggie his phone.

"Call an ambulance," he said.

"There's no service," Maggie said.

"Maggie?" Beth said in a small voice.

Laurent looked up at her.

"Who is that?" he asked.

"Nobody," Maggie said firmly, as Beth covered her face again with her hands. "Nobody at all."

By the time Maggie had raced to the entrance of the cemetery and called for an ambulance, the volume of the sirens was nearly overpowering.

"I believe those are for you," Laurent said to Maggie as she hurried back to where he waited with Monica. "Antoine called them."

"He's okay? Antoine's awake?" Maggie asked breathlessly. "How did you—?"

But that explanation would have to wait. She could already hear several police officers running down the path toward them, the powerful strobes of their flashlights crisscrossing and cutting through the darkness. Antoine had called for backup! At least that explained the sirens. Maggie knew the police would never have responded so quickly to just the air horn, no matter what she'd told Sophie.

Monica moaned, and Laurent patted her shoulder.

"The ambulance is coming," he said to her. "Just lie still."

Then he turned to Maggie as the police charged into the clearing.

"It looks like you didn't need me after all," he said.

"That's where you're dead wrong," Maggie said, moving into his embrace. "I don't think I've ever needed anyone so much in my whole life."

50

The sterile scent of the hospital was nearly overpowering as Maggie stood by Monica's bedside. Monica lay with her eyes closed and a faint frown across her forehead. A bandage was wrapped tightly around her head. The steady beep of the heart monitor filled the otherwise silent room.

Jason was there too, in a chair near the bed. His earlier drunken bravado was replaced with a haunted look of guilt and worry. The sight of him, so vulnerable and remorseful, stirred a wellspring of sympathy in Maggie. He held Emily in his arms. For the first time since Maggie had seen her, the child looked alert and engaged. It confirmed to Maggie that Sophie had likely drugged her to keep her easy to manage. Maggie realized that she had never really seen Jason interact with Emily before. Now that she did, she could see he loved her. Emily was his granddaughter. And that clearly meant something to him.

Laurent was in the other room talking with Antoine. Maggie stepped out of Monica's hospital room and called Zouzou. When she didn't pick up, she left her a long voicemail.

"Look, I get why you're not taking my calls," Maggie said in the voicemail. "But you need to know that when Pierre was threatened with the safety of his loved ones—you and the baby —he left town to ensure nothing happened to you. He was threatened by a crazy woman who killed a person in my reunion group. It's all over now and the people who threatened Pierre are mostly in custody. If you can reach him, tell him it's okay to come back. And if you can't, just trust that he'll eventually reach out to you. I'm so sorry about all this, Zouzou. Call me when you get this. I love you."

When Maggie came back into Monica's room, she saw that Jason was holding Monica's hand. He turned to her when she entered.

"She doesn't remember what happened," he said. "She won't be able to testify against Beth."

"Her memory will come back," Maggie said to him.

But even if it didn't, Maggie was confident that Beth could be prevailed upon to confess what she and Sophie had done. Maggie walked over to Monica whose eyes were open and watching Maggie.

"I'm sorry," Monica said.

Maggie nodded.

"Me too," she said. "I'm sorry I thought you were involved in Christie's death. My only defense is that you seemed to have so much to gain by it."

Monica turned her head away without answering. But before Maggie left the room, she saw Monica reach out from her hospital bed to touch Jason's hand and took the child's hand instead.

51

An hour later, Maggie and Laurent had settled back in Maggie's room at her hotel. At this time of early morning, the room was bathed in a soft, diffused light filtering through the sheer curtains, painting a muted watercolor of pastels on the vintage wallpaper. Laurent sat on the bed and poured from a bottle of brandy into two glasses.

"I can't believe you came," Maggie said as he handed her one of the glasses. "How in the world did you know?"

He shrugged.

"After our last conversation, I could not settle." He shrugged. "I called you back, but your phone was turned off. Then I called the hospital and spoke to Antoine's wife who told me what happened. But I should have heard it from you."

His gaze was steady, an unspoken but firm admonishment lingering in its depths.

"Once I knew what had happened," he said, "I dropped Amèlie off with Grace and headed to Paris."

"I didn't want to worry you."

Maggie sipped her brandy and looked at him over the rim of her glass. The truth was, he'd been too far away to help her or stop her at that point. All telling him would've done would be to ratchet up his anxiety. As it was, once he was nearly to Paris, he called the hospital again and this time Antoine was awake. He told Laurent he didn't know why Maggie wasn't answering her phone, but he thought he could find out. He hung up and called Lisa and found out that Maggie was meeting the killer at Montmartre Cemetery. After that, Antoine called the police and Laurent drove straight to the cemetery.

"Except I changed my mind about confronting the killer," Maggie insisted. "Lisa didn't know that I intended to just hide and video tape them."

Laurent snorted as if unconvinced.

"She also said you thought the killer was the husband?" he said.

Maggie sighed.

"I did until I saw Monica lying on the ground. Then I realized who the killer had to be."

"But why did Beth Robinson want to kill Christie?"

"That is a long story. Pour me another brandy and I'll tell you the whole thing."

Maggie settled on the bed next to Laurent, feeling exhausted but finally relaxed.

"Back in high school, Beth was always the quiet one of the group. She was the one constantly with her nose in a book. But she had a secret, one that tortured her for decades and one that Christie—who had a knack for uncovering the truth—had discovered."

Laurent nodded and punched the bed pillow to get more comfortable.

"Beth's father was a high-ranking police officer," Maggie continued. "He'd been involved in some kind of corruption scandal—taking bribes and manipulating evidence to protect influential criminals. Beth had overheard some things when her father was talking on the phone and when she was approached by undercover police agents, she told them what she'd heard, not realizing they were hoping to get evidence against her father."

"And he was arrested on the strength of her testimony?"

"Yes. He was tried and sentenced, and killed himself in prison."

Laurent shook his head.

"It is a terrible burden for a child to carry," he said. "To believe she was responsible for her father's death."

"It is. And then Christie comes along saying she was going to write a book exposing Beth as the secret informant who caused her father's downfall and death. I don't think even Beth's mother knew Beth's role in getting her father imprisoned."

"*Elle est despicable*," he said solemnly. "And the teenager's part?"

"Well, there's no doubt Sophie was the instigator and accomplice to Christie's murder rather than the actual killer but without her Beth would never have done what she did."

"No excuses, *chérie*."

"I'm not letting her off the hook. Beth is guilty. She'll be tried for Christie's murder. As is right."

"But how did she do it? I thought it was *pas possible* with the unopened can of soda."

"It was clever, not impossible. It seems, at one point in the weekend, Sophie was sent upstairs to get Monica's reading glasses. Once there, she slipped into Christie's bedroom and hid a slow-release aerosol of valerian. By the time Christie went to bed that night, the scent was nearly undetectable, but she still became unconscious."

"So when you discovered the body the next morning..."

"Right. Beth said she was dead, and I didn't question her."

"Do not blame yourself, *chérie*."

"What else can I do? If it wasn't for my stupidity—which the killers counted on—Christie would still be alive."

Laurent pulled her into his arms.

"I will not have you think such things," he said. "When you do, you let the guilty win twice. If not for you, they would have gone unpunished."

"I know," Maggie said as she laid her head against Laurent's chest. "And I'm working really hard on telling myself that that is what matters."

52

L aurent left early the next morning to get back to Domaine St-Buvard in time to start prepping his pickers for the upcoming harvest and to get Amèlie ready for her first week of first grade. Maggie would have gone with him, but there was a conversation she needed to have with someone she hoped to then never lay eyes on again.

After checking out of the hotel and leaving her bag to be picked up later, Maggie went to the hospital as Antoine was in the process of checking himself out.

"Leaving so soon?" she said as she saw him packing a sack with some clothes.

He turned to her and smiled.

"I wondered if you would come and say goodbye."

Maggie leaned a hip against his bed and crossed her arms.

"We did it, Antoine. And thanks to you, nobody had to die in the process."

He arched his usual eyebrow at her at the remark.

"You know that planning to meet the killer in the cemetery was foolhardy, yes?" he asked.

"How many times do I need to say I wasn't going to confront

the killer?" Maggie said with a frustrated laugh. "I was only going to videotape them."

"Does your husband believe that?" Antoine asked.

"Yeah, okay, no. But that's only because he's so cynical."

"Or perhaps because he knows you so well?"

Maggie grinned fondly at him.

"I don't know what you think you owe Laurent," she said. "But I'm pretty sure you're even now. If it hadn't been for you, Antoine, things would've gone down very differently at the cemetery."

"We will never be even," he said. "But I am glad for the chance to see him as he is today. You were right. In the big ways he has not changed. Except of course for the fact that he is happy."

Hearing him say that made Maggie feel pretty happy herself.

"Is you wife coming to collect you?" she asked.

"*Oui*. She just stepped out to run an errand."

"I'm sorry not to get the chance to meet her. I imagine anyone you chose to be with must be pretty amazing."

"She is. And perhaps someday we will meet again, and I will introduce you."

"Can I hug you?"

He laughed and held out his arms which Maggie stepped into as naturally as if she'd known him for years.

An hour later, she was walking toward her meeting with Monica at the café around the corner from their hotel. They both had decided mutually that this conversation needed to be held on neutral ground—or at least away from the hotel which had been the base for so much recent discord and enmity.

The vibrant colors of Montmartre seem to glow in the morning light as Maggie walked down the street. But despite the sunshine, there was a distinct chill in the air. It was a sharp contrast to the recent mild days and a reminder that fall was indeed coming. It would be a few more weeks before such a cool harbinger would present itself in Provence, but here in Paris, the sudden dip in temperatures had people already wrapping their scarves tighter and hastening their steps as they walked.

Maggie slowed when she approached the café, spotting Monica at an outdoor table. She was alone, as they'd agreed, but she had Emily's stroller parked next to the table. As Maggie watched, Monica offered the baby one of the *sable* cookies that came with her coffee. Just then, Maggie's phone rang. She pulled it out and stepped out of the flow of pedestrian traffic.

"Hey, Lisa," she said.

She'd already spoken to Lisa earlier and imagined they'd talk again in the coming weeks. Lisa had apologized for bailing on her the night of the cemetery rendezvous and Maggie had once more forgiven her. Lisa had already left to go back to the States. It seemed her daughter had called and asked if she could babysit this weekend and she didn't want to miss the opportunity.

"I just wanted to say sorry again," Lisa said.

"It's fine, Lisa," Maggie said. "It all worked out."

"I know you're probably busy. I remember you saying you were having coffee with Monica this morning and I was just wondering...you know the things that keep you up at night? Did you ever find out about the paint that was found under Christie's fingernails? I've been wondering about that."

"Funny you should mention it," Maggie said as her eye went back to Monica and the baby at the café. "It turns out that that night Monica was with Christie in her room—"

"When she got the black eye?"

"Right. She said while they were arguing, Christie was digging with her fingernail under the top layer of the painting she'd bought because she'd read an article somewhere that said millions of famous paintings stolen by the Nazis were hidden under touristy kitsch paintings."

"So Christie was a little crazy."

"I think the real question," Maggie said, "is why, when the autopsy detected paint under her fingernails and the cops discovered the painting in her closet, they didn't examine it more closely."

"I'm not sure scraping away at the top layer of a painting you just bought is really an immediate go-to for most people."

"I suppose not."

"How is Antoine doing?"

"He was released from the hospital this morning and will be recovering at home. I'll tell him you asked about him."

"Good. Thanks. Listen. I have a sort of confession," Lisa said. "It's been bothering me the whole flight home and I wanted to set the record straight."

Maggie found she was bracing herself for whatever it was that Lisa had to say.

"I think that whole thing with Christie and Beth getting together—you know, that one night stand I was telling you about?"

"Yes?"

"Well, I think that was just gossip. I'm not sure who started it or why."

"You don't think it was true?" Maggie asked.

"I guess I don't. I feel bad for spreading gossip."

"Okay, well, anyway," Maggie said. "It's over and done with, and in the end, it didn't add up to anything. Beth killed Christie for her own reasons and those had nothing to do with you or Monica or being in love with her or anything else."

"I still can't believe she did it," Lisa said. "Beth was always so quiet. And Sophie! I was floored when I heard the news. Did you ever find out *why* they did it?"

But Maggie had already decided that gossip and shame had taken enough of a toll for one month. Beth's guilt over her father's death would now mesh with her guilt at having been talked into killing Christie. She didn't need more, and it wouldn't make anyone's life better to know the truth.

"It doesn't matter why, Lisa," Maggie said. "Just enjoy your grandbabies. I'm glad we reconnected after so long. I'm glad to see things are looking up for you."

"You too, Maggie."

As Maggie approached Monica's table, she wasn't surprised when Monica didn't look up to greet her. Even for mortal enemies, such behavior between French women would have been considered at least a little rude. But of course they weren't French, and Maggie was way past caring about rudeness at this point.

"How is Lisa?" Monica asked as Maggie sat down at the table.

"She's fine," Maggie said, impressed that she knew who she'd been speaking to on the phone.

"Any news on Sophie?" Monica asked.

"They haven't found her yet," Maggie said, signaling to the waiter to bring her a coffee. "But they will. She doesn't speak French and there's a citywide manhunt for her."

"You know, I thought I was doing her mother a favor by hiring her," Monica said. "I had no idea she was related to Beth. They have different last names."

"You and Beth weren't as close as I thought," Maggie noted.

Monica narrowed her eyes at her.

"I thought we agreed there'd be no finger pointing."

"I'm not blaming anyone," Maggie said. "But I've got questions."

"I have a few of my own, frankly," Monica said primly. "I

mean, was Beth really mugged or was that faked? I mean, I saw her head. She had a huge lump on it."

"It seems Sophie convinced her that if she presented herself as a victim, she'd be less suspicious."

"Sophie hit her on the head?" Monica's mouth fell open. "And Beth was okay with that?"

"I guess you really didn't know Beth as well as you thought you did," Maggie said.

"Well, that's certainly true if she was a murderer," Monica sniffed.

Maggie felt her stomach tighten as she heard Monica abandon every vestige of affection or bond she'd ever had for her lifelong friend. In the end, Maggie knew that Monica was no different than she'd always been. She was a mean girl in high school and a mean woman in middle age. There was no cataclysmic event or experience that was going to change that —and even if it did, it wouldn't matter to Maggie's life.

"I'm a little surprised you contacted me to join you for this reunion in the first place," Maggie said as her coffee was set in front of her.

"Well, we did hang out some in school. And you know French."

Maggie forced herself not to roll her eyes.

"No judgement," Maggie said. "But I'd like to hear how you came about adopting Christie's baby."

Monica sighed and pushed back from her chair, but she'd known this question was coming. Maggie had made it clear it was the main reason they were meeting.

"Jason already suspected that Christie's baby was his," she said. "He kept that to himself until right around the time she was due to deliver."

"He told you?"

Monica gave a harsh laugh.

"No. He told his father. I don't know how well you know

Jason but he's not what you'd call a go-getter. Unlike his dad who instantly tracked down Christie at the clinic in Switzerland and arranged for a paternity test. Now, in the late seventies paternity testing didn't give the same accuracy as a modern paternity test, but it was close enough. The antigen testing of T cells on Christie's newborn revealed an eighty percent likelihood that Jason was the father. That was all Jason's father needed to know. You know he was rich, right?"

Maggie shrugged.

"Anyway, Jason and I got married as soon as he graduated from high school. I was unable to have children. I'm sure you didn't know that. I've kept it secret so long I'm sure my own mother has forgotten. Jason's dad was able to pull strings to procure the child—who had every privilege and advantage and grew up to be a meth addict. End of."

Emily's big, baby-blue eyes sparkled with curiosity as she swiveled her head to take in the world around her. She had soft, wispy curls—light brown like Christie—that peeked out from under a little pink hat. Maggie wondered who had put the hat on her this morning.

"I wasn't a loving mother," Monica said as she watched Emily. "I'll admit that. Sometimes I think I hated Adele. When she got involved with drugs, a part of me was glad to see her go. I'm a terrible person."

Maggie didn't know what to say. But she wasn't going to argue with her.

"I have a lot of guilt about how I treated Adele," Monica said. "And when she turned out the way she did—drugs, aggression, thievery—well, who else was I going to blame? Bad genes? Half was Jason's. So, no, I took my lumps for that. Nature and nurture were neck and neck. I hadn't loved her, and she became who I'd made."

"That's a little harsh," Maggie said, although she wasn't sure Monica wasn't right.

"Anyway, I felt a lot of guilt about how she turned out, so I had ambivalent feelings toward this one." She glanced at Emily. "You'd think I'd be thrilled for a second chance." She shook her head. "But at fifty-four I'm too old to be raising a child. Besides, we have no idea who the other half of this baby is. I seriously doubt Adele had a one-night stand with a Rhodes Scholar."

"And that matters?"

Monica laughed.

"I'm sure it wouldn't for you. I envy you that. That, and that handsome hunk of yours who carried me in his arms to the hospital. My oh my. How in the world did you manage *that*?"

Maggie knew that Laurent hadn't carried Monica out of the cemetery. She'd been loaded onto an ambulance gurney at the scene. She wasn't sure whether it was the hospital drugs or wishful thinking that had Monica misremembering.

"You never mentioned anywhere on social media that you married a sexy hulk," Monica said. "And that accent of his! Dear Lord. And here I thought you leaned toward the bespeckled academic types."

Maggie bit her tongue to say that Laurent was probably the smartest man she ever knew. It wouldn't matter. Monica wanted her tropes. And at this point, she wasn't going to be talked out of them. Better to save her breath. Monica brushed away a leaf that had dropped on Emily's blanket and then handed the child a stuffed toy that had migrated to the bottom of her stroller.

"I wish I were good," Monica said, suddenly. "I hate who I am."

And right there Maggie saw the problem and also that there was no real solution to it. She felt a flicker of sympathy for Monica but a surge of compassion for the baby who continued to look around as if fascinated with the world.

"Does Jason know of your struggles?" Maggie asked.

"Mostly."

Maggie found herself praying that he was as loving with the

baby as she'd seen in the hospital yesterday. It wouldn't make up for having an unloving mother. But it would help.

"Have you thought about talking to someone?" Maggie asked.

Monica sighed. "I'm sure it couldn't hurt."

When they parted, Maggie watched as Monica pushed the stroller across the street to the nearest park. She'd said that Jason was waiting for her there. As Maggie walked back to the hotel to pick up her luggage, she thought back to the final excerpt she'd read in Christie's diary.

Diary Entry - June 8, 1978

Just a few more weeks now. The fear is all-consuming, but so is the love. I've started packing your things, little clothes, a soft blanket, and this diary. I want you to have a piece of me with you, always. I want you to know that you were loved, cherished, longed for. I want you to know that you were not given up but given a chance at a life I could not provide. I hope you understand, my darling. I hope you know that you are, and will always be, my greatest love.

It had made Maggie cry the first time she read it and then whenever she thought of it. Christie never married and her desperation to find the child who would always be her greatest love had, in the end, contributed to her death. She hadn't been a nice person, but she'd missed out on all the things that Maggie counted as the best parts of her own life—her husband and children.

In the end, Maggie hadn't given the diary to Monica. She couldn't trust her not to destroy it. She thought about sending it to little Emily one day but decided she would send it to Adele, Christie's daughter, instead. Drug addict or not, the diary had

been written for her. She needed to know how much her
mother had loved her and wanted her. Better late than never.

Maggie got out of the Uber with her luggage in the unloading
section of the Gare de Lyon, one of the busiest railway stations
in Paris. She loved the grand façade of Gare de Lyon, which was
a breathtaking blend of classic and modern architectural styles.
In her mind the train station stood as an icon of the city's rich
history as well as its vibrant present.

Inside, the station was a whirlwind of activity with travelers
rushing around, their conversations blending into a symphony
of different languages. She headed toward the platform for the
train to Aix-en-Provence, the closest station to St-Buvard.
Passengers clustered near the edge of the platform, their eyes
scanning for incoming trains, their bodies tense with anticipation. Like most train stations, the very air was filled with a mix
of excitement and anticipation.

She saw Pierre and Zouzou standing halfway down the
platform. They stood close together and touching, Zouzou's
forehead resting on his chest and Pierre's chin on the top of her
head. It was as if they were completely oblivious to the frenzy
of passengers and manic activity swirling around them. Maggie
smiled at the sight. Even more than her goodbye coffee with
Monica, this was the real reason that she had sent Laurent on
ahead. She knew that Zouzou could use the support before she
arrived home and told Grace all that had happened—and all
that she had not shared before now. Zouzou had taken a brief
leave of absence from her work and Pierre would join her later
in the week at *Dormir* to meet Grace.

As Maggie walked toward the couple, she saw Pierre kiss

Zouzou and Zouzou tighten her grip on him. Antoine had finally come back to Maggie with the information that Pierre's juvenile crime had been shoplifting when he was thirteen. Not the end of the world and not something that would impact negatively on the young man today.

They looked up as she neared and Zouzou smiled shyly at her.

What was it that Grace had said? Regret and redemption. The twin emotions and driving factors to any lasting peace. Maggie wasn't sure who regretted what in her five days in Paris, or who got redeemed, unless it was Maggie herself when she finally realized how little she had to regret from the last thirty years.

She smiled as she thought of Laurent picking her and Zouzou up at the Aix train station in a few hours. One thing was for sure, whatever her idea of friendship had been before she left on this trip was fundamentally fortified by the love and admiration she felt for Grace. Grace had been right about that too, she thought with a smile as she reached the couple and stepped into their embrace feeling Zouzou's tight grasp and Pierre's firm arm around her. There really was a place in life for Lemon Drop martinis and social media comparisons.

Especially when holding your life up against a perfect version of someone else's life helped you to see how truly blessed you were.

~

Be sure to check out the next Maggie Newberry Mystery, *Murder in Toulouse, Book 25* that will release this year!

~

Author's Note

In telling this story, I must say I took some creative liberties with the process of adoption from thirty years ago. Because I structured much of the mystery around the challenges that Christie faced in searching for her birth child from so long ago, I thought it important to mention that adoption in 2024 would not be anything like what happened with her.

My aim in this story was simply to craft an engaging plot, with lots of problems to overcome—not to provide any real adoption situations. For many women facing an unplanned pregnancy, adoption can be a compassionate choice that allows a child to be raised in a loving home. If you are considering adoption, I encourage you to research the supportive permanent family options that are available today.

LAURENT'S RECIPE FOR CROQUE MADAME

Croque Madame is a mainstay in the Dernier family weekly menu because the children love it as much as the adults. It's basically a Croque Monsieur with a fried egg on top and is always delicious—especially when served with a green salad on the side.

Ingredients (4 servings)
    8 slices thick sourdough or firm white bread
    2 TB all-purpose flour
    1-1/2 cup milk
    6 TB (3/4 US stick) unsalted butter, soft and divided
    1 tsp kosher salt
    ½ tsp black pepper
    8 slices (6 ounces) cooked unsmoked ham
    2 TB Dijon mustard
    ½ tsp ground nutmeg
    ¾ cup grated Gruyère cheese
    4 large eggs
    Fresh chives, chopped
    Flaky sea salt

Béchamel sauce

Melt 2 tablespoons of butter in a saucepan over medium heat and stir in the flour. When the mixture becomes bubbly, cook for one minute, whisking constantly until light golden. Whisk in ¾ cup of milk, stirring to discourage lumps; then whisk in the remaining ¾ cup of milk and ¼ cup of the grated Gruyère. Reduce heat and cook until thick and creamy. Remove from heat and stir in the kosher salt and nutmeg. Remove from heat and set aside to cool and thicken.

Directions for Croque Madame

Heat a large frying pan over medium heat. Spread one side of each bread slice evenly with butter and place butter side down in the skillet. Cook all bread slices until toasted and golden, 2 to 4 minutes. Arrange 4 of the 8 bread slices toasted side down on a work surface. On each slice, spread béchamel evenly. Sprinkle with 1¼ cup grated Gruyère and top with 2 ham slices. Spread mustard evenly on un-toasted sides of remaining 4 bread slices and place toasted side up on each of the ham-topped slices. Spread remaining béchamel sauce evenly on top of sandwiches, then top with remaining 1¼ cup grated Gruyère. Turn on the broiler. Transfer the sandwiches to a baking sheet and broil in preheated oven until the cheese melts. Meanwhile crack the eggs into melted butter in a large skillet over medium high heat and fry until whites are cooked but yolks are runny—about 3 minutes. Top each sandwich out of the oven with a fried egg and garnish with chives, flaky sea salt and pepper.

ABOUT THE AUTHOR

USA TODAY Bestselling Author Susan Kiernan-Lewis is the author of *The Maggie Newberry Mysteries*, the post-apocalyptic thriller series *The Irish End Games, The Mia Kazmaroff Mysteries, The Stranded in Provence Mysteries, The Claire Baskerville Mysteries,* and *The Savannah Time Travel Mysteries.*
    Visit www.susankiernanlewis.com or follow Author Susan Kiernan-Lewis on Facebook.

Books by Susan Kiernan-Lewis
The Maggie Newberry Mysteries
Murder in the South of France
Murder à la Carte
Murder in Provence
Murder in Paris
Murder in Aix
Murder in Nice
Murder in the Latin Quarter
Murder in the Abbey
Murder in the Bistro
Murder in Cannes

Murder in Grenoble
Murder in the Vineyard
Murder in Arles
Murder in Marseille
Murder in St-Rémy
Murder à la Mode
Murder in Avignon
Murder in the Lavender
Murder in Mont St-Michel
Murder in the Village
Murder in St-Tropez
Murder in Grasse
Murder in Monaco
Murder in the Villa
Murder in Montmartre
Murder in Toulouse
A Provençal Christmas: A Short Story
A Thanksgiving in Provence
Laurent's Kitchen

The Claire Baskerville Mysteries
Déjà Dead
Death by Cliché
Dying to be French
Ménage à Murder
Killing it in Paris
Murder Flambé
Deadly Faux Pas
Toujours Dead
Murder in the Christmas Market
Deadly Adieu
Murdering Madeleine
Murder Carte Blanche
Death à la Drumstick

Murder Mon Amour

The Savannah Time Travel Mysteries
Killing Time in Georgia
Scarlett Must Die
The Cottonmouth Club

The Stranded in Provence Mysteries
Parlez-Vous Murder?
Crime and Croissants
Accent on Murder
A Bad Éclair Day
Croak, Monsieur!
Death du Jour
Murder Très Gauche
Wined and Died
Murder, Voila!
A French Country Christmas
Fromage to Eternity

The Irish End Games
Free Falling
Going Gone
Heading Home
Blind Sided
Rising Tides
Cold Comfort
Never Never
Wit's End
Dead On
White Out
Black Out
End Game

The Mia Kazmaroff Mysteries
Reckless
Shameless
Breathless
Heartless
Clueless
Ruthless

Ella Out of Time
Swept Away
Carried Away
Stolen Away

Printed in Great Britain
by Amazon